Two Wolves for Soren

Copyright RK Munin, 2021
ISBN-13: 978-1-962699-01-3

Beta reading team: Mary Alegre, Martha Collins, and Lauren Meghoo

Professional Editing: Jenny Sliger, Owl Eyes Proofs and Edits.

Cover Illustration: Ryn Katryn Book Covers

Feel free to contact me with questions, requests, or comments: author@rk-munin.com

And, as with many writers, your reviews on Amazon, Goodreads, and/or Kindle help immeasurably, even if it's just clicking on the stars.

Thank you to all my readers!

Other books by RK Munin

-Science Fiction-

Hissa Warrior Series
Rescuing Halin (Mian and Halin)
Buying Tiran (Mara and Tiran)
Tempting Selon (Lara and Selon)
Defying Kilan (Deena and Kilan)
Healing Mavito (Raleen and Mavito)
Claiming Yopin (Mouse and Yopin)
Teasing Woken (Safena and Woken)
Defending Revin (Kamaril and Revin) – Coming soon

Human Pets of Talin Series
Loving Captivity (Sora and Searin)
Escaping Captivity (Lakin and Dalt)
Negotiating Captivity (Nalia and Derani)
Fighting Captivity (Zia and Palforma)
Tender Captivity (Jinna and Holian - This is a novella you can get for
free by signing up for my newsletter)
Craving Captivity (Lasha and Tamerin)
Stealing Captivity – Coming soon

Origins (A Human Pets of Talin Series)
Creating Captivity (Ari and Bazium)
Gossamer Chains – Coming soon

-Paranormal /Urban Fantasy-

Ours Evermore Series
Two Wolves for Soren (Soren, Kalli, and Quinn)
A Hacker, Vampire, and Chimera Walk into a Bar….(Tobias, Briar,
and Memphis)
When Darkness Meets Dawn (Imani, Lex, and Mac)
Kidnapping Their Third (Cora, Pike, and Kimble) – Coming soon

Alpha Series
Alpha Mage (Emma and Kade)
Alpha King (Cathleen and Lazlo)

New Clan Series
Stray Wolf (Steph and Eli)
Lost Lion (Maeve and Cyrus)
Reluctant Cervid (Tavi and Donovan)
Broken Thorn – Coming soon

-There is violence and fighting on page.

-There is no sexual assault on page, but there is brief talk about it. It is also used a threat.

-When Soren first meets Kalli and Quinn, he uses thrall (mind control) to hold them against their will. He doesn't sexually assault either, but one of them is naked during that scene.

-There is a mention of suicide, but nothing in-depth and no actions on page.

-This novel is a ménage that **<u>contains MMF scenes</u>** of an explicit nature (including MM interactions). If that bothers you or you're under eighteen years old, then this isn't the book for you.

To Lauren M.: You're my most favorite person in all of Georgia, maybe even the whole Southeast! Thanks for dealing with the "ogres" I send you. You manage to clean them up no matter how messy they are when they get to you. You've got talent woman!

October 1868: San Francisco

Soren comes back to himself slowly. The first thing he notices is the pain. His chest is on fire. When he looks down, he sees his shirt is only a few scraps of fabric and soaked in blood. He touches the fabric and only then realizes that his chest is covered in deep wounds. They aren't bleeding, but they hurt.

Something slashed at him. Did he get into a fight with a shifter? He's always had a calm, peaceful personality, so he had never gotten into any physical altercations before being kidnapped and turned into a vampire by his master. After being turned, he still didn't like to fight, but sometimes his master would demand it of him.

He has never refused his master.

Now, staring down at his bloody chest, confusion fills him. Why can't he remember what happened? The damage is grievous enough to be slow in healing. Shouldn't he remember how it occurred?

"Soren?" Looking up, he finds Rachel watching him with wary eyes. Except for a little blood on the hem of her dress, she looks untouched by whatever violence transpired.

"Rachel?" His voice isn't much more than a croak, and his throat hurts when he tries to talk. When he brings a hand up, he finds that there are more healing wounds on his neck too. Something tried very hard to kill him. "What happened?"

"You don't remember?" she asks, eyes wide.

To save his voice, he shakes his head. She bites her lip, and big, fat tears start falling from her eyes. Funny, he thought none of them could cry anymore. "Oh, Soren! You saved us."

"Is he back?" Samuel calls out as he comes running into the room from outside. His heavy riding boots leave a trail of dark mud across the room. Soren knows he should be concerned about the mess. Master doesn't like a messy house. He always insists that everyone be tidy all the time.

But Samuel knows Master's proclivities as well as Soren does, so if he's unconcerned about the mud, something more important must be going on. Maybe Master is out hunting for food or looking for his next slave to enthrall. He said something the other day about wanting one more slave. He'd gone on about wanting a small shifter like a fox or lynx. Someone he could force to shift and lock in a small cage for his amusement.

It had made Soren feel ill, but Master's control was too absolute for him to even verbally protest.

"He talked only a moment ago," Rachel tells him.

Samuel's expression is one of relief. "Finally! We need to get him into the secure room before dawn breaks."

He left the door open when he burst into the room so Soren can see the first glimmers of predawn light illuminating the horizon. Yes, Samuel's correct, he needs to withdraw to the dark room Master created for the two of them. He can already feel the fatigue that daylight causes tugging at him.

Rachel takes a half step forward. Her expression is kind but a little scared. "Soren, love, you need to come with me."

Soren doesn't move. "What happened?"

"We can go over that once you're safe from the sun," Rachel promises.

"Go with Rachel," Samuel orders him. "We've known each other for a long time, you and me. Have I ever led you astray?"

Both Samuel and Rachel are sobek, shifters whose animal form resembles a crocodile. Being sobek means they're eternal, like vampires. Alive until something deliberately kills them. The two have been with Master for a long time. When

Master managed to turn Soren, they were the ones that cared for him until he recovered.

The two of them have guided him when Master was too busy to teach Soren the art of surviving as a vampire. The couple helped him find blood donors. Both sobeks cheered him on when he learned to shift and use thrall. Rachel also taught him all the refinement a dirt poor farm boy knew nothing about. Samuel even taught him to read.

In turn, he's shielded them from Master's wrath as best he can. He's taken blows that might have killed Samuel. He's redirected Master's anger to allow Rachel time to hide. They are the only family he had after Master slaughtered his own family when he kidnapped Soren.

But where is everyone else? Master has twenty other servants. They are always bustling about, cleaning, cooking for each other, lighting fires or candles, and seeing to all the chores that a mansion requires. Especially at night. Master likes to watch them work, so they were forced to sleep during the day and be active at night.

If the sun is about to rise, they should all be busy securing windows for the day and getting ready to sleep themselves. His vampire hearing is as good as most shifters. That means when he concentrates, he can tell there isn't anyone else in the house. It is only him, Samuel, and Rachel.

"Where . . .?" he tries to ask, but Rachel's expression is becoming more alarmed by the second.

"No, Soren. No more questions. You need to come with me now," she demands. She rarely takes that tone with him, so the urge to obey is strong. He hates it when Rachel gets upset.

"You get him in the room," Samuel says. "I'll run to town and find donors."

"Hurry," Rachel urges her mate even as she takes hold of Soren's arm and starts pulling him toward the dark room.

Yes, donors, Soren thinks. He is so very hungry. Famished. He needs blood. He can't take from Samuel or Rachel. They are a rarity with blood that can make a vampire very ill. He doesn't notice Samuel leave. He's too busy concentrating on keeping himself upright as Rachel leads him into the dark room.

As they walk, he absently notes the mansion is in shambles. Broken furniture everywhere, ruined masonry, and torn doors. By the looks of both the mansion and himself, he must have participated in a fierce battle.

He isn't very aware of the rest of the trip to the dark room. He closes his eyes and lets Rachel guide him to his bed. The sun drags him into slumber the moment his head hits the pillow.

"Soren, wake up for me now, please. Soren!"

Samuel is yelling at him, and he sounds upset. As with Rachel, Soren doesn't like it when Samuel gets upset. It's only with a great force of will that Soren gets his eyes to open. Along with Samuel and Rachel, a stranger is staring down at him.

"Hello," Soren croaks out, unhappy to find that his throat still hurts. He should be healed by now, shouldn't he?

"Soren, this is Tad from the village nearby. He's a willing donor and you need the blood."

"Willing?" Soren asks, focusing his gaze on Tad.

Nodding his head, Tad grins down at him. "Samuel promised me money."

"Human?" Soren croaks out.

Tad nods. "I'm human, and so are my brothers. We're all going to donate and then we're going to have enough to start our textile business."

Soren knows he should be concerned that these humans know he exists, but he trusts Samuel. "Thank you," Soren whispers.

He reaches up to cup the back of Tad's head. He draws the young man down, unable to find the energy to even sit up. Tad is tense but allows Soren to guide him. He's so weak that if the human resisted, Soren wouldn't be able to do anything.

Focusing on being gentle, Soren sinks his fangs into Tad's neck. The moment the blood hits his system, he feels better. He pushes Tad away long before he's sated because he doesn't want to hurt the young man.

Another male who looks a lot like Tad takes the man's place. Then another. By the time Soren's done pulling blood from the third human, he's feeling the effects of being fed. Their service complete, Samuel ushers the humans out of the room and Soren can hear him paying them from Master's store of gold coins.

Rachel is smiling at him when he stands up, and she hands him a change of clothes. "You had me worried there," she comments.

That's when most of his memories return, and he freezes, fresh clothes held in a hand covered in dried blood that isn't his own.

It's Master's blood on his hands. Soren killed him.

"Are you sure you won't take more?" Soren asks as Samuel finishes hitching up the horses. The wagon is full of furnishings from the house. Although Samuel and Rachel claimed the house, they didn't want to keep it. Once it's sold, Soren will send them the rest of their portion of money from the proceeds.

He knows the swamps and humidity of New Orleans calls to the sobeks, but he's sorry to see them go. At least the goods in the wagon and the money coming to them will set them up with a good life.

Samuel scowls at him. "You divided up that bastard's wealth evenly among all of us that he held captive for so long. Why would we want your share on top of what we already have?"

"For the last two decades, you and Rachel are the only family I've had," Soren tells him.

Samuel's expression softens. "I know, Soren, but we have enough now. We all have enough. Now that Master—"

"Don't call him that," Soren growls out.

Samuel startles at first and then grins. "How about we use his name and title: Matthew De Chambre, the most malevolent vampire ever created."

That makes Soren chuckle. "Good title."

Samuel nods. "I thought so. As I was saying, now that he's gone, we can start living our lives again. That means you too. Fall in love. Find your flock. Enjoy your life, my friend. You deserve all the happiness in the world after setting us all free."

"I wish I'd done it sooner," Soren admits.

"You had to grow powerful enough," Samuel reminds him. "And you couldn't have known if you were strong enough until you actually challenged Mas . . . De Chambre. It was a gamble, Soren. He could have killed you instead."

"He was going to hurt Rachel again," Soren says. "I couldn't let him do it. Not even one more time."

"And that's what sets you apart from so many other blood suckers in the world," Samuel points out. "You still have human kindness in you. To keep that humanity, you need to find and bind your flock. I don't want you turning out like the rest of them."

"I won't," Soren promises. "I'd rather walk into the daylight than be like De Chambre."

"I know you would," Samuel says softly. "You would never do to someone else what he did to us. No beatings or threats. No one held against their will with thrall."

"Never," Soren readily agrees.

They chat about inconsequential things as Samuel works. When he's finished hitching the horses, he turns to Soren with an expression that is both excited and sad and holds out his arms for a hug. Without hesitation, Soren folds his much larger body down so that he can wrap his arms around the sobek.

"I'll act honorably," he promises Samuel. "And I'll never take another's free will away like De Chambre did."

He couldn't know how tempted he would be to break that vow many years later.

Present day: Wilderness a few miles outside Bend, Oregon

The young couple had built a small campfire, and that was their downfall. As Soren gazes down at them from his perch in a nearby tree, he realizes how lucky he is. It's obvious they've been camping in this spot for several days and, judging by their conversation, they plan to move on tomorrow. If they hadn't lit a cooking fire to enjoy a warm meal, Soren would've never known they were so close. They might have been safe if he hadn't decided to enjoy a night flight over the forest. Their fire caught his attention, and they drew him in.

Now he watches them finish their paltry meal, teasing each other as they eat. The couple's easy comradery and constant touching tells a story of friends turned lovers. Jealousy floods him as he watches. A primal need rises, very similar to when he goes too long between feedings.

But he's not craving blood. He's craving love.

It's not so simple as wanting to go down there and steal one of them as his maker might have done centuries ago. Clouding the minds of non-vampires is easy and even advisable. It's common for his kind to steal a few hours of affection along with a meal, leaving no one the wiser.

But these two are different. He doesn't want to steal either of them. He wants to seduce them. He wants them to desire him back.

He wants them without having to cloud their minds. He wants in on this love and affection without his power forcing them to his will.

This is a first. He's never had this impulse before. He might be gentler than his brethren when it comes to sex and food, but he's never felt this drawn. A strange tenderness overtakes him. He doesn't just want these two to adore him as they adore each other; he wants to protect and cherish them as well.

The male below barks out a laugh at something the woman said to him. Soren unfurls his wings and swoops to a lower branch to perch right over the two of them.

"I dare you to repeat that," the male says as he playfully wrestles with the female. "I dare you!"

She laughs as she wiggles under him. "You're getting a beer gut!"

He gasps in pretend outrage and starts tickling her. She shrieks and tries to get away from him.

"Take that back!" he orders with a mock growl.

Soren's raven form doesn't have the best sense of smell, but now that he's close, he can tell these two are wolf shifters. How odd for a couple so young to be out on their own. That rarely happens.

And by the worn state of their equipment, Soren guesses they've been on their own for some time. Their bags, tent, and other possessions are old and piecemeal. The rainfly doesn't match the rest of the tent, their coats are patched, and the food they just finished eating all came out of dented cans with sale tags. It's clear these two don't have a pack looking after them. That makes them vulnerable.

That makes them his.

Now the male has the female on her back and he's tugging up her shirt. Their playful wrestling has turned into something more salacious.

"Quinn," she sighs as he tugs her shirt off. She isn't wearing anything underneath, putting her voluptuous breasts on display. Soren watches with his keen raven eyes as Quinn latches onto one of her nipples, alternating between sucking and nipping at the beaded flesh.

He can't stand it any longer. Even knowing he shouldn't, he swoops down and shifts to his human shape as he lands. Unlike these two wolf shifters, he doesn't need to be naked to assume the form of a raven. His dark suit shifts with him, and he knows he's an intimidating sight, seeming to appear out of the darkness dressed in mostly black, and looming over them.

Distracted by his mate, the boy doesn't notice him at first. It's the girl who gasps, eyes wide and fearful as her gaze meets his.

"Quinn, run!" she cries out. At the same time as she's trying to shove her partner away, she lets her fur flow over her skin, ready to defend her mate.

But Soren expected this. Dropping to his knees next to the couple, he grabs the boy by his hair to hold him still and grabs the shifted female by the throat to keep her from trying to attack or run. Gold wolf eyes stare at him with horror, and both of them freeze. He's not hurting either of them yet, but his overwhelming strength and speed promises pain if they try to struggle.

Vampires are apex predators, after all.

"Please," Quinn begs. "Please don't hurt Kalli. I'll stay. You can drain me dry, but please let Kalli go."

"NO!" Kalli cries out, shifting back into her human skin. "No, Quinn!" She rolls her eyes to him, pleading. "Please don't kill us."

"I won't," he agrees, feeling tenderness fill him. This initial interaction needed to be fast and harsh. Capture is never a pleasant experience. But now that he has them, the seduction can begin.

He draws up his power, making both Quinn and Kalli flinch. He focuses on Quinn first. "Don't look away," he orders the young man. The moment Quinn meets his gaze, the young man's body relaxes, and his eyes become unfocused.

"Good boy," Soren praises him.

"What . . .?" Kalli begins, but Soren tightens his hold on her neck, and she stops talking with a little whimper. He feels bad for being brutal, but she needs to be quiet, and he can't look away from Quinn yet.

"You will not remember this," he tells Quinn, letting go of the boy's hair. Quinn doesn't move. He stays still, trapped by Soren's gaze. "You're not going to remember that I was here."

"Yes, sir," Quinn whispers.

"Where were you two going to go next?" Soren asks.

"South, to the desert. It's getting cold here. Snow will be coming soon. We can smell it on the wind," Quinn explains without hesitation. "But we miss the forests when we have to winter in warmer places, so we decided to have one more night."

"How long have you two been on your own?" Soren asks gently. He can feel the boy struggle against this question. He doesn't want to answer. There is deep pain there. Memories he doesn't want to deal with. He pushes more power into his question. "Tell me how long, pup."

"Three years," Quinn finally answers, a shudder going through him at the force of Soren's magic.

"How old are the two of you?" Soren asks next. That question doesn't evoke an emotional response.

"We're both twenty-three," Quinn answers easily. A loving smile unfurls across his face. "Kalli's birthday was yesterday."

"Then I'll have to make sure we celebrate it properly," Soren says, enjoying the uninhibited joy in Quinn's expression at the thought of his female.

Time for instructions. "You won't head south tomorrow. After I leave, you're both going to feel drained. The exhaustion is so bad that you're going to sleep for most of tomorrow. When you wake up, you'll be worried about an approaching storm. You're both going to walk northeast until you cross a private road. You're scared of the dark. You don't want to spend another night in the woods with only a tent for shelter. That means that you're going to follow that road to a house. The house is safety and security. Go there and ask for shelter. Don't be afraid. No one in that house is going to hurt either of you. Now repeat all that back to me."

Quinn dutifully repeats Soren's instructions, his brows furrow a little in concentration. As Soren has him repeat it a second time, he gives himself a moment to examine Quinn.

Both wolves have dark skin and black hair, which is common among wolf shifters. But Quinn's eyes are a beautiful cinnamon color with a ring of amber around the outside. He has sharp cheekbones and full lips but still carries the remnants of boyhood. A softness that even the harsh living of the last few years hasn't erased.

His black hair is cut close to his head, probably to make it easier to keep clean. It's practical but upsetting for Soren. There's barely enough there to grab onto. Quinn should have lovely long hair that gleams blue-black in the light.

The boy also has worry lines that someone so young shouldn't have. It angers Soren that these two were forced to fend for themselves. He vows to find out what happened and make those that hurt these two precious wolves pay.

". . . and no one in that house is going to hurt us," Quinn finishes.

Soren smiles and leans over to lay a gentle kiss on the boy's forehead. He rubs a soothing hand up and down the boy's back. "Very good. Now you're so very tired, aren't you? And sleeping long into the day won't be enough. You're going to feel tired and worn down when you wake up. I'm sorry tomorrow is going to be a strenuous hike, but I promise there's a reward at the end. Now go to bed. Kalli will join you in a moment."

Already yawning, Quinn nods and stumbles to his feet, barely able to get his boots off before he collapses inside the tent. Soren turns his attention to Kalli.

She's shaking in terror. "Please," she whispers.

"Shhh," he soothes as he brings his power to bear on her. It takes more power than with the boy, but after a minute, her body goes limp and she blinks slowly up at him, completely under his thrall. Soren smiles down at her, and she smiles sweetly back up at him.

"Very good, *cariad*. Now tell me your full name, sweet girl," Soren orders.

"Kalliope . . ."

"Kalliope what?" he pushes.

She frowns and moves her head in agitation, as if trying to shake off his control. That surprises him. She's stronger than he thought. He pulses more power at her. "Kalli, what's your last name?"

"Brown," she says, but that doesn't feel right.

"Your real name. What is your real last name?" he pushes. Maybe these two weren't ejected from their pack. Maybe they ran away. She fights him, but she can't win. He's much too powerful. Although her attempt at resistance makes him proud. She's a strong one. Stronger than Quinn.

He releases her throat and picks her up. Sitting back, he arranges her in his lap, enjoying the feel of her lush, soft body.

She's naked now because she ripped out of her clothes when she shifted, and he takes a moment to admire her. Just like her breasts, all of her is soft, round, and perfect. Like Quinn, her skin is a beautiful brown and her hair a dark, shining black that only reaches to her shoulders. Unlike Quinn, her eyes are almond-shaped, and her face is more round. She doesn't have the sharp cheekbones or cinnamon eyes of her lover. If he had to describe her eye color, it would be dark like deep water at night. Not true black, but close enough to fool the casual observer. And like an abyssal darkness, her eyes hold mystery and the promise of hidden depths.

The two of them take his breath away. They are that perfect. He wraps his arms around her, hugging her tight, catching a faint smell of her earlier arousal.

He's been half-hard since the two of them started making love, but now he goes rock hard. Her scent invokes images of the two wolf shifters, naked and in his bed. It takes more control than he wants to admit to keep from carrying her into that tent, waking Quinn, and enjoying everything the two of them have to offer while they're under his thrall.

But he wants them to be his. Truly his. And a thrall won't do that. His power makes mindless minions. He wants lovers and eventually partners. Not slaves.

"I'm not going to hurt you," he whispers to her as he places a gentle kiss on the skin behind her ear. He runs his lips along the shell of her ear, breathing in her delectable scent. He needs to finish and send her off to bed with Quinn before he does something he'll regret.

"Tell me your last name, beautiful Kalli. You can trust me with that information. I'd never betray either you or Quinn. You don't know this yet, but both of you are precious to me."

"Volk," she mumbles. The name means nothing to Soren, but she whispers it as if that single word will draw boogeymen from the shadows. She must be terrified of her old pack. Her tense body shakes in his hold.

"You've pleased me by answering," he praises her with a hug and another kiss behind her ear.

"No tell . . ." She fights to speak despite the thrall, but only gets out those words before she gives up. He pushes more power at her, not to force her will but to ease her fear. Her body relaxes again.

"No, I won't tell anyone. What is Quinn's last name?" He wouldn't be surprised if it's the same as Kalli. Wolf packs often share the same last name, even if they aren't related by blood.

"Dawson," she answers easily, telling him that Quinn's name probably won't reveal much when he does some research.

"Very good. Now, do you remember the instructions I gave Quinn?" She nods her head. "Then repeat them for me."

She dutifully repeats everything. He only has her do it once more, pushing the message deep into her subconscious to make sure there's no chance the two of them will wander in the wrong direction. Not that he wouldn't find them, but it will work out so much better if they come into his home believing they found him by happenstance.

Once he's satisfied, he guides her to the tent himself. Quinn is snoring softly on top of their two zipped together sleeping bags. The state of their bed is deplorable. The sleeping bags are old, and they don't even have any pads between them and the ground. If they weren't shifters, they'd both probably have frozen to death in the lightest frost long ago.

He gets both of them snuggled together and bundled up as best he can, content knowing that by this time tomorrow, they'll have access to all kinds of luxuries. They only need to endure this life one more night; then they'll be under his roof. Under his protection.

And maybe even under his body.

That thought makes him smile as he gathers up Kalli's ripped clothes and burns them. The less evidence of the night, the better his instructions will hold. Then he cleans up the small mess from their pathetic dinner and banks the fire. He checks on them one more time, then shifts and wings his way home.

His instinct is to stay and guard them until the pre-dawn light forces him to seek shelter, but he has things he must do to prepare for their arrival.

Landing and shifting at the same time, he walks into his home, surprised at how cold and empty it feels after spending time with Kalli and Quinn. To ward off the chill that has nothing to do with temperature, he does something he rarely bothers with, turns on the heater. He hears the furnace roar to life as he settles down at his desk to work.

His call is answered on the second ring by a very gruff voice. "What the fuck?"

Soren can count on one hand how many friends he has, and this man is one of them. "Memphis, I need a favor."

"It's ten at night. I was about to go to bed," Memphis complains. Soren can just see the tall, broad man, probably at one of his favorite dive bars, pretending to be some kind of human outlaw biker.

Soren will never understand why Memphis likes to hang out with a bunch of lowlife humans. But he knows one thing for sure, it's nowhere near Memphis' bedtime. Even though he's a chimera, and the sun isn't an issue, Memphis leans toward vampire habits. Insofar as he stays up all night and sleeps during the day.

That is, when he needs to sleep. Chimeras require little sleep and Memphis pushes the envelope of how much sleep chimeras can do without. It's that very fact that makes him perfect for what Soren needs.

"I think I've found my flock," Soren says simply. Memphis's sharp intake of breath tells him that his good friend understands the gravity of that statement.

"Shit, that's great!" Memphis nearly shouts, and Soren can hear people around the chimera asking him who he's talking to and what's going on. "Fuck off. I'm on the phone," Memphis growls at the inquisitive humans without pulling the phone away at all. Soren sighs. He adores Memphis and trusts him implicitly, but sometimes wishes the man were a little more refined.

"They're camping in the national forest land near my territory," he explains. "I put both of them in thrall. They'll be coming to me tomorrow. But I need you to watch over them as they sleep and then travel. I can't have anything happen to them."

"No, of course not," Memphis agrees readily. "Can you send me GPS coordinates, or do I need to hunt them down the old-fashioned way?"

Because the couple set up camp near a spring, it's easy to give Memphis directions to find them. Chimeras tend to be good at tracking and Memphis excels at it. He'll have no issue homing in on them the moment he gets within a few miles. It's one of the reasons he's so good at his job as a bounty hunter with the human authorities.

"Don't let them see you," Soren orders after he explains the instructions that he gave the couple while they were under his thrall. "Don't scare them. They'll be suffering from low-level anxiety and worry from what I did. I don't want them stressed any further."

"Hey, I know how to track and guard without being seen," Memphis comments, and the noise around him quiets. He must be walking away from the bar. "I'll look after them, Soren. Don't worry about that. Just concentrate on your part. A real flock can't be linked with thrall. This kind of thing can't be forced. None of you will thrive if their free will is compromised."

"I know that," Soren snaps, feeling a little defensive. "You'll notice that I didn't pick them up and carry them off. I'm letting them come to me."

"With instructions under thrall," Memphis points out. "That's almost as bad."

"Once they get here, I won't do that again," Soren announces, and then winces. He might be lying to himself as well as Memphis. If anything goes wrong and they try to leave, he's probably not going to be able to stop himself from putting them in thrall to make them stay.

It's a testament to their friendship that Memphis doesn't argue. But his sigh into the phone tells Soren everything he needs to know about what Memphis is thinking.

"You might be the only decent vampire out there. If anyone deserves a loving flock, it's you. But for fuck's sake, keep your instincts in check. They'll probably challenge you at some point so don't go off the rails." With that, Memphis hangs up.

Soren sets his phone on the desk in front of him. He's relieved that his friend will guard Quinn and Kalli. Now he needs to concentrate on making his nest appealing.

It takes several hours of online shopping to find and order everything they'll need for the next week. Then he sets about preparing the house. He ignores the kitchen for now. There's nothing to be done about the empty refrigerator or bare shelves until after the deliveries arrive.

His house is always neat, but over the years, dust and cobwebs have accumulated in areas he doesn't use. He does his best to make the place as neat as possible and takes heart in the fact that after camping in the woods, a stray spider or two probably won't bother the wolves.

There's a moment of indecision as he thinks about where Quinn and Kalli will sleep. His room is the largest in the house, boasting a massive bed and an enormous en suite bathroom. But two things stop him from trying to house them there at first. One, his bedroom is in the basement. It might look like any other large bedroom, but it lacks windows and has fortified doors at the bottom and top of the stairs. That might frighten his wolves.

And the second issue is that moving them right into his bed might be much too upsetting right away, even if he sleeps on his couch or the floor. To them, he's a stranger they'll be meeting for the first time. Even with masking his power, they will eventually figure out he's a vampire. He needs them to come to love him before that. Or at least learn to trust him.

He prepares a room on the second floor for them. Like the basement, the entire first floor has no windows either, a safety measure in case he rises early and wants to leave his bedroom.

The two bedrooms on the second floor both have windows and the room he's putting the wolves in has a small balcony with glass doors. He smiles as he opens the doors and lets the crisp air of the night clear out the musty smell of a room left unused for too long.

By the time he's done, the night sky is giving way to the sun. Pre-dawn light floods the room, making everything look soft and welcoming and forcing him to retreat downstairs. He wishes he had thought to bring in flowers from the garden, but he's out of time

He grabs his phone and retreats into his basement room. There are several texts from Memphis.

The first one is time-stamped from hours ago: *Found them. They're both sleeping the night away.*

Then a second text was sent only a few minutes earlier: *Dawn is here. I'll be with them all day, guarding and guiding. Sleep, my friend. Your flock is safe.*

That makes him smile, and he no longer fights the sleep pulling him under.

Quinn wakes up feeling like crap. Rubbing gritty eyes, he yawns and struggles into his clothes and then out of the tent. Kalli's already up and by the time he emerges, she's thrusting a cup of steaming coffee at him. He takes it gratefully, sipping the harsh brew. A quick look at his watch tells him it's already afternoon. He slept over half the day away.

"You look horrible," she comments.

He eyes her over the rim of the battered tin cup. She looks pale, and her eyes are red. "You don't look so great yourself."

She huffs out a little laugh. "Are we sick?"

He looks over to the fire and sees the tin cans they ate out of last night. The sales sticker on the side is half torn off one of them, and the other is dented.

"Maybe we shouldn't have bought those cans of stew," he says. She follows his eyes to the empty cans.

"But we didn't throw up or anything," she points out. "I feel hungover, like we drank a bunch of Crescent Moon Wine. But we didn't. We only had that one can of beer. And I didn't drink any of it."

Quinn winces at her comment. He shouldn't have been so adamant about the beer. They should have used that bit of money to buy food that wasn't on the discount rack. But after spending hours hiking into town and knowing it was going to be more hours of grueling hiking to get back to their secluded camping spot, adding a cold, crisp beer to dinner sounded irresistible.

"I'm sorry about the beer," Quinn says, dropping his eyes down to the cup in his hands. Kalli is on him in a second, wrapping her arms around him in a powerful hug.

"I didn't say that to make you feel guilty. I don't think it was the food. Or if it was, maybe there was something in there that didn't agree with us. You know there are some human spices that make us sick. I looked at the can, but the labels were torn or too old to read, so I can't check the ingredients. I'm sure that must be why we feel so bad."

"You think there was saffron in that stew?" Quinn asks, holding his cup in one hand so he can hug her back with the other.

"Maybe? Weirder things have happened. But whatever it was, we need to get moving. It was cold last night. I think winter is moving in earlier than we thought."

Quinn looks up at a patch of clear, blue sky he can see through the canopy of trees. "I thought we had more time, but it sure feels like there's one heading in right now."

Kalli nods in agreement. "I know we slept almost all day, but I feel like we should get moving. Here," she holds out a peanut butter and honey sandwich. "You eat. I'll start packing up."

Wordlessly, he takes the food and finishes it in several bites, washing the sandwich down with the last of the bitter coffee. Then he helps Kalli. They work well together, and everything's ready to go within twenty minutes.

They don their backpacks and start walking. For some reason he's not sure of, they head northeast instead of south. Maybe it's because that direction is away from Bend.

Yesterday, they found out that a clan of naga, giant snake shifters, live in Black Butte. It's not the closest town, but it's not far enough away to make either of them feel safe. They got lucky and didn't run into any members of the clan when they passed through Black Butte, but they don't know if there might be another naga clan in Bend. Both of them were looking over their shoulders all the way back to camp.

Suddenly, it seems like a fantastic idea to put as much distance as they can between them and the nagas.

They hike in companionable silence, matching each other's stride without conscious thought. Quinn walks behind Kalli. She's better at picking out clear walking paths. Not to mention he enjoys watching her ass as she moves. It always makes long hikes more pleasant.

Several hours into their hike, they stumble across a paved road. Even though they haven't covered much ground, both of them are far more tired than normal. Quinn can tell by the way Kalli's moving that she's only got another mile to two in her. He feels the same level of exhaustion. Whatever made them sick last night is still affecting them.

Rubbing the back of his neck, Quinn looks around. "I don't think we're in the national forest anymore."

"Probably not," Kalli agrees, eyeing the road. "This might lead to a town, a main road, or a private house. Do you think we should follow it?"

Quinn doesn't know. His brain feels like it's full of thick grease and turning over slowly. "Maybe?"

Kalli sighs at his non-answer. "I'm tired."

That's her way of saying she doesn't know where to lead them next. They have three options. Cross the road and keep going straight into more woods. Follow the road to the left. Or follow the road to the right.

Then they both smell it. A whiff of something that smells like a predator. Neither of them knows what it is, but it smells strongly of magic and danger. It only takes one quick look at each other and with no further discussion, they link hands and start down the road to their right, away from that smell.

The scent disappears soon after they start walking, making both of them breathe out in relief.

"What do you think that was?" Kallie whispers, casting a worried glance over her shoulder.

"Let's not find out," Quinn says determinedly. For two wolves on their own, the world is full of perils.

It's twilight by the time the two of them stumble past a cattle guard and find themselves staring up at a mansion. A mansion in the middle of the woods at the end of a paved private road miles long.

"Did we end up in a horror movie?" Kalli asks, trying for humor. Quinn works up a smile, but barely.

"There are lights on. We could go ask if we can camp out here for the night."

They've done that before with varying degrees of success. Sometimes the humans shoo them along, sometimes the humans give them food and let them pitch their tents in a backyard or in the nearby woods. But they've never approached a house this isolated.

That same scent they caught after discovering the road comes again, making both of them jump and gasp. Something big moves in the woods.

"It followed us," Kalli whispers, gripping his hand tightly in hers. Quinn stares hard into the gathering darkness, hoping he can spot whatever is stalking them.

"This doesn't make sense," Quinn mutters and wishes he could get his tired brain to think.

"Come on," Kalli urges as she tugs him to the house.

He follows her, noting that several windows on the upper floor are lit up and the porch lights are on. The massive house should be intimidating, but he feels a wave of welcoming hit him. Almost like he's coming home.

The strange smell fades away as they get closer to the house. Hurrying up to the front door, Quinn boldly bangs the big, antique, iron door knocker. The door opens almost immediately as if someone was standing there waiting for them to knock.

A man fills the doorway. Quinn stands a little over six feet tall, but this stranger towers over him, making both Quinn and Kalli gasp. He isn't just tall, but wide as well. His dark, three-piece suit does nothing to hide powerful shoulders and a broad chest. Ice gray eyes stare down at them while a half-smile curves the man's pale lips. Actually, everything about him is pale. Quinn isn't sure he's ever met anyone with skin this colorless. His face looks young, which means he must have been born with his white hair.

Quinn takes a sniff, but all he smells is human. That can't be right. There's something about this guy that screams magic and power.

Before he can pull Kalli away and make a run for it back into the woods, the stranger pins him with those ice-gray eyes and the urge to flee fades. Quinn realizes that this man isn't menacing. He isn't intimidating or terrifying. Quinn's suddenly very sure that this man poses no threat to him or Kalli.

As all those thoughts sweep through Quinn's brain, the man's smile brightens. "Who do we have here?"

"We're, uh, hikers," Kalli says with uncharacteristic hesitation. "We were hiking."

"And you found my home," the man states. "You both look rather travel-worn. Perhaps you could use a break and some refreshments?"

"Maybe," Kalli mumbles.

Quinn looks over at her. Something's off about the way she's staring at this stranger, but he can't put his finger on it. Then he looks back and loses himself in the man's ice-gray eyes.

"Let me be a good host and welcome you in," the man says and steps back, inviting the two of them into his home. "I don't get visitors often and you both look like you could use a break from your hiking and camping." When neither of them moves, the man makes a beckoning motion. "Come in, come in."

Almost as if their legs have a mind of their own, he and Kalli step over the threshold. For some reason, that last step feels significant and profound.

Perhaps even life changing.

Soren silently curses himself. He spots Memphis smirking at him from the woods, a witness to his quick use of thrall to quiet the couple's initial fear of him. He casts a scowl at his old friend. Memphis gives him a small salute with two fingers and a sardonic smile, then disappears into the darkness.

Memphis herded the two to him. Now it's up to Soren to keep them here.

"We were wondering if we could camp on your land," Kalli says as her wide eyes take in the large foyer of his house.

"Follow me," he insists. Fearful that they're both feeling intimidated, he rushes them through the house and into the kitchen, hoping that will make them feel more at ease.

"Nice place," Kalli comments as they fall into step behind him.

"It's home," he says dismissively as they reach the kitchen. "Are you two local?"

Eager to feed his wolves, he pulls out food that arrived only an hour ago. His kitchen is now fully stocked with enough provisions to feed two young, hungry wolves for at least a few days. He's eager to learn their likes so he can better tailor the grocery order in the future. For now, it will be steaks and potatoes. After a diet of canned stew, he knows they'll be thrilled with the fresh meat. They probably haven't had anything real since the game migrated earlier in the season.

"Uh, no, we're not local," Quinn says. "I'm Quinn. This is Kalli. We were doing the Pacific Coast Trail, but I think we're a little lost."

Soren admires their ploy. The Pacific Coast Trail is a hiking trail that stretches from Canada to Mexico and is popular with both avid long-distance hikers and tourists. It's easy to see these two as eager youths tackling a trail too advanced for them. It's an excuse for the sorry state of their gear that will most likely evoke sympathy. Everyone in the area has run into at least one ill-prepared hiker. Several times a year, major searches are conducted for missing hikers who wandered too far off the trail.

A young couple in dirty clothing and carrying big backpacks wouldn't raise eyebrows anywhere along the notorious route.

"The PCT?" Soren murmurs, pretending to be surprised. "Then you're very lost. That's miles west of here. It's a good thing you stumbled across my place because there's no one else around here, and I think a storm is due to hit in the next few days."

It's not cheating if he uses a compulsion he set up in an earlier thrall, right? At least that's what he tells himself.

"Yeah, we had the feeling the weather was going to turn," Quinn murmurs.

"Let me fix the two of you some dinner. You can use my guest room. As you can see, this place is enormous. And it's only me here. It would be nice to have a little company for a change."

They huddle together, staring at him wordlessly. It's as if they aren't sure what to do with his offer. He gestures to a back door.

"There's a mud room through there. Why don't you set your stuff down for now? Eat first, then decide what you two want to do. I promise I only murder people on Mondays. Today is Tuesday, so you have an entire week of safety." His attempt at humor falls flat, and neither of them moves or cracks a smile.

He tries again. "My name's Soren Bowen. Sorry about how stuffy this place looks. It was my father's. After he died, I didn't want to change anything." His second ploy works and both wolves relax a bit.

"I'm sorry about your dad," Quinn murmurs and takes a half step toward him. Both of them have sympathetic expressions on their faces.

"It was years ago," Soren states. "I should probably look into redecorating. Making this place a little more contemporary."

That's the truth. Besides a few furnishings, like the bed downstairs, the house is very similar to how it was when the house was first built.

In Soren's defense, the house actually reflects its original owner. The robber baron who built it made his money off supplying gold miners in the 1850s and 1860s. Wanting to acquire property on the West Coast, Mathew put the man in thrall and forced him to sell the house and extensive property for a song.

It wasn't the first or last time Mathew would do that. After a few years, he owned property all up and down the coast. But even after obtaining numerous estates, Mathew rarely bothered to leave urban San Francisco.

At most, he would stay a night or two at his various homes, mostly to reassure himself that his wealth was a real and tangible thing. As far as this property outside of Bend, Oregon, is concerned, Mathew only viewed the place once and never inhabited it.

The fact that he never stayed here is the reason Soren picked this property to claim when he divided everything up. Nothing in the house or the grounds reflects Mathew. It was one of only several properties where he didn't bother to change anything. That means that there was no taint of his old master to mar the place for Soren.

He's made some changes over the years, mostly things to update the house as humans invented conveniences like indoor plumbing, electricity, and gas furnaces. Of course, the kitchen was redone also, but he kept almost all the rest of the place the same as it had been when it was built in the 1850s.

Looking at it through the eyes of these young wolves makes him realize he's let the place go stale. It doesn't look classic anymore. It looks old and stodgy. Time has dulled everything as well. He should have at least had it repainted and the floor refinished.

"It's very nice," Kalli offers.

"It could be nicer," Soren declares, enjoying the idea of gutting the house and starting fresh. Making it something new for his flock.

Or perhaps they would like to live elsewhere. He doesn't want to move into a town or city, but he could make it work if that was what they would like. But that's in the future. Right now, he needs to focus on gaining their trust. Then their passion. And finally, their commitment.

One step at a time.

"It does feel a little formal," Quinn comments carefully, then starts backtracking. "But this kitchen is nice. My pac . . . uh, family had a stove like that. That's top of the line. Really great for doing big, complicated meals."

Soren raises a brow at him and ignores his slip of the tongue. "Do you cook?"

"I used to," Quinn admits. "But nothing fancy."

"Quinn is an amazing chef," Kalli pipes up, the pride in her mate strong. "We keep it simple while camping, but when he has access to a kitchen, he can whip up some fabulous meals."

"I look forward to it," Soren says. He's not eager to pretend to eat, but his magic is strong enough to keep food down until he can expel it in privacy. For these two, he'll eat and smile while doing it. He pulls items out of the fridge and frowns as he tries to remember everything he'll need. He works to keep his movements casual, but it's been so long since he cooked anything, he's afraid he might be moving stiffly or with undue awkwardness.

"I can cook a nice breakfast before we leave tomorrow," Quinn volunteers with a genuine smile, eyes still on the stove. Kalli's eyes are on Quinn, so neither of them sees the flash of panic that crosses Soren's face at Quinn's words. He's smiling pleasantly by the time Kalli's eyes turn back to him.

"That sounds nice," Soren intones distractedly as he fishes a skillet out of a cabinet. That's when he realizes that for all his cleaning, he didn't even think to worry about the dishware and cooking implements. The skillet has a thick layer of dust on it.

Trying to be unobtrusive, he moves to the sink to give the pan a quick rinse. Thankfully, neither Kalli nor Quinn seems to think this is odd, and relief makes him slap down the skillet with a bit too much force. It clangs loudly on the stovetop, making both wolves jump a little.

"Sorry about that," he says. "Quinn distracted me with his French toast description."

Kalli chuckles. "If you think that sounds good, wait until you taste it. It's melt in your mouth amazing!"

He nods with enthusiasm. "I can't wait." He knows he should let them banter back and forth a bit longer, but he can't hold back his impatience. Trying for nonchalance, he launches into his carefully prepared speech. "You know, you two are the first faces I've seen in almost six months."

Both wolves startle at his words. Shifters like wolves are used to living in communities. Lone wolves don't do well and often go insane quickly. These two must love each other deeply to survive without a pack for three years.

"Six months?" Kalli's horrified voice matches Quinn's expression.

He gives them a rueful smile and shrugs. "I guess after my father died, I became somewhat of a recluse, and over the years, it's gotten worse. I used to go into town at least once a week, but now I have everything delivered." Most of that is true, if a little exaggerated. He pauses, letting his true self shine through in the next sentence. "My life has gotten unbearably lonely. I think it might be fate that you two stumbled onto my place. I'm not sure I could go even another night by myself."

Kalli and Quinn make a move toward him but stop. They look at each other, then back at him, and then back at each other. Wolves aren't able to communicate telepathically, but it almost feels like they are having a conversation with each other that he can't hear.

"We can't stay long," Kalli finally says. "We need to go south soon. But we could stay for a few days. You have some nice flat area where we could pitch our tents and—"

"No tents are needed. There are rooms upstairs," Soren cuts her off, then realizes he was much too eager when her eyes narrow suspiciously. "I mean, there's a guest room upstairs. I don't think it's ever been used. At least not in this decade," he jokes, trying to undo the damage his hasty words caused.

Suspicion is clear on both their faces. Neither of them has even taken off their backpacks yet. He wants them to relax, eat, and talk to him. But they don't feel comfortable enough to even shed their burdens.

He's doing this all wrong. He knows they're starving, so he should have offered a snack and then access to a shower before he began cooking. He drops the platter he was holding, and it hits the counter but doesn't break. Where the hell is all his normal calm?

Oh, that's right, his entire future happiness rests on convincing these two wolves to stay in the home of a stranger who's acting like an idiot!

They're both watching him now with twin expressions of concern.

"Are you feeling okay?" Quinn asks. "When Kalli gets hungry, she gets super clumsy. She'll drop things or knock herself over. Maybe you should have a snack, and I can cook."

"I do not," Kalli protests, but she doesn't move her eyes away from Soren. "But we can help if you're feeling off."

Summoning up a self-deprecating smile, he tries for some honesty. "I guess it's been so long since I've tried to interact with anyone new that I'm nervous. I'm afraid you guys will think I'm a creep or weird and leave."

"Oh, well, you're the one who joked about murdering people on Mondays," Quinn points out with a small grin.

"Should I tell a knock-knock joke?" he offers and that works. Both Quinn and Kalli laugh.

"Do you know any knock-knock jokes?"

With a perfectly straight face he says, "Knock-knock."

Quinn bites. "Who's there?"

"Interrupting cow."

Both Quinn and Kalli give the next line. "Interrupting cow w—"

"Moooooo!" After a youth spent around livestock, Soren can do an excellent impersonation of a loud bovine. Kalli startles when his noisy "moo" cuts into their line of the joke; then both she and Quinn break out in laughter.

"You got us," Kalli allows. "That was a good interrupting cow sound."

"Thank you. I fooled a few cows with it in the past," Soren says with a grin. "Now, does a good knock-knock joke mean I'm not so creepy?"

"We never said you were creepy. You said that," Quinn points out.

"Okay, does that mean you're willing to at least take a look at the guest room?"

"Sure," Kalli agrees. "Why not?"

"This way," he says eagerly and leads them out of the kitchen. They follow, expressions cautious but interested. "If you want to stay, even for just tonight, the guest room is all yours. It's very nice. I was just checking it over today. Again, it must have been fate that you ended up here because I seldom go upstairs. But today I got the urge to change the sheets and freshen the room up."

He's babbling. He hasn't been like this since he was a human youth. If he gets any worse, he might even end up blushing and stammering.

"Sleeping in a bed does sound nice," Quinn states, his tone gentle.

He leads them through the main room and up a wide set of stairs, turning on every light as he goes so there are no dark corners. He wants his wolves to feel safe and secure. By the time they make it down the hall to the guest room, the house is well lit but still looks formal and stuffy.

Perhaps Memphis is right, and he should sell the place. Dispose of all the old and start fresh. Maybe he has been wallowing and didn't even realize. It's not as if he doesn't have the money. It's only that he met Memphis, and the rest of his family, and they make this area seem like home more than anything else.

He opens the double doors to the guest room with a flourish and walks in. "Here we are!"

Kalli and Quinn have identical expressions of astonishment, and they freeze in the doorway. He hoped they'd be impressed, but they look overwhelmed instead. He tries to look at it from their perspective.

The room is large because it was the original master bedroom. All the furniture except the bed are old, finely crafted wooden items. The desk, dresser, table, and chairs are all antiques and original to the house when it was built. One wall is covered with oil paintings, mostly depicting ships and rough seas. The wood floor under their feet gleams from his quick polishing job, and the white curtains framing the glass doors to the balcony ripple in the cool night breeze.

That's when he understands that this room looks like it belongs in a gothic novel. Or perhaps a horror movie. To his wolves, this room probably appears at least intimidating, if not slightly eerie and maybe even menacing.

He stands stock-still in the middle of the opulent room, unsure what to do. How should he go about assuring Kalli and Quinn that they could trash the room and he wouldn't care? That if they wanted, he'd single-handedly carry everything outside, dump it into a big pile, and set it on fire. That they could paint the walls turquoise and hang posters with thumbtacks and he would be happy.

Suddenly, he feels defeated, and they haven't been in his house for more than ten minutes. He can see it all now. They're going to run away. He'll have to use his thrall, and they'll never be a true and loving flock.

Dejection must have shown on his face because Quinn steps forward and lays a gentle hand on his shoulder. His touch helps ground Soren, making his dark thoughts calm.

"The room looks comfortable," Quinn offers. "Way better than the woods. Thank you for letting us use it."

"You can do anything you want," Soren blurts out. "Move the furniture around. I can take things out if you want me to. Or we can go to the other room on this floor. It's not as big and doesn't have a balcony. That's why I thought you might like this one. The sheets on the bed are fresh. Wait, I told you that already. Well, uh . . . yeah, tell me if you don't like anything."

"So it's okay if we sleep in here?" Kalli teases him. "We'll shower first, I promise."

"Sleep on the bed, the floor, or the ceiling. It doesn't matter," Soren says honestly. "Feel free not to care about the sheets. Shower if you want to, but if you don't feel like it, then climb into that bed dirty."

An image of the two of them, naked and filthy from love making flashes in his mind, and his cock fills with blood. He shifts on his feet, hoping they don't notice. Where the hell is his control? His emotions are sweeping from dejection and insecurity to lust in seconds. If Memphis could see him now, the chimera would be laughing his ass off.

"This is the bathroom," he says, opening another door. They peek in, and both sets of eyes go wide at the large shower. But their expressions are everything eager now instead of intimidated. Relief floods into him at the sight of their straightforward reaction.

"Make yourselves comfortable. Come downstairs when you're ready. I'll finish making dinner." With that, he practically runs from the room before his control can be tested any further.

Soren Bowen is lonely and sad.

Kalli watches him disappear out of the room and all she can think is that this man desperately needs companionship.

"Was that weird?" Quinn asks as he shrugs out of his backpack. He sighs with relief as he lets it fall to the floor with a soft thump.

"A little," Kalli agrees, as she does the same. She stretches as Quinn digs through his bag for their toiletries. "I think he had a little freak out a minute ago. When he showed us the room and neither of us said anything right away."

"You caught that too?" Quinn shakes his head in confusion. "I mean, this is a fancy room. Dude's gotta give us a minute to look around before we can react, right?"

Kalli eyes one of the oil paintings. It's a ship being tossed around on a stormy sea. It's clear that the ship is only moments away from going under. While that one is the only painting where a ship is about to get swamped by angry waves, all the paintings have a darkness to them. As if a kraken is getting ready to surface and drag everyone down to a watery grave or sirens are about to appear to lure sailors to their death. Whoever picked out all this artwork liked three things: boats, the ocean, and a sense of doom.

Quinn comes up behind her, wrapping his arms around her waist and resting his chin on her shoulder. She turns her head to give him a little kiss on the cheek.

"Fancy," he mutters.

"Fancy but depressing."

"Agreed," Quinn says. "Do you think he's depressed? Like clinically depressed? I know humans can live alone, but most of them don't like to. Maybe he fell into one of those, what are they called? When you just keep getting more depressed and can't be happy anymore?"

"Downward spiral?" Kalli guesses.

"Yeah, that's it," Quinn agrees.

"You'd be a better judge than me," Kalli comments. "You're always better at reading people than me."

"And cooking," he teases. That makes her laugh.

"And cooking," she repeats. They go quiet, staring at the oil paintings.

"Want to paint some rainbows in a few of them?" Quinn suggests as he straightens up. "He said we could do anything we want to the room."

"Defacing a bunch of old paintings seems drastic," Kalli comments dryly. "Maybe we could take them all down and stack them in a closet? We can put them back up before we leave. But having them all hanging there feels, I don't know . . . dark?"

"They are kind of disheartening," Quinn agrees with a small nod. "Like they were painted by someone who wanted to off themselves." It's obvious she's not the only one affected by the paintings. "But we can do that later. Let's shower first."

"Hell, yeah," she says with an eager grin. "Last one to the shower has to go down on the other one!" she calls, already halfway across the room.

Quinn meanders after her. "Oh no," he deadpans with a grin. "I'll never beat you. You're so fast. Now I'm stuck eating out your sweet pussy."

They make quick work of getting clean in the massive tiled shower, even using some of the products already in the bathroom. Once the dirt of the past few days has been washed away, Quinn pushes her against the shower wall and roughly kisses her. Kalli loves this. Quinn lets her take the lead on a lot of things, but he likes to be the aggressor when it comes to sex, and that's more than fine with her.

Moving away from her mouth, he bites a path down her jaw to her neck. They exchanged mating bites soon after running away, leaving matching scars on their necks. For Quinn, the bite healed quickly and never troubled him again. But for some reason, the bite on Kalli's neck took a lot longer to heal and even now, years later, it's sensitive. When she's aroused, it becomes an erogenous zone that Quinn loves to exploit.

Quinn scrapes his teeth over it, making Kalli shudder as sharp needles of lust hit her. He teases her like that until she wraps her legs around his waist and tries to wiggle his hard cock into her needy heat.

"Not yet," he murmurs, dropping to his knees and carefully setting her down on the wet tiles. The shower rains hot water down on them, making her feel decadent.

Languidly, he kisses down her body. She makes a frustrated sound, and she feels him smile into the soft skin of her belly. He likes to torment her. If it were up to her, sex would be a race to orgasm. But Quinn likes to take it slow and draw everything out. She has to admit his way is better, but she's never learned to curb her impatience.

Thank the goddess that he's patient enough for the both of them.

"Hands behind your head," he orders, nipping at the flesh near her belly button.

Making a low, whining sound, she laces her fingers behind her head and lies back. He works his way down to the soft black curls at the apex of her legs. He grabs her behind the knees, draping her legs over his strong shoulders.

For a moment, she pictures Soren there, his big body between her legs. Quinn would kneel over her, feeding his beautiful cock into her mouth. While she took Quinn down her throat, Soren's hands would be—

A nip on the inside of her thigh gets her attention and makes her blush from letting Soren into her thoughts. What is she doing even thinking about another male? She's mated and in love with Quinn. She's never felt desire for another male besides Quinn. He has been her everything since they were both old enough to walk and talk. And now this man they've only just met has wormed his way into her thoughts.

Determined to keep her mind from wandering, she refocuses on Quinn. Knowing how he'll react; she grins as she pulls her hands out from behind her head and sits up. She plants her palms on the tiles behind her to support herself. Quinn lets out a growl of disapproval and surges forward. Because her legs are still over his shoulders, he practically bends her in half.

With a little challenge growl of her own, she tries to brace against him but only puts up a token effort. With a hand around each of her wrists, he tugs her arms out from behind her. Without her hands to support her, her back meets cool tile while Quinn forces her hands over her head. He locks both wrists together in one of his hands and glares down at her with mock ferocity.

"Bad girl," he says and slaps her on the thigh. It has enough sting to it to make her shudder. Seeing her reaction, he does it again. Her eyes close, and she uses her legs on his shoulders to arch her back.

"Quinn," she whines. "Please."

"What are you begging for?" he demands and grips her hands against the tile. He takes his free hands and tugs one of her legs off his shoulder. With one foot on the tile and one resting on his back, her sex is fully open to him.

He runs a finger through her folds, much too lightly. "Do you want me to touch you here?"

"More, please. Harder," she begs. She loves giving up control in this area. Early in their relationship, even when they were fumbling pups going at each other during stolen moments in hidden places, Quinn was always the sexually dominant one of the two of them. She might take charge everywhere else, but here she likes him this way.

A small slap here. Teasing there. Sexy words spoken in a commanding tone. She responded to it all.

"What if I want to touch you like this?" He runs soft fingers over her sex again, brushing his fingertips lightly over her clit. "I could do this for hours," he taunts.

"Nooooo!" she wails, and that makes him chuckle evilly.

"Yesssss!"

"I'll suck you off," she offers. She's come before with him in her mouth and her fingers rubbing hard on her clit. It isn't her favorite. She likes his mouth on her and his fingers inside her for the first round. Then him pounding away inside of her. But she wants to come so bad, she'll take it anyway she can get it.

He shakes his head at the offer. "I know what you'll do with these sneaky hands."

"Please, Quinn," she begs again. He parts the folds of her sex, holding them open and exposing her heated flesh to the warm water raining down on them. The sensation is novel and as horribly provoking as his light touch. She struggles a little, not putting much effort into trying to get free, but wanting him to know she's not happy about her current treatment.

When she thinks that she might need to struggle for real, he dips his head down and sucks that throbbing nub of flesh into his mouth. The move is unexpected and makes her give a little cry of surprise and pleasure. He uses his teeth a little, giving her a bit of pain with her pleasure.

She is so close, but he's not ready to let her come yet. He alternates between licking, sucking, and nipping, backing off every time her orgasm gets close. The third time he does it, she curses him with the few Russian words her grandmother taught her, making him laugh.

"Don't move those hands!" he growls at her.

She moans and laces her fingers together behind her head to help keep them there. "Please Quinn!"

When he starts on her again with that talented mouth, he doesn't stop. She goes rigid as her orgasm hits her, sobbing at how good it feels. When her body relaxes a little, Quinn pulls his face out from between her legs and rearranges her pliant body. He hooks her knees over his shoulders, fits his cock at her entrance, and thrusts in. His expression is fierce as he pauses for a moment, both of them shuddering at the feel of him buried deep inside her.

Then he starts moving. Hard.

Eyes fluttering shut; she lets herself enjoy his brutal movement. He couldn't do this if she hadn't already come, but now that she's relaxed, his rough treatment feels wonderful.

"Goddess, Kalli, you always feel so good," he grunts out as he works himself in and out of her body. She can feel another little orgasm building.

Nothing will ever be as perfect as every moment she gets to be with Quinn. She feels bad for her parents who will never know or understand this kind of happiness.

It doesn't take long before his breathing becomes uneven, his movements less coordinated. He's close and Kalli helps him along by tightening her muscles around him. Not only does that make him gasp, but it feels good for her as well. She tilts her pelvis a little, her expression pleading. He leans over, knowing exactly what she wants. Now the length of him is dragging on her sensitive clit enough to push her into a small, second orgasm.

As she convulses around him, he moans and goes still, body held rigid as he shudders through his own climax.

"How are you so perfect?" he murmurs in a ragged whisper.

"Because I got lucky enough to have you," she answers, her love for him feeling as perfect and overwhelming as it did the first time that they had sex at fifteen. "If I'm perfect, it's because you taught it to me."

He mutters something she doesn't get but knows its words of love.

They stay that way for a few precious minutes, wrapped up in post-orgasmic bliss as the hot water rains down on them. With obvious reluctance, Quinn pulls away from her.

"We should finish before we use up all the hot water." As if prompted by his words, the water suddenly turns frigid, making Kalli screech and hurry to her feet.

"Too late!" she declares with a laugh. They rush through the rest of their bathing.

Even with the freezing rinse making her teeth chatter, Kalli wouldn't have traded that moment for anything. Every moment with Quinn is important, even the uncomfortable ones.

Someday their time together will be over, either because their pack catches up with them or because they'll eventually grow old and die. That means she's not willing to waste even a second with Quinn.

For some reason that thought brings their host's face to mind. How odd? She loves Quinn with all her heart, so why does Soren keep popping up in her thoughts?

When Quinn and Kalli join him in the kitchen together, they're clean and smiling. He can tell by the way they are both more relaxed and slightly flushed that they had sex, probably in the shower. It's too bad. If they fucked after the shower, he might smell a hint of their passion on them now.

Patience, he reminds himself. Soon enough he'll be able to know what they're like himself. No more moving in close and hoping to catch the fleeting scent of spent passion.

"Can we help?" Kalli asks.

He's getting a feel for these two. Kalli is the more driven one, ready to take the incentive and lead. Quinn is more laid back and empathetic. They're a good foil for each other, balancing aggression with caring. Action with contemplation. And suspicion with sympathy.

"You could set the table," Soren suggests, pointing to a drawer. The food has been ready for a while, sitting in the warming drawer on the stove. He deliberately didn't set the table to give them a task once they emerged from their room. Kalli moves to the drawer and pulls out silverware while Quinn looks at him with questioning eyes.

"Why don't you see if there's anything you guys like to drink in the fridge, Quinn." He made sure the food delivery included the same brand of cheap beer that they had splurged on for Quinn, as well as some higher end beer, sodas, fancy sparkling water, and various juices.

"I also have a nice wine selection in the wine refrigerator and the rack next to it," he comments as Quinn peruses the fridge. Both wolves throw him quizzical looks.

"You have a fridge just for wine?"

He smiles back at them. "Doesn't everyone?"

That makes them laugh and start teasing each other about who's going to carry the "wine fridge" in their backpack.

When he had the kitchen remodeled after a small electrical fire gutted it, he picked an appliance package that included all kinds of high-end amenities including the wine fridge. Vampires have little use for a kitchen, so why bother paying attention to what was installed?

He brings the plates to the table and Quinn brings drinks, a higher end beer for himself, and a bottle of sparkling water for Kalli. Soren resists the urge to fetch glasses for the drinks. If Quinn didn't think of it, he'll let it go. He doesn't want to embarrass the pup.

The three of them settle down at the table and, almost in unison, Kalli and Quinn frown at the empty spot in front of him.

"You're not eating?" Kalli sounds affronted. "We can redivide the food so you can have some too. There's more here than either of us will probably eat."

She's lying. He kept the portions modest so his wolves wouldn't make themselves sick eating rich food after probably subsisting on a meager diet for so long. One of Memphis's texts informed him that all they ate the entire day was a couple of peanut butter sandwiches. No fresh fruit. No veggies. No meat. Quinn alone could probably eat his and Kalli's portion in one sitting. Soren looks forward to being able to give them full portions in the future, but for now he wants to be cautious.

He smiles at them, prepared for this question. "I ate before the two of you got here."

It isn't a lie at all. He gorged himself on bagged blood the moment he woke from his daylight slumber. He's going to need to be careful about his feedings during these early days. Suffering hunger pangs around these two delectable wolves would be a disaster waiting to happen.

Quinn looks down at his plate, then back up at Soren. "Are you sure you don't want some?"

Neither of them is eating yet. It's heartwarming to have both of them hesitating because he has no food. They're both so hungry he can practically hear their stomachs growling, but they remain steadfast. Maybe this is a sign that they're already seeing him as part of their little pack. That will make the transition from pack to flock much easier.

"Tell you what," he says, rising from his chair. "I'll get myself a glass of wine to enjoy while the two of you eat. Would either of you like some?"

Both wrinkle their noses, making him chuckle. He goes to the refrigerator and digs way in the back where he stored a bottle full of blood. He thought it could pass for a dark merlot, but Kalli looks at him suspiciously when he pulls it out and shows them.

"Why was that in the regular fridge and not the wine fridge?"

He blinks for a minute, caught off guard by her question. Clever, quick-thinking wolf. "It's a special type of wine. It needs to be chilled lower," he ad-libs.

Both wolves nod their head thoughtfully as he grabs a wine glass and rejoins them at the table. Her question made him realize this whole ruse could easily be discovered long before he has a chance to make the two of them his. He needs to tread carefully. This is too important to mess up because a silly detail got overlooked.

They're still watching him with unblinking eyes, waiting for him to pour his wine and take a sip so they can start eating. But they'll smell the blood the moment he pulls the cork out.

There's no help for it, he's going to have to use thrall on them to keep the blood scent from making them upset. He consoles himself that it will only be this one time. And all he's doing is keeping them from getting upset. He's not forcing them to stay against their will or anything like that.

"Kalli, Quinn, I need both of you to listen to me carefully," he says. He pushes power into his aura until it flares out and touches them both. He watches the two fall under the influence of his magic. "I'm about to drink some wine. It's going to smell odd to you, but it's probably because you don't like wine anyway. You'll ignore the smell because you don't want to make me feel uncomfortable. Understand?" They both nod their heads. "Good, now why don't you two eat."

As they sink their forks in, he pulls back his power. Both glance up when he pulls the cork and pours himself half a glass. Quinn cringes, but then blushes and shoves a big bite of steak in his mouth, covering up the fact that the "wine" stinks enough to have caused him to make a face.

Soren sips slowly as the wolves devour their meal. He's not hungry in the least, and he doesn't like his blood cold like this, but he's thankful for the foresight to have the disguised blood on hand.

It's not long before the plates are empty, every morsel consumed by his hungry wolves. It was satisfying to watch them eat what he provided, and he looks forward to getting to do it again. There's something fundamentally satisfying in providing sustenance for his flock.

Of course, once they're all bound together, they won't need as much food because they'll be feeding off his magic. But he'll always get to feed them something. That thought makes him happy.

Kalli yawns, making Quinn yawn a moment later. They're both looking sleepy, and Soren has a moment of panic. They can't go to bed yet. If they decide to go to bed, they'll retreat to the guest room, shut the door, and leave him to face the rest of the night alone. He's not ready for that. He can't bear even one more solitary night.

"Let me show you the garden," he says abruptly, startling both wolves. When they eye him, he realizes that most people would want to show guests a garden during the day, not after the sun is gone down.

"It's a garden specially meant to be viewed at night," he explains, trying to rein in his alarm at the thought of them going to sleep so soon. "It's a hobby of mine. I'm rather very proud of it."

That makes them give him matching, indulgent smiles. "We'd love to see it," Kalli says. "Let me and Quinn clean up, and then you can show us."

Before he can protest that he can do the simple task of washing up, they are already jumping up to clear the table. Working in tandem, they wash, dry, and put away the few dishes they ate off of as well as the cooking implements he used.

Carefully corking his "wine," he buries it back in the fridge and washes his wine glass himself. Then he leads the two through the mudroom and out the back door.

Before he took control of the property, this area had been bare. After a few years in residence, Soren decided he wanted to see things grow and develop. He doesn't do much now, but for almost a decade, he was obsessed with the garden. Kalli and Quinn make him want to show off a bit.

He points to a few raised flower beds, where white and pink flowers glisten in the moonlight. "Those are full of evening primrose. They don't normally bloom this late, but it was unseasonably warm a few days ago and the entire garden came back to life for a last hurrah."

He leads them around the winding brick path, pointing out each plant and giving both its common name and Latin name. Most are dormant, but a few are showing off their last blooms. They end the tour by sitting on a garden bench next to a large bed of Lamb's Ear softly glimmering silver in the moonlight.

"This is amazing, Soren," Quinn comments. "I didn't know there was anything like it."

Soren's not surprised. Night gardens are an uncommon hobby, even among vampires. "I stumbled onto it a few years ago. I was feeling . . ."

How does he finish that statement? He was feeling morose. Lonely. Forlorn. Gardening alleviated it for a while. Going out and finding fights or having sex helped too.

"Hey, it's okay," Quinn murmurs. Somehow, the wolves ended up on either side of him on the bench. Quinn wraps an arm around his back and gives him a side hug. Kalli drops her head to rest on his shoulder. Both of them radiate heat, and it feels like he's basking in the sun.

Slowly, tentatively, he brings his arms up and stretches out, one arm around each wolf. Wolves are used to giving each other comfort through touch, so neither pulls away from him. They nestle closer to his bulk, enveloping him in warmth.

"You're cold," Kalli murmurs, worried. "Maybe we should get you inside."

If he were human, his low body temperature would be an issue to worry about. While wolves run hot, vampires run cold. But he can't tell her that yet.

"I'd rather sit here a little longer, if you two don't mind," he says. "I feel warm enough at the moment. It's such a pretty night. I'm not ready to abandon it yet."

They murmur agreement, and the three of them fall silent as the night moves around them. Stars slowly make their way across the sky, night bugs flitter from leaf to leaf, and small scavengers search the underbrush for goodies.

Quinn is the first one to fall asleep. Kalli giggles softly when his head droops and he ends up leaning heavily against Soren, breathing deep and even.

"He can fall asleep anywhere," she comments.

"Oh?" They keep their voices low, so they don't disturb Quinn.

She nods her head. "We were waiting in a checkout line once, and he leaned against a candy rack. It only took, like, twenty seconds, and he was out. The rack wasn't that sturdy, so the moment his entire weight was on it, everything fell over. The mess was intense, candy bars and small boxes of gum everywhere. But the best part was his expression. He was so shocked to find himself on the floor, along with the mess. It was priceless."

She chortles at the memory. He wants to ask what was going on that Quinn was that exhausted but refrains.

"I'm sure it was," he says with a chuckle of his own. "When I was young, it was my job to care for our herd of sheep. We had a few dozen, and they needed to be walked to the grazing area, watched, and then walked home in the evening."

"How old were you?" Kalli asks.

"About seven, I think," Soren says, trying to remember his childhood after so many years.

"That's young. Didn't you have school during the day?"

"I was homeschooled," he lies. At the time he was a child, formal education for the dirt poor didn't exist. His mother knew how to read a little, and she taught him as much as she knew. But reading and writing weren't considered important life skills when he was growing up. "My parents didn't believe much in 'book learning,' as they called it."

"I'm surprised. You seem so refined. So educated."

"I pursued knowledge later in life," he says, and then gives her a little squeeze with his arm. "Now do you want to hear my funny story or not?"

She giggles again. "Sorry, please continue."

"So there I am, watching sheep eat. And yes, it's about as boring a job as you can imagine. I've skipped all the stones. I defeated all the pirates—"

"Were there a lot of pirates?" she teases him.

"Many," he retorts, enjoying their banter. "I was forced to fight them off with my wooden sword on almost a daily basis. Now hush and let me finish. Where was I? Oh, yes, I had done everything there was to do for a young lad, and I ended up falling asleep on a nice patch of shady grass. While I slept, I dreamed of my mother pouring warm water on me in the bath, but it didn't smell right."

Kalli clamps a hand over her mouth to stifle her laugh. "No!"

"Yes!" he answers with a grin. "I woke up to find one of the sheep pissing on me. She must have had a massive bladder because she soaked both the bottom of my shirt and most of my pants. I learned my lesson that day."

"Don't fall asleep near the sheep?"

"Oh no, I took naps all the time while watching the sheep. I learned to always claim the high ground when stealing some sleep. Boulders and trees became my favored napping spots."

She laughs again, and that rouses Quinn for a moment. But he settles back down and falls right back to sleep with his head nestled on Soren. Giving into temptation, the vampire tucks the wolf tighter against his bigger body. Quinn makes a soft, appreciative sound.

Kalli tries to reach across Soren to touch Quinn, but Soren is a little too broad and her position too awkward to make it work. Worried she'll get up and reposition herself to get closer to Quinn, Soren moves his arm from around her shoulder and picks up Quinn's arm to lay it across his lap so she can easily twine her fingers with her mate. Quinn's eyes don't even flutter and Kalli makes a soft, contented sound.

Soren marvels at how wonderful it all feels.

Eventually, Kalli falls asleep too. Soren wraps his long arm around her, drawing her close and making sure her relaxed body doesn't slide away from him and off the bench. She makes a soft sound and nuzzles into his side, cuddling close.

He keeps them there, sitting with him in the garden for as long as he dares. When he judges the air too cold for his wolves, he gently wakes Quinn.

"Wha . . .?"

"It's time for bed, *annwyl*," Soren tells him softly.

"Kalli?" the young man mumbles as he gets to his feet, eyes barely open.

"I've got her," Soren assures him, standing with Kalli held securely against his chest. "Here, hold on to me. I'll walk you to your room."

Trustingly, Quinn clings to Soren. The vampire's able to guide him to the bedroom while carrying Kalli.

Once in the bedroom, he holds Kalli with one arm and pulls back the covers with the other. He lays her out, intending to at least pull off her shoes, but then gets distracted. Movement makes him look up in time to watch a sleepy-eyed Quinn strip nude and crawl under the covers, pulling a fully dressed Kalli tight against him. He murmurs something and then drops back into a restful slumber.

Straightening up, Soren stands there and watches his wolves sleep. Time stops registering and he immerses himself in the sight that fills him with peace. He's loathe to move, and it's only when he feels the pressure of the sun about to rise that he reluctantly departs the guestroom.

He writes a note and leaves it for them to find in the kitchen, then retreats to his basement bedroom.

Lying on his massive bed, unwilling to take off his clothes because they smell faintly of Kalli and Quinn, he messages Memphis.

It went well tonight.

Memphis's reply comes almost immediately: *How well?*

He smiles, thinking of all three of them sitting together in the garden: *Better than I expected.*

Memphis: *Did you get to be the meat in a wolf sandwich?*

Soren snorts out a laugh: *Not yet. But they fell asleep in my arms. I regret to inform you that we were all fully dressed at the time.*

Memphis: *Then you're doing it wrong.*

Memphis: *But seriously keep it up. These two feel pure to me. Like what I imagine it would feel like to meet a fated mate. And they're both cute. If you hadn't already staked a claim, I might have stolen them away for myself.*

That makes Soren scowl at his phone: *Mine!*

Memphis: *You know I wouldn't do that. Stupid fucker.*

Neither of them texts for several minutes, then Soren writes: *The sun is coming up.*

Memphis's answer makes it clear that he heard all the subtext in Soren's words: *I'll come over and guard. I'll be there to persuade them to stay if they think about leaving.*

Soren: *They shouldn't want to leave yet. They promised to remain here for a few days.*

Memphis: *Doesn't matter. I'm coming over anyway. Just to warn you, if they want to leave, I'm going to let them go, but I'll do my best to talk them into staying.*

Soren: *I wouldn't have it any other way.*

It's late afternoon by the time Kalli wakes up alone in bed. Stretching out on the luxuriously soft bed, she pulls the covers off to find she's still fully dressed. She even slept with her shoes on.

Rubbing the sleep out of her eyes, she looks around, trying to figure out how late it is. The glass balcony doors are shut, but the curtains aren't drawn. The sun is high in the sky, telling her it's probably somewhere close to noon.

Slightly embarrassed because she slept so late, she hurries to clean herself up in the bathroom. Then she makes her way downstairs in search of Soren and Quinn. She finds Quinn in the kitchen, but there's no sign of their host.

"Hiya, sleepyhead," Quinn greets her, holding out a cup of coffee. She takes it with a grateful smile as she notes he looks well rested and a far cry from the exhausted and mildly sick wolf of yesterday. Whatever made them feel bad is out of their system, thankfully.

With his hands free, Quinn points to something behind him with his thumb over his shoulder. "This guy has one fancy-ass coffee machine. Thank the goddess the instructions were in the drawer under it or that cup would've been full of Turkish coffee."

Kalli wrinkles her nose. They were forced to make Turkish coffee for almost six months until they picked up an attachment for their cooking pot to make percolated coffee. She doesn't miss the days where they had to sip the coffee carefully to avoid chewing on coffee grounds first thing in the morning.

"Ugh, thanks for figuring it out," Kalli comments, sipping from her cup. "Where's Soren?"

"He left a note," Quinn says, tapping a piece of paper on the island countertop. There's a shiny new cell phone sitting next to it. "I guess he needed to run into town."

She leans over to read it herself:

Dearest Kalli and Quinn,

I had to leave for a bit. Here's a phone if you need to contact me while I'm gone. I should be back just before dark. Please make yourselves at home. There's an entertainment center on the third floor. You can watch movies or play video games. Eat anything you want. But save room for dinner. I look forward to cooking for both of you again.

Yours sincerely,
Soren Bowen

"I don't think I've ever seen handwriting that fancy," Kalli comments, looking up from the note to see Quinn grinning.

"I know, right? He has an old-school feel to him." Quinn nods his head toward the living room and front door area. "Heck, this whole place has an old-world vibe."

"Including our room," Kalli points out with an exaggerated shudder. "And all those ships about to sink."

Quinn chuckles. "Right, except here's the good part. That entertainment room on the third floor is fully stocked. He's got all kinds of great stuff up there, and I think almost all of it is brand new."

"Maybe it's his latest hobby," Kalli guesses, picking up the cell phone. She hits the power button, and the main screen displays only a few icons. It's probably his spare phone. He might be one of those guys who's always going out to get the latest model. She sets the phone down and grins at Quinn. "I'm thinking he picks up hobbies to pass the time."

"Probably." Quinn holds out a heaping plate of food. "Here, eat this so we can go play GTA! He's got the latest one."

She takes the plate from him and rolls her eyes. "What are you, twelve? I thought you outgrew Grand Theft Auto when you hit puberty."

"No, I got distracted by sex when I hit puberty," he says with a smirk. "Now that I get all the sex I want, I wouldn't mind playing video games occasionally."

She makes a sound of mock outrage. "After a comment like that, I hope you're not expecting sex from me anytime soon!"

That makes him laugh. "If you can beat me at GTA, you can pick the next game we play," he offers.

"How about I just—"

The sound of the knocker on the front door ends their playful banter, making both of them fall silent.

"Should we answer it?" Quinn whispers, even though there's no way the person at the door can hear them way back in the kitchen.

"I don't know," Kalli answers. She chews her lip for a moment, then decides. "We should at least tell whoever is there that Soren isn't home."

"Yeah, we could even take a message or something," Quinn agrees. He follows her through the living and stands right behind her as she opens the door enough to see who's outside. Before she can even get a word out, the smell hits her, and she slams the heavy door shut, gasping in fear.

Pale, Quinn looks at her with wide eyes. "Is that . . .?"

Wordlessly, she nods her head. Whatever followed them yesterday is out there.

Oh shit! What if she just closed the door on someone innocent and trapped them out there with a monster?

But what if whoever is knocking is the monster?

She can tell by the look on his face that Quinn followed her thought process because he's shaking his head. "We can't leave someone out there to get eaten by whatever that thing is."

"We don't know who's standing there," she points out quickly. She smelled and reacted but didn't have time to look at whoever knocked on the door.

"What the fuck!" the guy on the other side of the door shouts, outrage clear in his voice. "Who the hell are you two and where the fuck is Soren?"

"He sounds pissed," Quinn whispers.

"Of course he's pissed. I slammed the door in his face," Kalli hisses. "Should I open it again?"

"Yes, you should open it and invite me in," the voice calls out dryly. "My name's Memphis Granger. I'm a good friend of Soren's. As long as you haven't murdered Soren and buried him in that stupid night garden, you're safe from me."

Kalli exchanges a guilty look with Quinn, then slowly opens the door. The man standing in front of her isn't anything like what she expects a friend of Soren to look like. Short-cropped, deep brown hair covers his head. A thick, bushy, russet-colored beard covers most of the man's face. If that wasn't enough to give him a rough look, his leather pants, black t-shirt, and leather vest are doing the trick.

Trying to be subtle about it, Kalli leans forward and takes a sniff. The scent is gone. Whatever monster is out there has moved away or is smart enough to move downwind.

If it's smart enough to stalk them for miles, then it's probably still out there and masking its scent. Reaching out, she grabs the guy's forearm and pulls him in, slamming the door behind him.

"Whoa there, little girl," he says as he gets his balance back after almost running into Quinn. Memphis eyes her appreciatively. "You're awfully strong for your size."

"Runs in the family," she mutters. There are long windows on either side of the door, only a few inches wide. The glass is distorting, but if Kalli presses her face close, she can see a small portion of the area. Nothing in her restricted field of vision moves, but she can't relax.

Memphis's motorcycle is parked right in front of the house. She's surprised they didn't hear it earlier. This house must have superb sound insulation. Memphis is lucky that the lurking beast didn't make a snack out of him as he rode up the long drive to get here. She knows she smelled that thing again. The scent was strong, so it must be close.

Shaking her head, she gives up on seeing anything and straightens away from the narrow windows.

"Everything okay here?" Memphis asks, eyeing her with concern.

"I, uh, thought I saw a bear," she stammers out.

Memphis's eyes go wide. "No shit? Huh, well I guess I'll stay indoors for a bit. Might even crash here for the night. I've got no interest in tangling with a bear. Especially not one around here." Memphis looks around as if searching for something. "Hey, where is Mr. Tall-And-Pale anyway?"

Quinn laughs, and Memphis's eyes move from one to the other. His smile goes from friendly to flirtatious. "You guys are like a matched set. Kinda cute. Are you two staying with Soren?"

Kalli moves to Quinn's side, wrapping her arm around his waist, clearly staking her own claim on her mate. This isn't the first time one or both of them have been hit on. She isn't insulted, but she is quick with a rebuttal.

She holds up her free hand with one finger up. "We're together, not siblings. That would be gross." She holds up a second finger and gives him a cheeky grin. "Hell yes, we're cute. You can look, but don't touch." That causes Memphis to bark out a laugh as she brings up her third finger. "We haven't seen Soren today. He left a note saying he had to go to town, and he'll be back soon. But we're here so don't try to steal any of his shit."

Memphis cocks his head thoughtfully. "You can't have been here long and you're already being all protective of Soren's stuff? That's sweet."

Something about Memphis makes Kalli wary. Quinn must feel the same way because he moves to stand a little in front of her, half blocking her from the large biker. Memphis might not be as tall as Soren, but he's wide and so densely muscled that she's not sure he has a neck. He makes her think of a bull, solid and dangerous.

Neither of them fear him. If he gets violent, then all they need to do is run into the woods and shift. He'll never catch them.

Except there's something out in the woods. Something powerful and frightening.

With an impatient sound, Memphis walks past them, heading to the kitchen. They follow him silently. It doesn't escape Kalli's notice that once they're in the kitchen, Quinn positions himself next to the knife block. Memphis ignores both of them in favor of opening the fridge.

"Nice, he's got the good stuff," he mutters as he pulls out a bottle of beer, then opens it with his bare hand, flipping the cap on the counter. He takes a long draw of the beer, swallowing half the contents in one go. Then he regards the two of them, smirking when he sees Quinn next to the knives.

He leans back against the counter and strokes his beard. "I know you have no reason to believe me, but I'm no threat to either of you."

"How did you and Soren meet?" Kalli asks. "You two seem very . . . different."

"Naw, we're fucking doppelgangers," Memphis retorts with a grin. "My three-piece suit is at the fucking cleaners." Quinn gives him a half-smile, but Kalli doesn't bother.

"No, really, how did you two become friends? Did you guys grow up next door to each other or something?" Quinn pushes.

Kalli's not surprised at Quinn's questions. She wants to know more about this guy so she can better find out if Memphis is a threat. Quinn wants to know because people fascinate him.

Memphis's expression hardens. "When we met, it wasn't my finest hour. I got myself in over my head, and Soren helped me out." Before Kalli can ask what kind of trouble, Memphis shakes his head. "Nope, that's all I'm saying." He finishes the beer, sets it on the counter with a click, then gets another out of the fridge.

"Hey, those are Soren's," Quinn protests a moment before Kalli can. Both of them are thinking the same thing:

resources are meant for family and pack, not outsiders. Until Soren says differently, this man is an outsider.

"It's a beer. Trust me, it won't break his bank," Memphis says. Then his eyes narrow a little. "What are your guys' names, anyway? Or should I just call you Boy and Girl?"

"I'm Kalli, and that's Quinn," she tells him.

"Last names?" Memphis pushes.

"Smith," she tells him without inflection.

Memphis grins. "Ha, that's funny. I guess that's fine if you don't want to tell me. Just so you know, I'm not a criminal or anything. I work in law enforcement, kinda."

"Kinda?" Quinn asks.

"I'm a bounty hunter."

Kalli feels herself get tense. She's at Quinn's side without realizing she moved there. When the pack couldn't find them, they employed bounty hunters, claiming that Kalli and Quinn were underage runaways. Keeping ahead of those bounty hunters is one of the things that drove them into the forest.

She presses against Quinn's side. By the tension in his body, she can tell he's ready to run. "Keep your distance, Mr. Granger. We'll keep ours."

"Whoa there, I've never seen either of you before, Kalli and Quinn Smith. As far as I know, there are no warrants with your names or faces on them. I only hunt down the really bad guys. I'm not interested in penny-ante shit like shoplifting."

Kalli almost smiles at that. He thinks they're small-time crooks. She feels Quinn's body relax slightly.

"Just keep in mind that we're much stronger than we look," Kalli warns him.

"I won't dare forget it," Memphis states, much too seriously. She feels like he's trying to placate them. "What should we do while we're waiting for Soren? He's got some nice shit on the third floor. We could go play GTA or COD."

"I'm up for playing either," Quinn says with genuine enthusiasm. He nods his head at Kalli. "She only wants to play Mario Kart."

"Well, hell, son, let's get those games fired up and shoot some shit," Memphis says and strides off. Kalli and Quinn trail after him, still cautious but not scared. Memphis and Quinn chat about their favorite games and why they like them.

Quinn admits he loves ramming things with his car in GTA and Memphis explains how much he enjoys shooting Nazis in the original Call of Duty but gets a kick out of the Black Ops version. Especially Black Ops II, where there are multiple endings available depending on the choices the player made. Memphis even brags about a few high scores he's gotten playing later versions of Black Ops online in a last man standing Battle Royal. Their conversation makes Kalli roll her eyes and grin.

In the end, up playing Mario Kart.

Memphis watches the wolves carefully without trying to be obvious about it. As they did when they were out in the woods, the two work seamlessly as a team. With an ease that the military wishes it could duplicate, they effortlessly read each other's body language and facial expressions. When they felt threatened, Quinn stepped in front of his female without hesitation. But Memphis isn't fooled. Kalli is as big a threat as Quinn.

With that quick mind and shrewd eyes, she might be more of a threat than her larger mate.

The important thing is that he's not getting the impression that either of them are being held here under thrall. After watching the house most of the day, he'd started getting worried. Why hadn't either of them even peeked out a door or window? Sure, the temperature dropped today, but for a couple of wolves, weather in the forties is nothing.

Worries that Soren might have gone against his promise and either locked them up or stifled them with thrall had filled Memphis. Finally, his concerns pushed him to knock on the door.

Originally, he was going to get a look at them and leave, claiming he'd come back to visit Soren another time. His unease distracted him enough to make him forget to mask his scent. Catching the slight whiff of chimera, even if unfamiliar with his kind, is a clear signal of danger to any shifter. The female reacted faster than he expected, surprising him with her speed. Then surprising him again with the way she pulled him away from perceived danger. It's not something many would do for a stranger that looks like him.

"This is so much fun," Kalli sings out as she mashes her thumbs on the controller. "It's been years since we've gotten to play Mario Kart."

"GTA next," Quinn reminds her. That was the deal. A couple of games of Mario Kart, then on to GTA. It was interesting to watch the two negotiate. They never got upset with each other. They talked with a reasonableness far beyond their twenty-three years.

They also teased each other mercilessly. He can see why Soren mentioned that they act like childhood friends that became lovers. Chimeras are like vampires in so far as they don't pair off with their own kind. But unlike chimera, who don't mind the company of other chimeras, vampires almost never even hang out with other vampires. In fact, Soren was paying a rare visit to a powerful vampire named Darius when he ran across Memphis getting his ass kicked. Soren swooped in, slaughtered the whole nest, and carried Memphis to a safe place.

That was several years ago, and the two of them have been good friends ever since.

He's downstairs getting another beer when his phone buzzes, alerting him to a text. Returning to the third-floor rec room, he slumps onto the comfy couch to watch Quinn and Kalli play. His hands are free, and the wolves are distracted, so he pulls out his phone to check.

Soren: *I'm awake.*

It's about an hour until sunset. And although the first floor is safe for Soren, it's probably wiser that he stays hidden in the basement for a little longer. Kalli's a perceptive one and might notice if Soren has to dodge an open door or winces when he looks up the stairs to the brightly lit second floor.

Memphis: *The wolves are good. We're hanging out.*
Soren: *You're in the house?*

Oh, he can hear the outrage in those words.
Memphis: *Yup.*

Soren: *GET AWAY FROM THEM! MINE!*

Memphis: *We're playing fucking Mario Kart, fang face. Keep your cool. Nothing happening. Nothing fun anyway.*

"Ha! Take that." Kalli crows as she throws a fist up in the air. Quinn laughs and knocks her over. The controller goes flying, and Memphis snags it out of the air as the two wolves wrestle. Then Quinn is on top of her, tickling her without mercy until she's gasping and begging him to stop.

Feeling like a voyeur but unable to look away, Memphis watches the play turn sexual as they kiss. They're so focused on each other they've forgotten that he's in the room.

Somehow their kissing is both sweet and sexually raw at the same time. The smell of Kalli's arousal hits his nose. It's subtle but there.

He needs out of this room now. Forget worrying about Soren's secret being discovered. The vampire needs to take over with these two before Memphis does something they'll all regret.

Memphis: *Meet you on the first floor. Now. Sun is almost set so the first floor will be safe at the moment.*

"I think I heard the garage door," Memphis comments, startling the two lovers. Yeah, he didn't even exist during their little make-out session. Fuck his life.

The sad fact is that he has a woman. He has a mate. But damned if she'll let him get close to her. He doesn't even know her real name. Only her voice and the nickname he gave her— Baby Doll Hacker. He's getting so desperate to find her that he might even resort to asking one of his brothers if they can help, although the thought of Lex doing anything in connection to Baby Doll makes his skin itch with aggravation.

"Oh, uh, sorry," Quinn says, scrambling to his feet, face flushed and a hard-on straining against the fabric of his pants. He holds his hand out to help Kalli to her feet.

"I didn't hear anything," she says.

"You were distracted," Memphis points out wryly and enjoys her blush. Now both wolves have matching red stains on the dark skin of their cheeks. The last hour spent in their company hits him hard. His chimera has been itching to hunt down Baby Doll. His patience is worn thin and being around so much love and intimacy is making him want to bed everyone and anyone just to see if he can make the pulsing need inside himself stop.

The urge is so strong he has to turn and get away from them before he betrays his only genuine friend, Soren, and his future mate, Baby Doll. They aren't even his and he's not that interested, but his chimera mating reflex was triggered a few months ago the first time he talked to the mysterious hacker, and now it's clambering to claim and fuck.

He's already down the first flight of stairs before the wolves catch up with him, concern on their faces. "Yup," he declares a little too loudly. "I know I heard the garage door. It's got to be Soren."

Dressed immaculately, Soren meets them at the bottom of the stairs. Memphis watches his friend's face light up with happiness at the sight of the wolves.

"Hi, Soren," Quinn calls out as he jumps down the last few stairs, Kalli right behind him. "You've been gone all day."

"You hungry? We could make you something?" Kalli offers. She also jumps down the last few stairs. Instead of hitting the wood of the first floor, she lands on her lover's back. Quinn grunts, and then reaches back to help support this mate even as he teases her.

"You mean I can make something, and you can sit there and look pretty?" he questions, looking at her over his shoulder.

"Well, we all have our talents," she shoots back.

"Unfortunately, one of my meetings included an early dinner, so I'm stuffed," Soren tells them. It's an easy lie, but it makes Memphis want to growl.

He wants Soren to tell them. Stop pretending to be human. Stop playing around. Show them his power and mark them. Right now, they're vulnerable. Soren's mark or Memphis's scent would stop everything but the most determined predator from coming anywhere near them.

Stifling his discontent grumbling, he realizes where his mind went and feels a bolt of shame go through him. Looking up, he meets Soren's knowing gaze.

"You were right," he mumbles, making the two wolves go silent. They'd been chatting away about the third floor, unaware of the silent dialogue between him and Soren. Oblivious to the two powerful males, one who wants to claim them and the other who wants to fuck them, hoping to fill a void. Soren gives him a sympathetic but knowing look, making Memphis feel like he has to repeat those damning words. "Fucker, you were right. I should've kept my distance."

"You can stay for dinner too," Quinn offers, looking concerned. "You definitely shouldn't try to ride your bike anywhere. You've had, what, an entire six-pack?" Quinn looks over at Soren. "He should spend the night, right?"

Soren grins. "Inviting people into my house and offering one of my guest beds for me now?"

When her mate goes silent with worry that he's overstepped, Kalli jumps in. "He's your friend. You should look after him."

Her words and tone are aggressive, and Memphis feels touched. Kalli is coming to Quinn's defense and demanding hospitality on Memphis's behalf. This one is a caretaker.

"Perhaps," Soren says, looking between the two wolves and Memphis with barely concealed hostility. "The three of you seem to have become fast friends while I was gone."

Kalli rolls her eyes. "Guy comes to your door looking for you, but then there was a bear, and we didn't want him to get mauled. Now, he's guzzled down a bunch of your fancy beers and probably shouldn't ride his bike. Up to you if you want to toss your buddy out in the gloom and see if he makes it home in one piece."

Quinn winces at her mildly aggravated tone. "Kalli, it's not our place to tell anyone what to do." His admonishment is gentle, and instead of getting upset, Kalli shrugs, unconcerned.

"Whatever. Come on Quinn, let's go make dinner. Let these two hash out their weirdness on their own."

Quinn grins, walking away with no problem from his added burden as his mate remains clinging to his back. They disappear into the kitchen and Soren's warm smile disappears.

"What do you think you were doing with my flock?"

"Not your flock yet," Memphis taunts. You would think he'd know better by now, but old habits die hard. The "yet" is barely out of his mouth before Soren has him by the throat, lifting him several feet off the ground with ease. Magic saturates the air around them, making his skin feel like it's being eaten alive by ants.

"They. Are. Mine." Soren grits out.

"Yours," Memphis gasps out. Soren lets go, dropping him to the floor.

It takes more than a chokehold and rough magic to cow a chimera, but Memphis feels honestly guilty over the taunt. Soren is walking a very fine line between keeping the two wolves with him and not taking away their will. Honestly, the vampire is doing a good job of seducing Kalli and Quinn. It's easy to tell when others are being held under thrall. They look dazed and drugged, reacting sluggishly or not reacting at all.

Soren might have used his power to get them to travel to his estate and help them calm, but he's certainly not using it to compromise their free will. He shouldn't taunt the man.

Once he gets his balance, he shakes his head ruefully. "Sorry, Soren. I didn't mean that. They are your flock. It's only a matter of time."

Soren pulls him into a rough hug, and Memphis returns the embrace. "Thank you for looking after them, my friend."

"There's something else I need to tell you," Memphis warns as they separate. "Stephen Marks is on the West Coast. I think he might be heading here."

Soren's reaction is predictable. Anger takes over his features and his hands curl into tight fists. "When?"

"Got to the US sometime last week. Landed in Seattle, but after that, I don't know where he went. I thought you should know."

"He's risking a lot," Soren comments. "Coming anywhere near my territory."

"Look on the bright side. Maybe someone else will take him out for us," Memphis says. Although he's pretty sure that the two of them could take down Marks if they had to, it's not something Memphis is eager to try. "I'll keep in touch with the clans and flocks in the area. If he comes near here, we have plenty of people to call for backup. He's made a lot of enemies over the years."

"You're right. This isn't all on me," Soren says, almost to himself.

Along with the sounds of Kalli and Quinn talking, the smell of food drifts out from the kitchen. Memphis realizes he's starving. Seeing his hopeful glance in the direction of the kitchen, Soren's tension breaks.

"Come on, let's see what my wolves are cooking up," he says with a pat on Memphis's back that almost sends the chimera into a wall.

With friends like these . . .

Quinn feels odd.

Odd and a little guilty. The source of the guilt is easy to figure out. For so long, it's only been Kalli. The perfect girl. His best friend. His mate. But now he keeps staring at Soren. Staring and feeling a strange longing twisting his gut. He's never felt attracted to anyone but Kalli. Not even another female. When his parents paraded eligible girls through the house hoping to break his adoration of Kalli, he didn't give any of them a second look. None of them were right. They didn't look right. Or smell right. Or sound right. Only Kalli was right.

But now he's sitting across from Soren, and he keeps finding himself staring at the man's hands. He might be wearing a three-piece suit. His hair might be perfectly styled and his manners impeccable. But he's got scars on his hands. The kind of scars someone gets from doing repetitive hard labor day after day.

Soren's past isn't one of wealth and privilege. How did he go from sheepherding and being homeschooled to owning so much? He mentioned his father owned all this, but a man that owns this wouldn't be herding sheep for a living.

Could it have been a lover, not a father that lifted Soren from poverty to wealth? That would make more sense. And it would explain why Soren is being so secretive. Among humans, there's still a lot of prejudice against same-sex couples. And don't some humans call their partners Daddy? He's not familiar with that kink, but he isn't naïve either.

Wolves are more liberal concerning sex and sexuality because more often than not, mating is about political and social connections, not love. Enjoying many lovers and engaging in a lot of different kinds of sex is expected while young because once they're matched with a mate chosen by their family, cheating isn't just a strict taboo, it can be a death sentence. That means that young wolves are encouraged to have fun while they can.

Despite the tradition of taking multiple partners and trying anything and everything out, he never explored his sexuality with anyone but Kalli. He's never felt aroused by anyone else. But for the first time, he feels drawn to someone besides her, and it's low-key freaking him out.

"Hey," Kalli whispers, nudging his shoulder. "What's wrong?"

"Nothing." He winces the moment the word comes out of his mouth sounding defensive.

He drops his gaze to his empty plate to avoid seeing Kalli's expression. They all finished dinner recently and Memphis and Soren are chatting about some kind of festival scheduled to start next weekend. Quinn's been mostly silent during the meal. Probably because he's been trying not to stare at Soren.

When Kalli doesn't respond to his one-word answer right away, he risks a glance up. She doesn't look angry. She looks . . . interested? Then she leans close, putting her mouth right up to his ear.

"You want him too, don't you?" Both her whispered words and the feel of her soft lips against his ear make the erection he was mostly keeping in check rage out of control. He pulls in a sharp breath and goose flesh breaks out all over his body. Kalli knows what she did because when she moves away, he sees a satisfied smile on her face.

Then her expression turns serious. "Me too," she admits, sliding her eyes over to Soren and then back to him.

"Yeah?" Quinn breathes out, feeling relief roll through him. Thank the goddess, it isn't only him.

"There's something here," she says.

"Did you hear something, Kalli?" Soren asks, worry on his face.

Quinn watches Kalli blush a little and shake her head. She wasn't exaggerating when she said she's feeling something too, because Kalli isn't one to blush easily. He's the blusher of the two of them, not her.

"Nothing like that. Quinn and I were talking about something."

"Judging by the naughty look on your face, I want to know what it was you two were talking about," Soren teases. His tone and smile are lighthearted, but Quinn can see something more in his eyes. A kind of longing.

Could he want them too? Or maybe he only wants Kalli.

But if he had a male lover before, maybe he only wants Quinn?

Quinn feels himself scowling at that idea. No, they do everything together or not at all. If Soren wants to fool around, then he gets both of them or nothing. He and Kalli won't be separated or played against each other. Their families already tried that, and it failed. This man they barely know doesn't have a chance.

"Quinn?" Soren's gentle voice brings him out of his thoughts. He focuses on the large man to find everyone at the table staring at him. Kalli is rubbing a hand on his back and even she looks a little concerned. "Are you okay? You look upset."

"Kalli is the love of my life," Quinn blurts out. Everyone at the table has a different reaction to those words. Kalli's expression turns tender and loving. Memphis snorts out a laugh, and Soren blinks in confusion.

"It's okay, Quinn," Kalli murmurs to him, accurately following his thought process. "No one's going to separate us." Her words must have been a revelation to Soren because his expression goes from confusion to resolute.

"Of course, no one's going to separate the two of you," he announces. "Who could be so cruel? You two share a unique bond. A kind of love that endures no matter the obstacles. Yours is a relationship to be admired, cherished, and protected, not torn asunder."

There's a beat of silence after Soren's heartfelt words; then Memphis says in a scoffing tone, "Torn asunder? That's some Shakespearean shit right there."

That makes both Kalli and Quinn laugh, while Soren casts an annoyed look at his friend. "I'm sorry if these two make me wax poetic and your small brain can't comprehend my brilliant words."

Soren's retort only makes them laugh harder. Memphis's expression goes from smirk to frown. "I think that was an insult."

"I wouldn't do that if I were you," Soren mocks with a half-grin. "Thinking isn't your strong suit."

The banter continues until Kalli gets up to clear the table. Then Soren jumps up with an expression that looks almost panicked. "Oh no, *annwyl*. I can do that."

He and Kalli startle at both Soren's quick actions and the unfamiliar word. Before either of them can say anything, he's swept up the dirty plates and hurried to the kitchen sink.

"What does that mean? *Annwyl*?" Kalli asks.

"And while we're on the topic, what does *cariad* mean?" Quinn jumps in to ask. "You've used that word a few times too."

To Quinn's surprise, Soren seems embarrassed. The big man makes a show of running water in the sink as he mumbles. "They're both terms of endearment in Welsh. *Annwyl* is beloved and *cariad* means love or sweetheart."

"You're from Wales? I don't hear an accent," Quinn presses. Maybe if his parents immigrated to the US with no funds or support network, they ended up deep in the countryside, working the land to eke out the most bare bones existence.

Or maybe they were criminals, hiding off-grid to keep from being found. Fearful that any misstep would bring them to the attention of local authorities, and they would be deported back to Wales to stand trial for their crimes.

And if that happened, Soren could have been adopted by an American couple. That would explain how he started poor and ended up with a rich father!

Yes, Quinn can see it all now. Soren's father got into an impassioned argument with his brother. Suddenly, there was a gun and a struggle. It goes off. One brother is dead and the other must flee. The scene unfolds in his head like a movie, including Soren's shocked mother, clutching baby Soren to her chest, and sobbing with the horror of it all.

Kalli nudges him and smirks. "Come back to reality."

She knows where his mind goes, and she's reminding him that reality is usually far more mundane than his rampaging imagination leads him to believe. He's asked some odd questions in the past because his brain found a random path to follow instead of being logical and sticking to plausible explanations.

That strange shape in the distance was a rock worn down by weather, not a sasquatch foraging for food.

The scream turned out to be birds mating, not a woman being murdered.

When hearing hoofbeats, he's one to think about zebras, not horses. He'd be embarrassed by his thought process if it didn't keep him so entertained, despite Kalli constantly trying to interject realism.

As usual, when Soren explains, the truth isn't exceptional.

"My parents immigrated from Wales, but I was born here in the US," he explains easily, his earlier awkwardness and embarrassment evaporating. Whatever triggers they stumbled on moments ago that made him jump up from the table don't appear to be tied in with his family because he's relaxed as he gives them that tidbit of information.

When Quinn opens his mouth to ask more questions, Soren shakes his head. "I'd rather not waste time talking about them or my childhood. It was all very mundane, including the small farm I grew up on. My parents liked to live a simple life and be self-sufficient as they had lived back in Wales. To them, America represented opportunity, but they soon found out you can be just as poor here as you were back home."

"Sounds like it might have been idyllic for some," Kalli offers carefully.

His expression shutters a little, but then it's gone, and he smiles. "Perhaps. But enough of that. Why don't you two start a fire in the den? I'll be there in a moment after I've cleaned up here," he suggests before either of them can ask any more questions.

"Sure, I guess," Kalli answers hesitantly, eyeing Soren with confusion. Quinn feels the same. He doesn't feel threatened by Soren, but he feels like he's missing something. Something more than this gorgeous male lusting after one or both of them.

"Come on, you guys. I'll show you where the den is and help you get a fire going," Memphis offers as he stands and stretches his bulky arms over his head. The man is built like a brick shithouse. Any female or male who ends up under him in bed might accidentally get smothered if they aren't careful. That thought makes Quinn grin and Memphis catches it.

"What the hell is so funny?" Memphis asks with a smile of his own.

"You're going to teach two seasoned campers how to build a fire?" he teases.

Memphis makes a *harrumph* sound. "Fine, then I'll show you the den and where the damn lighter is. Or do I need to go searching for a flint and striker?"

The den turns out to have the biggest fireplace Quinn has ever seen. He's pretty sure Kalli could walk into it without ducking. There's plenty of paper and kindling, along with good sized logs sitting on the stone hearth. Memphis leaves Quinn and Kalli to "build the damn fire," claiming he needs another beer.

The moment they're alone, Quinn and Kalli talk in hushed tones as they work in concert to lay everything out on the fire grate.

"You feel it too?" Kalli asks right away.

Quinn doesn't need to ask her to elaborate. "I think I'm attracted to Soren. It feels weird."

"It's like a draw, right? Like you want to snuggle up to him and start kissing. A little like . . ."

"Like it was for us, yeah," Quinn admits. "It feels like when we were fourteen and we first started fooling around but different."

"I know what you mean," Kalli agrees. "I feel a pull to him. Not in the same way as I feel for you, but similar. It's hard to describe."

"We talked about leaving at the end of the week, but do you think we should stay longer?" Quinn asks. That idea has been running around in his head ever since Soren casually mentioned the winter celebrations in the area and that they should stay so they can experience them.

"I want to," Kalli says slowly, as if considering it from all angles. "But if he kicks us out in the dead of winter, it's going to be tough to get somewhere warmer. I don't want to hitchhike unless we have no other choice."

Her caution is justified. The first year they camped, they got caught by an early first snow. They were forced to hitchhike south and ended up having to defend themselves against a couple of men who thought the young couple would be easy prey. Humans can be deadly when they're armed, and one man had a gun. Quinn broke his arm before he got to the weapon, but that entire episode made the two of them reluctant to try hitchhiking again.

"I don't think he'd kick us out," Quinn states with more confidence than he feels.

"Probably not, but it's still a risk," Kalli warns him. "We've got to decide if we want to take the risk. I borrowed his computer to check out the weather. They're predicting snow next week. We either need to leave by Friday or we're staying."

"Okay, that gives us two days to decide," Quinn says. "That's cutting it close, but with all the food and rest we're getting, we could do the miles."

"What are you two discussing with such serious expressions?" Soren asks as he walks into the room with Memphis right behind him with a half-empty beer. "And where's the fire? I thought it would be roaring by now."

"Almost ready," Kalli says brightly as she touches the lighter to some paper.

"We were talking about that winter stuff you told us about at dinner," Quinn says. He watches Soren's face light up with delight.

"Does that mean you two are considering wintering here? I promise you won't regret it. This place is beautiful in the snow, and it would be much safer to spend your winter here than on the trail."

"We haven't decided yet," Kalli warns him. "But we're thinking about it." It makes Quinn's heart break a little when Soren's expression deflates.

Then Memphis speaks up. "Quinn and Kalli might be worried that they won't be able to leave after it snows. Hiking in those kinds of conditions is dangerous, even for . . . uh, skilled backpackers."

Quinn gets the feeling that Memphis was going to say something else but stopped himself. A fission of worry goes through him. Is Memphis more than he seems? Or does Memphis know what he and Kalli are? Or maybe he was going to reference their youth and then got worried about offending them.

The idea that Memphis might be trying to be diplomatic makes Quinn grin.

Soren's expression lightens at Memphis's words. "Oh, is that what you're afraid of? Then let me alleviate that fear!" He hurries out of the room. When he returns, he shoves a wad of cash into Kalli's hands. She holds it stiffly, staring first at the roll of what looks like hundred-dollar bills and then up to Soren.

Memphis was taking a sip of beer when Soren shoved the cash at Kalli. He ends up choking on his sip and sputtering. "Soren, man, you can't do that."

Soren looks confused. "What? Why? There's enough there so that they could purchase tickets to go south if they decide to leave before winter is over. It solves the problem of them feeling trapped."

Kalli holds the money out to him. "We can't take this."

Crossing his arms, Soren frowns at her and takes a step back. "You have to accept it. It's a gift."

Those words make Kalli flinch. Among wolves, it's a deadly insult to refuse a gift. There are ways around it, but outright refusal is considered highly offensive.

"What if we don't end up leaving?" Quinn asks, trying to find a way to give the money back without directly refusing it.

"Then you can use it to buy things," Soren says dismissively. "I have plenty of wealth. That cash is just something I keep on hand."

Quinn eyes the roll of money. There are probably several thousand dollars there, and Soren's treating it like it's the dollar bills Quinn's family kept in a jar next to the front door, for when someone found miscellaneous money in a pocket.

"Maybe they could work for you. Earn the money," Memphis suggests. "You've been thinking of doing stuff to the garden. They could help you."

"During winter?" Kalli questions, the dubious expression on her face probably mirroring his own. They exchange a quick look, and he knows they're on the same page.

"The garden is already going dormant," Soren dismisses with a thoughtful look. "But you make a good point. I want to redecorate the entire house. If you two stay, you can help me."

Quinn likes this idea. They might not be skilled labor, but both of them are strong and eager. They could strip wallpaper, paint, and haul furniture around. He glances at Kalli, and they have one of their quick, wordless conversations. She likes the idea too.

"You take this back now," Kalli says, waving the roll of money in the air. "Then you can pay us when the work is done."

Memphis leans over, plucks the money from Kalli's hand, and sets it on the table next to the chair he's lounging in. "We'll leave it there. If you guys need it, you take it. Problem solved."

Kalli stares at the money, then looks at Memphis. Finally, her gaze moves to Soren. It surprises Quinn that neither Kalli nor he feel the need to get to their feet, even with the tall man looming over them. He might be big, but neither of them feels threatened at all. He feels . . . familiar. Safe.

"We're willing to stay and help for room and board," she tells him.

He doesn't give the money another glance in favor of looking back and forth between the two of them, excited. "Very well. But Memphis is right, take the money any time. We can leave it there and either of you can use it as necessary." He pauses and gives the two of them a brilliant smile. "I'm so happy you're staying."

Something in Quinn shifts and calms. Almost as if there was a tension that was suddenly released. That feeling tells him this was the right decision to make. That they are meant to be here. Meant to be with Soren.

For the first time in three years, he's looking forward to winter.

Soren is ecstatic. They've decided to stay. The first hurdle has been overcome. Then he catches Memphis's expression, and his excitement dims a little. They're going to get suspicious quickly when they never see him in the daylight. He's going to be forced to reveal himself sooner rather than later.

And their reaction to finding out he's a vampire will probably go badly.

He takes a seat on a large, dark-brown, leather wingback chair next to Memphis and rubs a hand over his face. Quinn and Kalli remain sitting in front of the rapidly growing fire, talking seriously about what colors he might like best. Later he can fetch his laptop and they can look at colors and furniture. For now, he's enjoying the two of them arguing over shades of blue.

"It might be fine," Memphis whispers to him.

"Or they might run away screaming," Soren whispers back. "But I can't let them leave. I can't."

"Control yourself," Memphis orders, and Soren knows his eyes are turning red. It happens when he's feeling powerful emotions. He takes a few deep breaths and focuses on getting his emotions under control. Memphis reaches out and smacks his shoulder. "It's only the second night. Calm the hell down."

"You have a point," Soren agrees.

Memphis's expression turns conniving. "I'll tell them I'm dog tired and hide out in the second guest room. That'll give you all some privacy down here. Get the seduction going. Some petting. Kissing. Don't go too far. Leave them wanting. Leave them needy. I know the boy is already responding to you. Use him to draw the girl in."

"That is a brilliant plan," Soren says, making Memphis laugh and drawing the wolves' attention.

"Let us in on the joke," Kalli demands with a grin.

"Soren's favorite color is pink," Memphis declares.

Soren groans. "No, it's not. Don't listen to a word he says. Look at him. The man has no taste."

Soren isn't surprised when Quinn jumps in to soothe ruffled feathers. "He might not be our style, but I'm sure someone out there would find him perfect."

Memphis pretends to look down at himself, examining his outfit. "I'll have you know that my style is 100% unfiltered, unadulterated, pure bad ass."

"It's bad something," Soren mutters. Even Memphis laughs at that one.

Standing up with his empty beer bottle dangling from his fingers, Memphis gives an exaggerated yawn. "I'm hitting the sack. See y'all tomorrow."

"Night," the two wolves chorus together. Memphis gives them a nod and walks out.

"I think I might like to get some contemporary artwork," Soren tells them after Memphis closes the door to the den behind him.

Kalli's eyes light up. "That would be great! I know many people see art as a good financial investment, but you should collect things you enjoy."

"Investment?" Soren asks.

"Kalli knows all about that stuff," Quinn says proudly.

But Kalli shakes her head. "I know a little about that stuff."

"She's smart," Quinn states and looks over his shoulder with a little frown at Kalli, as if admonishing her for being overly modest. "She wanted to go to college and study business and finance. She would have been brilliant at it." There's a hint of regret in his voice.

"Eh, it all probably would have ended up the same," Kalli tells him with a grin. "It's not like I would've been allowed to run anything, even after I got a fancy degree. You know how it was. Besides," she scoots closer to him and wraps her arms around his waist. Leaning her front against his back, she gives him a tight hug, then relaxes into that position. "I'm right where I want to be."

While the two of them are distracted, Soren takes advantage of the opportunity to move closer. Kalli was leaning against an ottoman before she moved forward to rest on Quinn. He moves to sit on the low ottoman right behind her. Carefully, he stretches his long legs out on either side of the two of them. Bracketing the two of them with his legs.

Kalli turns her head slightly so she can smile up at him. "Wanted to get closer to the fire?"

"Yes, I was cold," he responds honestly. He's been cold for decades.

Kalli scoots back and drags Quinn with her. She doesn't stop until her back is against the ottoman and Soren's thighs are even with her shoulders.

He expects that to be the end of her movement, but Kalli surprises him. Quinn remains still while she reaches up and grabs Soren's hands where they're resting on his knees. She drags his arms out until they're draped over Quinn's shoulder, forcing Soren to lean over. Now his upper body looms over Kalli, and between his torso, legs, arms, and Quinn's body, she's completely boxed in.

She wraps her arms back around Quinn and snuggles tightly against him. "This is nice."

Quinn was stiff when Kalli first put Soren's arms on him, but he relaxes a little and tilts his head to rest one cheek on Soren's forearm. "Yeah, it is."

Soren thought he was going to need to seduce these two, but it looks like they've already started the process.

Craving more contact, he forces himself to lift his arms so he can stand up and kick the ottoman away. Then he sits on the thick rug behind Kalli and reaches forward, wrapping his arms over where Kalli's are wrapped around Quinn's torso. He pulls the two of them back, so Kalli is slightly squished between him and Quinn.

Kalli squeaks in surprise, and Quinn grunts. Worried he might have used too much pressure, Soren relaxes his hold a little, ready to retreat completely if either wolf protests.

"You're strong," Kalli comments.

Had he used more strength than an average human would have? "I'm a big guy."

"True that," Kalli says as she wiggles against him.

His half-hard cock takes notice and floods with blood. Now it's his turn to grunt as his pants suddenly become much too tight.

Kalli gives a little sigh of contentment once she gets comfortable. She slides her hands up until they're covering Soren's on Quinn's chest. Quinn jerks and makes a little choking sound.

"Is this okay, Quinn?" Soren asks.

"Yeah, very okay," Quinn assures him.

There is a needy quality to Quinn's voice that makes Soren grin. "Excellent."

They sit like that for a bit, watching the crackling fire. Just like on the bench in the garden, the warmth of these two wolves chases away the cold. He should be content with this, but a small set of scars on Kalli's neck draws his attention.

He knows they're claiming bites. He's seen them on Quinn's neck as well. They're a physical manifestation of the couple's bond. The marks are beautiful, and he wants to touch them. Giving in to temptation, he tips his head down and places a butterfly kiss on Kalli's mark.

Kalli gives a little gasp, and the sudden smell of her arousal fills his nose. It couldn't be clearer that the mating marks are a strong erogenous zone for the young wolf. Eager for more, he opens his mouth and bites down gently on the mark. She jerks as if touched with a live wire, then moans. Quinn pulls away so he can turn around and see what's going on.

Soren raises his gaze to meet Quinn's eyes, half expecting to see outrage on Quinn's face, but there's nothing there but eagerness and lust.

"Me too," Quinn demands as he gets closer. He bites down gently where Soren's teeth were a moment ago and Kalli jerks again and whimpers.

"Please," she whispers.

"Please what, *cariad*?" Soren questions. Quinn abandons her claiming scar in favor of kissing a line up her jaw. When he takes Kalli's lips in a deep kiss, Soren licks his own lips in anticipation. "May I join you?" he asks when they separate.

"Yes," Kalli whispers, but she doesn't offer him her lips. She nudges Quinn toward Soren. "I want to watch."

Quinn looks hesitant but lustful, so Soren takes the invitation and captures the young man's lips with his own. He's careful at first, keeping his natural dominance in check for fear of frightening Quinn. But he shouldn't have worried. The wolf reacts with eagerness and when Soren pushes the kiss a little further, it causes Quinn to sound a muffled moan.

When they part, Kalli is there, claiming Soren's mouth before he can even open his eyes. Her soft lips are demanding at first, but then yield when he takes command of the kiss.

He feels Kalli jerk a little and breaks off the kiss to find Quinn is wrestling with the opening to her pants. She moves her legs and lifts her hips to help him. Because Quinn didn't remove her shoes first, her jeans and panties end up gathered at her ankles. Quinn lays down between her legs, his belly pins her pants to the floor and traps her.

"You smell so good, Kalli," he whispers. Soren has to agree. Both wolves smell delicious. He wishes he could be forward enough to demand Quinn strip out of his clothes, but contents himself with making Kalli the bridge between them for now.

"Both of you are beautiful," Soren comments.

Kalli turns her head and lays a gentle kiss on Soren's chin. He ducks down to capture her mouth, one hand moving under her shirt to cup a breast. She's not wearing a bra and her warm, soft flesh fills his hand.

She whimpers against his mouth and moves restlessly. He stops kissing her and thinks he should move away because she's upset. Quinn's voice stops him.

"She's impatient," he says, looking up at Soren from his place between her legs. His pupils are blown, and his wolf canines are peeking out a little. A testament to how aroused he is. "Don't stop or let her go." He reaches up and grabs her chin, forcing her to meet his eyes. "You'll come when we want you to come, understand?"

She whimpers again and nods her head.

He licks his lips. "Good girl."

Soren is delighted by this revelation. He knows better than to judge someone's sexual preferences by the way they interact in public, but he wouldn't have guessed Kalli would be a submissive bed partner. All kinds of images of things he could do to her fills his head.

But not yet. For now, he follows Quinn's lead as they dominate Kalli together.

Quinn lets go of her chin and drops his hand back down between her legs. Soren watches as he parts her wet folds to reveal glistening pink flesh. Quinn dips his head and makes a quick pass over her with his tongue. She bucks, trying to get her hips up to follow his mouth.

"So impatient," Quinn murmurs playfully.

Finally understanding this game, Soren circles his long arms around her and holds her tight against this chest. "I can see she's never learned the fine art of delayed gratification."

Quinn shoots him a lustful grin. "She always needs practice."

Soren drops his lips to Kalli's ear. "I wish I could be in Quinn's place," he whispers. "I want to be lapping at that sweet pussy. I want to taste and torment you."

As he talks, he gets his hand back under her shirt. This time, when he finds her breast, he isn't as gentle. He squeezes until he gets a reaction, then backs off, only to do it again. Quinn continues to torment her sex with light touches and quick strokes. Soon she's bucking, panting, and sweating, begging both of them for release.

"Does she deserve it, Quinn?" Soren asks. "Does she deserve to come, or should we keep her on the edge all night?"

His question makes her cry out in protest and struggle in earnest for a moment. Quinn punishes her with a nip to her inner thigh.

"Quiet you!" he orders her, voice heavy with need. "But even if she doesn't deserve it yet, I do," Quinn answers, getting on his knees and frantically pulling at the closure of his pants. Soren watches with appreciation as Quinn's cock springs free.

He's not as big as Soren, but he's perfect. Lovely brown flesh, turgid and throbbing. Soren fights the urge to wrap his hand around Quinn's erection and see if he can make the boy moan and writhe just like Kalli.

But he ignores the impulse, worried that he might spook the young man. He contents himself with tormenting Kalli's nipples.

Quinn grabs her legs and pulls her, so she ends up sliding out of Soren's grip until her back is resting on the rug under them. He rips away her shoes and pants, then hooks her legs over his shoulders. Restlessly, she moves her hips up and down in the air, trying to urge him to go faster. He positions himself at the opening of her sex. Soren watches with envy as Quinn slides into her heat with a moan of pleasure.

Although he wants to keep touching them, Soren holds himself back. It's one of the hardest things he's ever done. Then Quinn reaches up and grabs him by the back of the neck, drawing him close for a kiss.

Surprised and excited that Quinn wants to include him in more than the early seduction phase, Soren lets Quinn control the kiss, startled by the level of aggression in the young man.

Quinn tastes and feels so good that it makes Soren groan. When Quinn drops his hand away from Soren and tries to withdraw, the big vampire isn't ready for the kiss to end yet.

He grabs Quinn by the back of the neck, his broad hand almost completely covering all the flesh there. His grip is firm but not hurtful. The young wolf could easily pull away if he wanted to. Quinn doesn't even try. He gasps in a little breath, but then relaxes into his hold, letting Soren take charge.

That tells him that Quinn might be interested in submitting to him. How amazing would it be to have both of them doing as he ordered? Both of them at his mercy—to torment and pleasure at his leisure.

The thought fills him with excitement.

Under them, Kalli whines. "I want some too!"

They break apart with a chuckle. Soren releases Quinn's neck, letting the wolf lean back. Quinn pulls away from Kalli, then grabs her legs. Easing them off his shoulders, he uses his grip on her thighs to drag her away from Soren a little, then flips her over with ease. Now on hands and knees, she wantonly thrusts her ass at Quinn with a pleading whine. "Quiiinnnn!"

"None of that," Quinn says with a smack to her ass. "Now kiss Soren so he doesn't feel left out."

Kalli looks up at him and smiles. "Hi, Soren," she says.

"Hi, beautiful," he whispers and leans over to kiss her. She tastes like a warm summer day. Like honey and fresh spring water. He attacks her mouth, forcing the kiss deeper. She moans low in her throat, and he withdraws just enough to nip at her bottom lip.

"I love the sounds you make," he tells her.

"More," she demands, trying to lean closer to him, even though Quinn has a firm hold on her hips. Her eyes move down, and she sees the bulge in his pants. "Or I could kiss that beast. Bring him out to play, and I'll lick him all over and slide him down my throat."

He wants it. He wants it almost as much as he wants his next breath. But Memphis's words about leaving them wanting filters through his head.

"Not yet, sweetheart," he tells her. She pouts, but then cries out as Quinn pushes into her hard.

"Fuck yes!" she nearly screams, and Soren almost comes in his pants. Quinn's face is tense with concentration as he works himself in and out of his mate. She lowers her head and braces her forearms on the rug to gain hold against Quinn's thrusts. But he doesn't go wild. He keeps his thrusts slow and measured, making her beg and buck under him.

"Touch her," Quinn pants. "Touch her, Soren. See what sounds you can make come out of her mouth."

"With pleasure." Soren moves to her side and reaches under until he can feel the soft curls at the apex of her legs. He slides his finger along her folds, feeling her flesh pulled taut around Quinn's cock. Quinn gasps as Soren takes a moment to run his fingers over that firm, velvety flesh of Quinn's shaft as the young man moves against his mate.

"Oh Goddess," he mutters as Soren adds a little pressure by pinching his thumb and first finger around Quinn at the opening of Kalli's sex. Quinn's pace picks up a little, and Soren enjoys the way the wolf's hard cock slides through his hand, coating him in Kalli's natural lubricant.

Then he twists his hand enough to use the heel to put pressure on her sensitive clit, making Kalli buck. Both wolves grind against his hand, and his head fills with all kinds of dirty things he can do to them in the future.

Quinn's pace turns frantic, and Soren knows he's close. Moving a little, he finds Kalli's little nub of pleasure with his other hand. Now he has one hand on Quinn and the other on Kalli. The position is awkward, but he doesn't care because both of them are moaning from his efforts.

When he lets a little magic flow through his hands, they both jerk and gasp. Quinn's shocked eyes meet his.

"Please," Quinn whispers, and his pace falters for a moment. "Please, goddess, move like that again."

They're so far gone they don't realize he used magic. Grinning, Soren does it again. And again. And again. Both Quinn and Kalli are making needy noises and begging him for more. He puts a little more power into the next pulse and makes it last longer. The wolves' reactions arc immediate and exhilarating. They both scream as they orgasm. Soren can't see Kalli's face, but Quinn looks like he's feeling pleasure so intense it borders on painful. Both go rigid as they shudder and sob through the bliss. He dials down the magic and keeps sending tiny bursts of power, trying to draw out their orgasms as much as he can.

It's with great reluctance that he withdraws his hands after he's sure that he's wrung out as much pleasure as he can from these two.

Kalli collapses down on her stomach with a groan, leaving her mate on his knees, shiny cock slowly softening. Without Kalli to support him, a stunned Quinn teeters on his knees. Hands that had been holding his mate's hips are now grasping air. Dazed, he almost falls backwards, but Soren grabs him up and pulls him tight to his body.

"Easy, I've got you," Soren murmurs as he sits back and pulls Quinn into his lap. Kalli rolls over and curls at the waist until her head is resting on Soren's leg. She makes a contented sound and rubs her cheek on his pants leg as if he's a pillow. Quinn's eyes have also fallen shut, and his head is resting on Soren's shoulder.

Satisfaction is coming off both wolves in waves. Ignoring his own unrequited lust, he remains there, petting Kalli's head and holding Quinn against his chest. It's not until the fire dies down and a chill invades the room that he gently wakes Quinn.

"Bedtime, sweetheart," he whispers to the young man. "If you can walk, I'll carry Kalli."

He helps Quinn to his feet without disturbing Kalli's head on his lap. Then he gathers Kalli in his arms and stands.

Kalli murmurs something but doesn't open her eyes. Quinn leans against him, his eyes mostly closed. One hand holds up his undone pants and the other is wrapped around Soren's waist. This is so similar to that first evening in the garden that Soren can only hope it becomes a trend. What could be better than putting his wolves to bed each night, sated and sleepy?

Except perhaps joining them in that bed each night.

It's an awkward journey up the stairs to their room, but they manage without incident. He lays Kalli out on the bed and strips off her shirt that got bunched up around her neck and one arm. It's the only article of clothing she's still wearing. With absolutely no grace, Quinn flops down next to her. At least he's more helpful when Soren strips him of his shoes, sagging pants, and shirt.

When they're both naked, he tucks them in. He watches with longing as Quinn curls himself around Kalli and snuggles her close. She makes a soft, cheerful sound.

"You two are going to sleep now," he says, pushing a little magic into his words. He's not using thrall. His words will only have an effect if it's something they're willing to do. "Sleep late into the day. Wake up slowly. Make love. Shower. Take your time. It will make me happy if you don't end up coming downstairs until late afternoon. Memphis will be here to keep you safe. I'll be with both of you as soon as I'm able."

He kisses each of them one last time and then leaves the room, closing the doors quietly behind him.

Memphis is standing in the hall wearing his boxers and nothing else. He smells strongly of liquor, and his expression is both fatigued and tense. "I had to jerk myself off three times," he says to Soren, his tone grumpy but teasing. "Next time all that fucking needs to be done down in your basement or I need to leave."

Soren gives him an unabashed grin. "Only three? I'll try to do better next time."

Memphis shakes his head and runs his hand through his short-cropped hair. "Asshole. I'm going back to bed."

Apprehension hits Soren. He grabs Memphis's arm in a light grip. Memphis gives him a questioning look. "You're going to be here tomorrow, correct? To look after them while I sleep?"

"They're going to stay," Memphis points out gently. "They already agreed to stay through the winter. You don't need me to babysit anymore."

"One more day," Soren begs. "Give me one more day of you guarding them. Then I'll figure something else out."

Memphis sighs and nods his head. "Sure, I'll stick around another day. I have nothing else going on. But I don't think it's necessary."

"Thank you, my friend," Soren says and lets go of Memphis.

The chimera shoots him a lazy grin. "But you better order more of that fancy ass beer. I'm not a cheap date."

Smiling, Soren nods. "I'll put in another grocery order. It'll arrive tomorrow."

"Good," Memphis grunts and heads back into his room with a jaw-cracking yawn. "'Night, bloodsucker."

Soren isn't even paying attention to the chimera any longer. He's thinking about his wolves. Along with the groceries, maybe he should order a few things for the pups from the local stores. New shoes. Some better coats. Things they'll need for the coming snow.

He spends the rest of the night online, ordering everything that catches his eye and looking forward to making his wolves happy.

Memphis wakes up feeling like shit. It's not the first time and probably won't be the last. Squinting at the bright, late afternoon sunlight streaming in through the window, he fumbles on the nightstand for his phone. It's not there.

Then he remembers he stayed up most of the night watching porn on his phone and jerking off, trying very hard not to let Kalli or Quinn's face pop into his mind. Then he thought of his faceless Baby Doll and her perfect voice and things only got worse because then he was horny and frustrated.

Eventually, he'd given up and found a bottle of high-end vodka.

His phone is on the floor next to the bed, the empty vodka bottle resting against it. Chimeras have a good alcohol tolerance, but polishing off an entire bottle is a lot, even for him. He groans as he gets up, rubbing his face, and tries to figure out if his head really is splitting in two or only feels like it.

Stumbling to his feet, he hits the shower, feeling marginally better after soaping off the smell of alcohol from his skin. Brushing his teeth takes away the taste of roadkill and gulping down at least a gallon of water straight from the sink helps the headache.

He puts on the same clothes, which even he is getting tired of, and checks his phone. The thing's dead, so he plugs it in and heads out of the room. Seeing the wide-open door to the wolves' room stops him cold. They should still be asleep, shouldn't they?

Several long strides put him in the room and cursing as he takes in the empty room with a neatly made bed. Their packs are still on the floor, so they haven't taken off. That's good news. But where the hell are they?

He thunders down the stairs, calling out loud enough to wake the dead. Maybe not the dead, but he rouses the undead because Soren meets him on the first floor.

The vampire is nude, hair mussed and eyes hazy from being woken so abruptly with the sun still in the sky. "What's going on? Why are you yelling?"

"They're gone," Memphis says and doesn't stop moving as he heads to the kitchen. He knows even before he gets there that they aren't in the house. He can feel it.

He sees a piece of paper on the counter and grabs it.

Soren and Memphis,

You guys must be real night owls because you sleep so late! We woke up and decided to go for a hike. We'll be back before dark.

-Kalli and Quinn
PS: Somebody else needs to cook dinner tonight. We'll clean.

Memphis takes a deep breath, trying to calm his racing heart. They didn't run off; they went for a hike. That's all.

Impatient, Soren snatches the note from Memphis, but he doesn't stop scowling. "You let them leave on their own?"

"They're wolves. They can't be stuck inside all day. They need to get out and roam. Explore the area. They'll be fine," Memphis assures him, meandering to the fridge to look for a snack.

Soren grabs him before he can pick out anything and shoves him roughly toward the back door. "Go out and find them. They're out there alone! Anything could happen."

Memphis is about to push him away when he sees the absolute panic on Soren's face. "Easy, they're smart wolves. They've spent a lot of time in the woods on their own."

"But Marks could be out there. Or a naga from Black Butte could be in the forest hunting. A couple of young wolves on their own would be easy pickings."

Soren's eyes are blood red, and a dark tear slides out of one of them. It leaves a black trail down Soren's face.

Memphis has never seen a vampire shed a tear before. The sight of that lone tear is as startling as it is heart-wrenching.

"Calm the fuck down. I'll go out and find them. I'll even herd them back if they're straying too far north. But nagas aren't a threat this late in the season. You know they only go out in summer."

"But there are so many other things," Soren says, and Memphis can tell a reel of gruesome images is flashing through the vampire's brain.

Resigned, Memphis grabs a bottle of water and a small block of cheese, then heads out the back door. "Order me some damn clothes," he calls out over his shoulder. "It looks like I'm going to be here a while if you're going to go all protective every time they try to step out of the damn house, so I'll need a change of wardrobe."

"Hurry!" Soren yells after him.

It only takes Memphis a minute to pick up the wolves' tracks. They followed a narrow footpath until they got to a well-used trail that skirts the western edge of Soren's property. Memphis munches on his cheese as he follows them, regretting not grabbing more food. There better be something damn good for dinner or there'll be hell to pay.

Then he runs across their clothing. The two must have stripped and bundled up their clothes to tuck them high in a tree. After hiking and sweating in them, the clothes smell too strongly for him to miss. They must have stripped and stored their clothes so they could shift and run the forest on paws instead of feet. That makes sense. Wolf shifters don't like going too long in their human skin. That can make them grouchy and antsy.

This makes his job harder. It's unlikely they stayed on the path while in their wolf forms. And in their fur, it will be a lot easier for them to notice his presence. He doesn't want to shift himself because then it will be harder for him to hide his scent.

Frustrated, hungry, thirsty, and feeling unusually indecisive, his next move is decided for him when he hears rustling in the undergrowth.

He barely has enough time to scamper up a nearby tree before two enormous wolves burst onto the path only ten feet from where he was standing. They shouldn't smell him. He's in the habit of masking even his human scent when he's tracking, but if he's not still, they would see him. It's not like he's small. If they look up in the wrong direction, there will be no mistaking his bulk for a bird or a squirrel.

The two wolves are panting, tongues lolling out the side of their mouths. The smaller one gives the bigger one a nip on the rump and then dances away. He bets that one is Kalli. Mellow Quinn ignores her in favor of a whole body shake to clear sticks, leaves, and dirt from his coat. Then he shifts, standing up to stretch after he's done.

"Come on, Kalli. We should head back. And because you're the one who tucked our clothes up so high, you get to go up and get them."

Kalli shifts, grinning up at him. "Give me a boost?"

Stepping up to her, he circles her with his arms and reaches around to grab her butt and lifts her a few inches off the ground.

She laughs and slaps his hands away. Then lifts her foot. He crouches and links his hands together and she slides her foot in. He lifts as Kalli jumps. They move in perfect concert and Kalli flies up, landing gracefully on a high, thick branch. She reaches up, grabs the bundle, and tosses it back down to Quinn. Then she follows the bundle, landing soundlessly on dainty feet next to her male.

"Do you want to talk about last night?" Quinn asks as he picks up the bundle and starts unwrapping it.

"Do we need to?" Kalli responds. Both are avoiding each other's eyes. Now Memphis is glad Soren pushed him out the door. There might be hurt feelings or jealousy that needs to be dealt with.

Quin nods. "I think we should."

"Okay."

Neither speaks. They both stare at the clothes in Quinn's hands. With a huff, Kalli grabs the bundle and separates her clothes, shoving the rest back at Quinn.

"I liked it," she states, and Memphis can hear the challenge in her voice. "I thought you were into it too."

"You're not upset?" Quinn asks softly, making Kalli look up with a startled expression, her pants still unzipped.

"Of course not. Why would I be upset?"

"Because I let him touch you and you're my mate," Quinn says finally. "And I let him touch me and I belong to you."

"Oh," Kalli says as a relieved smile takes over from the earlier tension and she finishes closing up her pants. "Is that what you were worried about?"

"Well, yeah," Quinn says a little defensively. "It's my job to keep you safe, and I basically laid you out to . . ."

"Get laid?" she finishes for him. After a beat of silence, they both snicker.

"It was good," she says as she pulls on her top. "We both wanted it. I guess all three of us wanted it. Although I'm still sad I didn't get to see Soren's dick. I think he might be packing a monster away. With any luck, I'll get another chance."

"Does that mean we keep doing this?" Quinn asks, and Memphis can hear the hopefulness in his voice.

"Duh," she teases him, then sobers. "This is us. We don't do jealousy or insecurity. You've been my everything since we were five. Remember?"

"I remember you pushed me down and stole my ring-pop," he retorts, but then pulls her into a rough hug, letting his clothes fall to the ground.

"That was *our* ring-pop, and you were hogging it," she counters, and they both chuckle. "I don't know why, but Soren feels right. Adding him doesn't take anything away from us. If anything, it allows for more. More love. More affection."

"More cocks for you to play with," he adds, and she playfully shoves him away.

"Whatever. But don't think I didn't notice you liked his attention just as much as I did. I bet you're wondering what his mouth would feel like on your dick. Or maybe you're ready for it to go further?"

To Memphis's surprise, Quinn doesn't reject her suggestion outright. But then again, wolves are some of the randiest shifters he's ever met. If any male shifter is going to be open with experimenting, it's going to be a young wolf.

"Maybe," he finally says and scoops up his pants, shaking them out before he puts them on. "It's weird, but I feel relaxed here. Safer than anywhere we've stayed before."

"I know what you mean," she agrees. "Something about Soren and this place feels . . . right? Does that sound stupid?"

"No, because I've been thinking the same thing," Quinn admits. Then he gives her a playful shove while she's trying to button up her flannel over-shirt. Unprepared, she ends up hopping around for a moment, then gets her balance and sticks her tongue out at him.

They keep chatting about Soren and sex as they finish dressing and then start down the narrow path back to the house. It's obvious these two are already half in love with the big vampire, and Memphis couldn't be happier for him.

Now the thing Soren needs to do is get his butt in gear and claim these two, because Memphis isn't too keen about climbing any more trees.

Even though Soren knows he's being overly dramatic, he can't help himself. The moment Kalli and Quinn emerge from the mudroom at the back of the house, he grabs them up in a tight hug. He can feel their legs dangling as Kalli makes a surprised sound. Neither fights his hold, but they can't hug him back because he's got their arms trapped at their sides.

It's only when he hears Memphis bang his way in through the front door that he thinks about setting the two down.

"Yo! Where is everybody? I'm starving, goddamn it!" Memphis announces as he stomps through the foyer and down the hall toward them. By the time the chimera hits the kitchen, both wolves are wiggling in his grip and chortling.

"I can't cook like this," Quinn says, red-faced from laughing.

"You're not cooking," Soren announces, deciding what to do on the spur of the moment. "The note you two left specifically states that you do not wish to cook dinner today. That means we're going out for dinner." He looks over to Memphis. His friend looks sweaty, dirty, hungry, and, above all else, thoroughly irritated. "Would you like to join us?"

"Do I have clothes?" he asks sourly.

"Yes, you left a change of clothes here a while back and I had them laundered for you," Soren answers.

Memphis looks surprised and then grins. "In that case, I guess I can join y'all for dinner."

The reason Memphis had left clothes with Soren was because he'd gone into rut unexpectedly with no available females lined up to take care of his needs.

Soren's house was the only one far enough away from people, so he wasn't triggered into fucking or fighting some unwitting victim. Soren was glad to help since his power was strong enough to keep Memphis subdued. He was forced to keep Memphis in a stupor for three days, which wasn't fun for either of them. But at least he could help the chimera through a difficult few days.

Hopefully, next time, Memphis will find a partner, or four, to take care of him during his rut. Soren doesn't want to be forced to magically incapacitate the chimera again. Even though it saved both Memphis and others, it's not something the vampire wants to do to his friends.

"But right now, I need a snack," Memphis says, drawing Soren out of his memories as the chimera is fishing a beer out of the fridge. Does the man ever drink water? At some point, even a chimera's body needs more than beer.

"Dinner out?" Both wolves look apprehensively at each other, pulling away from him. He has to fight the urge to grab them back. Soren is at a loss to understand their reaction. Bend is a safe town full of humans. There are only a few single families of shifters and no large groups. As far as he knows, there isn't even a skulk of foxes living there.

"The snow hasn't fallen yet, but it's too cold for hikers, so the town isn't getting much in the way of tourists," Memphis explains to Quinn and Kalli. Soren gives his friend a confused look, but the chimera ignores him and continues talking to the wolves. "Soren is all about going into town often when there aren't enough tourists. He's probably the reason a couple of businesses haven't folded over the years. I know he loves my dad's shop. He pops in there to pick stuff up all the time."

While it might be true that Memphis's chimera father runs a small store, it's a tourist trap full of cheap, gaudy items Soren would never consider buying. But then Kalli and Quinn's expressions lighten, and they nod with more enthusiasm.

"We didn't think about the shop owners," Kalli admits. "The time between summer and snow season has to be rough."

"Right, exactly," Memphis says. "So, help Bend out and spend a bunch of Soren's money on a nice dinner and whatever else catches your eyes. The more you spend, the better off all the places are. Even if you don't end up in my dad's shop."

Now Soren understands. The wolves were uncomfortable because they lack the funds to buy dinners at pricy restaurants. They didn't want him to spend money on them.

"If you guys are worried, you can use the money on the table in the den," Soren points out, feeling flummoxed over the necessity of Memphis's subterfuge.

"That's for emergencies," Kalli disagrees, and Quinn's expression tells Soren that the young man agrees with his mate.

Memphis gives him an irritated look, and Soren realizes that with one clueless sentence, he undid some of Memphis's hard work. Both wolves are standing tall, facing him with unsmiling expressions. He realizes their pride is involved here. That makes his irritation evaporate.

"I don't go out to eat often," he states, keeping his tone soft, as if lamenting a missed opportunity. "I don't enjoy sitting in a restaurant alone, and Memphis won't go with me because he says I make it impossible for him to pick up women. They're always drawn to me instead."

"Asshole," Memphis mutters under his breath. "You aren't that handsome."

"But if you guys don't want to be seen with me, I understand."

He must have hit the right cord because Kalli hurries to comfort him. "We'd love to go out if that's what you want to do."

Quinn is quick to agree. "We can go wherever you like. We're not picky eaters."

Soren knows he's probably smiling like a maniac, but he can't help it. He's going to get to take his wolves into town and show them off. It will be good for the nearby humans to see the three of them together. Humans might not see auras or distinguish smells like the magical community, but they'll instinctively feel Soren's claim on Kalli and Quinn. That will keep the two safe if they ever have to go into town without him.

He makes a mental list of the places to visit so the three of them are seen together, while Quinn wrinkles his nose and glances at the small digital display on the stove.

"Do we have time to clean up?" Quinn asks as he slides his eyes over to Memphis with a teasing smile curving his lips. "Or are you going to die of hunger if we take a shower?"

"Shit, son, we all need to get cleaned up. But I make no promises about my table manners if I'm kept waiting too long," Memphis shoots back with an affable grin. "Off you go and hurry it up. Shit, shower, and shave. Y'all got ten minutes."

Laughing, the wolves bustle out of the room, promising to be down in five.

"I'll call and make a reservation for four of us at seven," Soren calls after them. They make confirmation noises that they heard him as their light footfalls disappear up the stairs.

"We need to talk," Memphis says, opening a second beer.

"You need to drink things other than beer occasionally," Soren replies, eyeing the beer. "I worry about you sometimes."

"Whatever, bloodsucker. You're not the one who should lecture me on only consuming one type of liquid."

"Fair enough," Soren says. "I'm assuming you found them and followed them back?"

"They hiked out past your property line to shift and run in their fur," Memphis explains. "It's getting darker earlier, so pretty soon you'll only need to suffer eight or nine hours of being cooped up downstairs."

"Thank you for going out and finding them," Soren says, feeling a little guilty for forcing Memphis out the door earlier.

"No worries. I get it, you know?" Memphis finishes the second beer and belches. Soren rolls his eyes but can't stop the smile on his face.

Memphis winks at him. "What? We can't all be refined and prissy like you. Anyway, I overheard some of what they were talking about, and I think you're doing it right. The whole slow seduction thing is working. Both of them really like you.

Getting them to stay for the winter wasn't a hard sell, and they mentioned they like it here."

"They did? They do?" Soren feels like a teenager talking to his best friend about a crush. If he had more blood in his system, he'd probably be blushing.

"Yes, and yes," Memphis says with a chuckle. "And they talked about the fact that you make them feel safe."

That makes Soren feel a hundred feet tall. He stands up a little straighter and squares his shoulders, making Memphis laugh. But he doesn't care because his wolves trust him. "They are safe. I'll keep them safe."

"Sure, sure," Memphis says and sets the second empty beer bottle down. "I'm going to get cleaned up. Wherever you're taking me better have proper food. None of that fancy shit that isn't even two bites and you're done."

"I thought I'd take everyone to that steakhouse in Bend — The Brickhouse," Soren says with a questioning lift of his eyebrow.

Memphis perks up at that. "Oh yeah? Good choice." Then he snags one more beer, slams the fridge door shut, and saunters out.

"I'll leave a five-star review for Soren's Love Shack Inn," he comments over his shoulder. "You know, 'cus we're supporting local businesses and all. Can't wait to take them to my dad's place."

"I'm lucky your father's shop is already closed for the day," Soren mutters to Memphis's back. Memphis flips him the bird over his shoulder and cackles out a laugh as he disappears out of the kitchen.

It probably looked odd, but when they are led to their table at the Brickhouse, it has three chairs on one side and only one on the other. The wolves look perplexed, but Memphis barks out a laugh and makes himself comfortable in the lone chair.

Holding out a chair for Kalli, Soren seats her and then indicates where Quinn should sit. Both shifters bow to his wishes, almost as if they are already a flock. As he planned when he called and made a very specific table seating request with his reservation, he ends up sitting between Kalli and Quinn with Memphis across from the three of them.

Perfect.

Lots of practice has made Soren an expert at looking like he's eating, when all he's doing is cutting his food into small bites and shuffling it around his plate.

Eating out is probably one of his least favorite activities. But it's all worth it as he watches his wolves devour their meals. He even gets away with sliding some of his food onto Kalli's plate, claiming he isn't very hungry.

She doesn't stop him but does cast a worried glance at him and then at Quinn. The two do their wordless conversation thing, making Soren feel left out.

"Um, Soren, I . . ." Kalli starts then slides her glance to Memphis. "No, never mind, we can talk about it later."

"It's okay, *cariad*," Soren says quickly. "Whatever you need to ask is fine."

"No, it can wait," Kalli insists and tries not to look over at Memphis again. Either she needs to say something about Memphis or doesn't want to ask Soren a personal question in front of the man. But he can tell by the expression on both their faces that his wolves are concerned about something.

He wants to push, but that could backfire. Magic in public can attract the wrong kind of attention. Besides, she must have a good reason to be reticent, even if it's only because she's feeling shy with Memphis present.

"That's fine," he assures her, wrapping his arm around her shoulder and giving her a squeeze. "You can tell me when you're ready."

To his credit, the chimera ends up being a perfect dinner companion. He keeps the conversation flowing and anytime the wolves look reluctant to answer an innocent question, he fills in with a funny story or tale of adventure. Soren has to admit, he hasn't heard even half of these bounty hunter adventures before. He hopes for his friend's sake that most of them are exaggerated.

Dinner is almost over when Memphis's phone rings shrilly, making everyone at the table wince. "Sorry," he mutters as he digs it out of his pants. "Not too many people have this number, so if someone's calling, it's got to be important. The ring makes sure I don't miss it." He answers the call as he steps outside to speak to the person. An efficient server arrives to deliver the bill, and Soren holds out a card before she can even put it down.

"I guess we don't have to do dishes to earn our food tonight," Quinn quips, reaching across Soren's chest to poke Kalli. She grins and pretends to nip at his finger.

"We don't have to do dishes here at the restaurant, but nothing says we won't end up doing dishes back home," she points out.

Home. She referred to his place as home. That fills Soren with warmth. Suddenly, he wants to gather up his flock and get them home right away. Strip them down. Worship their bodies. Make them sob and scream with pleasure. And then he wants to draw them close to hold tight all night long.

"Would that be okay, Soren?" Quinn asks, and Soren realizes he missed some of the conversation.

Clearing his throat, he focuses his gaze on Quinn. "Could you repeat that?"

"There's a bookstore down the street, I'd like to see inside," Quinn says.

"Quinn has a fascination for heavy objects made from paper," Kalli comments. "Even back when he had a phone and tablet with book apps, he was always buying actual books like a weirdo."

"If you're referring to Dudley's, then yes, it's a pleasant, cozy bookstore but small. If you can't find what you want, we can always order it online," he tells Quinn, then turns his attention to Kalli. "And don't tease," he admonishes her. "Books, stories, and writing are one of the highest achievements of civilization."

She isn't fazed at all by his rebuke as she grins up at him. "I wouldn't mind if he didn't complain so much that they're too heavy to carry in our packs."

"And what did you like to fill your shelves with, if not books?" Soren asks her as he stands. The server hurries up with his card and the receipt to sign. He includes a large tip and guides his flock out the door and across the street.

"Kalli was 100% girly!" Quinn says, excited to share this bit of information. "She collected all this crystal and glass stuff."

For the first time, Kalli looks a little hurt. "I liked how it sparkled," she mutters, and Quinn's smile vanishes. He ducks out from under Soren's arm and pulls her into a tight hug. Because they're standing just outside the restaurant door, Soren gently shuffles them sideways so they're out of the path of foot traffic.

"I'm sorry, Kalli. I forgot," Quinn murmurs and kisses her on the forehead.

She looks close to tears. "It's fine. I'm being stupid."

Her tears make Soren feel frantic. "What happened? Tell me right now! Why are you upset?"

Both wolves startle at his words, and he realizes that he spoke much too loudly. He takes a deep breath and tries again. "Did something happen to your collection?"

"Nothing," she says quickly, knuckling away a tear and giving him a smile that's obviously forced. "It was a long time ago, anyway. We should head to the bookstore. And I want a hot chocolate."

He focuses on her immediate wishes. "Hot chocolate is an excellent idea. Dudley's has a coffee bar, so we can get both books and drinks at the same place. But I need a hug first," Soren tells her, and wraps his arms around both of his wolves, pulling them close. As if he can protect them from past emotional trauma with his bulk. They sound twin contented sighs and burrow against him for a moment.

Moron, Soren chastises himself silently. Of course, there are going to be terrible memories associated with the impractical items they were forced to leave behind with their family and pack.

Whether they were thrown out or ran away, it would've been a heart wrenching experience. Living out of backpacks meant they probably couldn't take anything sentimental with them. No favorite, well-worn books. No beloved glittery figurines.

That makes him think he should spend some time researching. Or maybe send Memphis on a fact-finding mission. The Volk is an easy pack to find, and Memphis is an excellent investigator. Better to be prepared in case the pack comes looking for his wolves than to be caught by surprise.

"Hey, Soren, I hate to interrupt," Memphis says softly as he walks up to them from where he was leaning against a light post and talking on his phone. "I've got to track someone down. It's a missing person. A kid."

Soren doesn't even hesitate. "Go," he orders. Because he had planned to stop by his own place after dinner, Memphis rode his bike into town instead of riding in the car with Soren and the wolves. He gives a sharp nod and hurries off to where his big, black Harley is leaning on its kickstand, perpendicular to the curb.

"He finds missing kids?" Kalli asks as the three of them watch Memphis shove a helmet on his head, mount the bike, retract the kickstand with his heel, start up the motor, and roar away.

"Not often, but sometimes. He's an amazing tracker, either in the woods or city."

"I hope he finds him or her," Quinn comments.

"He will," Soren assures him. "Memphis excels at what he does. I don't know many who are better than him. Now, books and hot chocolate."

They end up staying until the store is ready to close many hours later. That's one thing Soren appreciates about Bend. Even in the off-season between summer and snow, the place doesn't shut down early.

And even better is that with winter comes snow and winter sports enthusiasts. If anything, the town becomes livelier as the days get colder and shorter. Something a lonely vampire can appreciate.

Ignoring Quinn's protests, Soren buys every book he looks at for more than a minute. He desperately wants to buy Kalli something, but she only flips through a magazine. Then she spends the rest of the time sipping hot chocolate and reading through a stack of discarded newspapers.

Watching her read through the broadsheets while the woman seated not far away is tapping away at her laptop makes Soren realize that neither of his wolves has any electronics. No phones, tablets, or laptops.

He'll fix that. With the newest electronics in hand, Quinn can buy books whenever he wants, and Kalli can have access to any news source she wants.

And he'll order some figurines for Kalli. But that makes him think about the guest room and how poorly suited it is for these two vibrant wolves. They'll need to redecorate that room first, before the rest of the house. Mold it into a space that will make his wolves happy. Eventually, he wants them sleeping with him in the basement, but it's also important they have a place to retreat to if they want alone time.

When they leave the store, Soren is carrying two bags full of books, while Quinn carries two more. The young man is still protesting all the purchases when a tall, statuesque woman dressed in high heels, a pencil skirt, white blouse with a deep red, knee-length wool coat steps out in front of them, blocking the sidewalk.

Because Soren and Kalli were looking up, they stop in time, but Quinn was looking into one of the bags he's holding and keeps walking. Soren drops one of the bags he's holding and grabs Quinn by the collar of his shirt before he plows into the woman.

Soren gives the woman an apologetic smile as he picks his bag back up. "Excuse us."

When he tries to guide his wolves around the woman, she sidesteps, blocking them again.

Large blue eyes set in an angular face plead with him. "Please, Master Bowen, I need your help."

Only someone who knows he's a vampire would call him Master. Soren pushes his wolves behind him, unwilling to underestimate this woman, even though he's sure she's human.

He gives the stranger an unwelcoming look. "I don't know you, Miss, and I can't help you. Kindly step aside so we can pass. Don't make me move you."

"You're the only one we can go to," she insists, clasping her hands in front of her as if praying. "Stephen told me you're the only one to ask. That you're powerful enough to do it, and that you would care for the person and be patient. We can pay you. We can find donors, so the blood is fresh. Please—"

He nearly hisses in frustration as he feels both wolves go tense at her words. Damn it, he's not ready for them to find out he's a vampire yet. And he absolutely didn't want it revealed in the middle of a busy street.

Anxiety makes him push his magic at her. She drops into thrall easily. Her expression turns blank, and her hands fall limply to the side.

"You will step away now," he orders her.

Wordlessly, she nods her head and steps to the side, pushing herself up against a storefront to allow as much room as possible for the three of them to pass.

Soren drops the books in favor of reaching back to touch his wolves but finds they've both backed away from him. He turns to see them gazing at him warily, bodies tense, eyes darting around as if looking for the best escape routes.

No . . . NO! This is not how this ends!

He's fighting the instinct to shove his power at the two when a familiar figure appears behind them. The man grabs them up, one in each arm, and holds them tight against this body. Both wolves struggle, but they're no match for a vampire's strength, and the man holds them easily.

"Stephen, release my wolves," Soren orders, fear spiking through him, making him careless with his words.

"Swear to me you will listen to us," Stephen demands, black eyes narrow and determined. "Swear to me you will at least hear what we need from you."

"I swear it," Soren says without hesitation, desperate to have his wolves free.

At his words, Stephen releases Kalli and Quinn with a shove. They both stumble forward and Soren grabs them, holding them close and breathing in the combination of their fear, anxiety, and confusion.

"Please don't panic," he whispers. "Please, *cariad*, don't panic and leave me. Let me explain first, my sweet *annwyl*. My hearts, let me—"

"Tell your pet dogs to go home so we can talk," Stephen orders, interrupting Soren's pleas. Soren lifts his head to hiss at the man who might have destroyed the fragile trust he was building in one fell swoop.

When Memphis told him Stephen Marks was on the West Coast, he assumed the vampire was here to fight him. To attempt to kill him. But with this woman in tow, Soren thinks Stephen may have a different purpose for seeking one of the few vampires strong enough to potentially kill him in a one-on-one fight.

But if there's love involved, Soren can understand why Stephen would risk death. Love makes them all do strange things.

But understanding does not make him sympathetic. Stephen has way too many skeletons in the closet for Soren to ever feel sympathy for the vampire. And any goodwill Stephen might have earned by sending this woman to talk to him first was gone the moment he touched Kalli and Quinn.

"I'll listen to you, then I'll stake you out in my garden to greet the sun," he hisses. "Your ashes will feed my soil so at least you will have been useful once in your miserable life."

Quinn pushes at him. "Soren, let me go."

Kalli is making discontent sounds and struggling to get out of his grip too. It's only with great reluctance that Soren loosens his arm so both of them can duck away from him. He's relieved when the two of them only move a few feet away instead of turning and running.

He half expected to be chasing them down the street the moment they were free.

"You know?" Quinn asks, his voice barely above a whisper. "You know what we are?"

If Soren were human, he wouldn't have heard Quinn. "That you're wolf shifters? Yes, I know," Soren confirms.

"But you invited us into your home. You fed us," Kalli states, confusion making her frown. She glances down at the bags of books discarded on the ground at their feet. "You bought us things." She looks back up, her expression hard. "Is it so we would have sex with you? Is that what this is about? We're not whores."

"No!" Soren says quickly. He tries to keep his emotions in check. He doesn't want his eyes turning red in public. "It's not like that. It was never like that. I lo . . . I wanted to get to know you." Is it too soon to tell them he loves them? That they're everything to him?

Quinn's expression isn't as devastated as Kalli's. He looks suspicious but more open.

"What were you going to say?" he asks. "You changed your mind and said something else. What were you going to say originally?"

Soren can only hope his eyes aren't turning red from the intense emotions rampaging through him. "I love you."

The moment the words are out of his mouth, he mentally braces himself. Closing his eyes, he lets his shoulders slump, and he hangs his head, ready for their rejection. Ready for them to call him a soulless monster incapable of love.

"Do you? After only a few days?" Quinn asks gently.

Soren looks up to see Quinn's hand halting in the air. He stopped himself from reaching out to touch him. But his expression tells Soren that he's fighting the instinct to touch and comfort.

Hope flairs in Soren's chest.

"I loved you from the first moment I saw you," he states simply.

Kalli makes a little sound and Soren lets his eyes slide to hers. He can see her mind working quickly. Ever the clever one, her next question is voiced in a challenging tone.

"When you first saw us?" she states slowly, as if working something out in her head. "You mean when we knocked on your door?"

"No, when I found you in the woods. You were in my territory and lit a fire." He watches as fuzzy, buried memories surface. They both gasp and grab at each other.

"You were there at our campsite. You came out of nowhere," Kalli accuses. "You did something. Something to make us tired. And to make us forget."

"Just that once," he explains quickly. "I only put you in thrall that once." His statement doesn't make the situation better.

"Thrall," Quinn repeats slowly, as if he's coming to a realization. "You're a vampire?"

Had they not realized before? He waits for the looks of horror on their faces.

"Yes, he is, children," Stephen drawls behind them.

The two jump, having forgotten he was there. They step sideways to stand against the wall next to the black-haired woman. Now they can keep both vampires within sight. The move is pointless. He or Stephen could easily put the two of them in thrall before they could run away.

Kalli glances back and forth between Stephen and Soren as she rubs her neck. "You never bit us." It's a statement, not a question.

"I never did," Soren agrees. "I'd never do such a thing without permission. To my shame, I did it when I was younger, before there was bagged blood. Before I had better control. But never again."

She regards Stephen. "What about you? Do you bite people without permission?"

Stephen scoffs. "I'm not here to talk to pups."

"Answer her," Soren orders. "If you want something from me, you'll give her anything she asks for."

Stephen casts all them an annoyed look, then focuses on Kalli. Soren feels power rise, and he quickly charges his aura to snuff it out. Stephen gives a choked gasp. He gives Soren a surprised look.

"Do that again, and I promise you'll regret it," Soren warns him. "There's a reason you want my help, Stephen, and it's not because I'm weak."

For the first time, Stephen looks a little cowed. "Yes, of course."

He meets Kalli's gaze, his earlier sneer gone. "I've forced humans," he admits. "I usually look for willing donors or use bagged blood. It's so much easier. But sometimes, I want the hunt. I want to feel the fear. I want to hear their heart pound away as I puncture their skin."

"Do you kill them?" Quinn asks, clutching at Kalli. He looks scared. She looks angry.

"Sometimes. I try not to," Stephen says with a little careless shrug, gaining back some of his earlier confidence. "But sometimes the blood tastes too good to stop. Especially when it's young, sweet, shifter blood. Lynx or puma are the best, but wolves are good too." He licks his lips suggestively.

"Monster," Kalli spits out.

With a mocking laugh, Stephen points at Soren. "We can't all be preoccupied with questions of morality like this one. The truth of it is the cow never wants to be eaten. But if they are not a source of food, why would the farmer bother raising it?"

"Did you just compare us to cattle?" Quinn asks. There are twin expressions of outrage on both wolves' faces. If the situation wasn't so dire, Soren might have laughed.

Stephen bristles "Ba, why do I bother talking to either of you? This is a matter between vampires." He looks at Soren. "Send them home so we might discuss what I need."

Then Kalli does something wonderfully unexpected: she grabs Quinn's hand. They exchange a quick look, then the two of them step between him and Stephen.

"You're not going anywhere with Soren alone," she declares.

Her expression is all things stubborn. Quinn nods his head in agreement, and the two young wolves widen their legs and face down a vampire almost as old and nearly as powerful as Soren.

And unlike Soren, this vampire is much more likely to hurt, kill, and destroy innocence without a second thought.

Looking over her shoulder, Kalli winks at Soren. "We're not done with you yet," she warns him. "You still have some explaining to do. But we don't trust this guy and except for that first night, you've been kind to us."

"Does that mean you forgive me?" Soren asks, and he can't keep the desperate hope out of his voice.

"Not yet," Quinn says. "But we won't run off either. You're important, Soren. Something worth taking a chance for."

"My *annwyl!* My darlings," Soren cries, and he wants to embrace them both, but holds back because he doesn't want to make either of them uncomfortable. He's determined to show them how disciplined he can be. How restrained.

"Are we done with this," Stephen makes a disgusted sound as he moves his finger to indicate Soren and the wolves, "this overly dramatic sentimentality?"

"Asshole," Kalli mutters. Stephen glares at her but doesn't respond directly.

"You swore to listen to what I need," he reminds Soren. "Send these two off so we can talk."

As much as he hates to admit it, Stephen might have a point. It's safer to send Kalli and Quinn somewhere else for the moment. "Very well. Perhaps the two of you should—"

Kalli cuts him off. Her expression is fierce. "Didn't you hear me earlier? You're not going anywhere with this guy by yourself."

Again, she and Quinn face off with Stephen, keeping their bodies between the two vampires. Stephen looks annoyed, but Soren feels elated.

Giving in to the need to touch them, he drops to his knees behind them, wraps his long arms around their waists, and hugs them tightly so their lower backs are against his shoulders. They don't take their eyes off Stephen, but both of them place a single hand on his head.

"Thank you, my hearts," Soren whispers, and knows he needs to keep his eyes tightly shut because if he opens them, they will be bright red and shining.

Unwilling to let Stephen anywhere near his home, Soren has all of them find an empty back booth at a nearby bar. The place is half full and most of the patrons are gathered around the large TVs hanging on the wall near the front. He and Stephen both order wine they won't drink. Tiffany, the black-haired woman who first stopped them, orders some kind of cocktail, and his wolves refuse anything, even water.

They never stop staring at Stephen with suspicion, and although there's nothing either of them could do to stop the vampire, they keep themselves between him and Soren.

Soren lets them. It's not because he trusts Stephen. But rather because he knows the other vampire will be on his best behavior until he gets whatever it is he wants. Unfortunately, Soren is pretty sure he knows what Stephen wants, and he has no interest in providing it.

"Tiffany is one of my flock," Stephen explains.

That puzzles Soren. He casts a glance over at Tiffany. "She doesn't feel like you."

She doesn't look up to meet his gaze. Once Soren released her from his thrall, she started pleading with him again until Stephen stopped her by using thrall to keep her calm and quiet.

Soren doesn't approve, but it's not as if he can teach Stephen how to build long-term, trusting relationships. He's trying to figure that out himself.

"Let me rephrase that. She will be my flock once we turn her sister," Stephen amends.

Soren blinks for a moment. There's a lot to unpack in that single sentence. Before he can start asking questions, Stephen curses in French and starts talking again.

"Tiffany has a sister, Delilah. I want Tiffany for my flock. As you know, I can't do that when she's under thrall and she won't permit me otherwise. She's holding out because she wants her sister turned so she won't age and die."

"Why not add the sister to your flock?"

Stephen looks uncomfortable for a moment. It's the most human he's looked in decades. "Having both sisters in the same flock is a bad idea. They'll fight. They love each other, but they fight. All the time. Even so, Tiffany doesn't want to watch her sister grow old and die. So, if she's not going to be part of my flock, then I need someone to turn the sister."

"Why don't you turn them both?" Kalli asks. "Make them both vampires."

Fear flashes across Stephen's face and he grabs Tiffany's hand, bringing it to his lips and breathing in deeply through his nose. Tiffany, still under a mild thrall, smiles vaguely at him.

"I couldn't risk that," Stephan whispers, his voice muffled by Tiffany's hand. "I can't lose her. I can't."

"Turning someone into a vampire is dangerous and has a low success rate," Soren explains.

"How low?" Quinn asks.

"Less than ten percent," Soren says with a wince.

"How many people have you turned?" Kalli asks.

"None," he answers honestly.

Quinn leans forward a little. "Is that how many people you've tried to turn or how many successes you've had?"

Soren decides to be very clear. "I have never turned anyone. Ever. It's an uncertain procedure, and most newly turned vampires die within the first year. It's a hard life to survive."

"The guy that turned you, how many did he do?" Kalli questions.

Old sadness swamps Soren as he thinks of all the lives lost while he waited to grow powerful enough to challenge his maker, Matthew De Chambre. "Too many. Far too many. And I'm the only one who survived."

"Is there any risk involved in being made into a flock member?" Quinn asks as he eyes Tiffany with pity. "Whatever that is."

Soren shakes his head. "Not really. To make a flock member, a vampire shares a piece of his soul with another. That sharing makes the other person stronger, faster, more powerful, and they live for as long as the vampire lives. But they don't share in our weaknesses. Sunlight and silver don't affect them like it does us."

Now it's Kalli's turn. "Does sharing your soul make you weaker?"

"In some ways, yes. But in other ways, having a flock strengthens us." Neither wolf is happy with that explanation, so he elaborates.

"Someone could use a member of my flock to hurt me. I'll feel their pain, so it can be a debilitating distraction. And I can be severely incapacitated if a member of my flock is killed. But flock members also bring light to a vampire's life. They bring joy and a type of happiness that we often lose along with our humanity. A flock is a source of great comfort and delight. They are the ones that keep a vampire from becoming a mindless, killing monster."

Kalli and Quinn exchange a look; then she asks the next question. "And you can't force someone to be in your flock?"

"Never. It's a gift that must be freely given and willingly received. And the magical binding used to create a flock member is permanent. There's no taking it back later. If a vampire and any member of his flock are separated for too long, they both suffer and can even die. There's no such thing as a divorce or annulment."

"How many?" Quinn asks. Soren gives the young man a confused look, so the wolf elaborates. "How many in a flock?"

"Oh, well, that depends on the vampire, but I've rarely seen flocks of over five. Two or three is most common."

The two share another look, and Soren wishes he could hear what the hell they were saying to each other with all those meaningful glances.

"Is 'show and tell' over yet?" Stephen quips with a sneer.

Soren shakes his head at Stephen's rudeness. "Why are you so set on having me turn her? There are plenty of vampires out there that would do it. Hell, Hildegard would be downright eager. She'd pay you for the privilege."

"Because I know you'll succeed," Stephen says simply, and real affection shows on his face when he glances at Tiffany. "For all their bickering, Tiffany and her sister love each other. I want her to be happy with me and to do that, her sister needs to live as long as we do. The only answer is to have Delilah become a vampire."

Soren feels a modicum of regret. "Your impulse might come from a good place, but I can't. It's much too dangerous."

Stephen's expression turns cagey. He focuses on Tiffany for a moment, and Soren feels the other vampire's power flare. Tiffany's eyes close, and she slumps back against her chair. Stephen catches her before her limp body tumbles to the floor. He pulls her into his lap and cradles her like a small child.

When Stephen returns his gaze to Soren, his expression looks as if he's a poorly trained actor trying for sincerity. "I won't blame you if Delilah dies."

Soren sits back, his eyes narrow with suspicion. "You wouldn't blame me, or you wouldn't mind if Delilah dies?"

Stephen's expression turns cold and calculating. "I wouldn't mind if Delilah was gone. The woman winds Tiffany up. Makes her act crazy sometimes. But I won't kill her. Once she's flock, Tiffany would know. But if you try to turn her and she dies, then I did everything in my power to give her sister longevity of life. I've explained the risks to both sisters repeatedly, so they know it's a bad idea. But they're both convinced that making Delilah into a vampire is the only way they want to do this."

"You don't care that Delilah will probably die?" Quinn asks, condemnation in his tone.

Stephen's expression turns stony. "I care that I get Tiffany. That's it. Whatever I have to do to make that happen, I will do."

Soren opens his mouth to refuse Stephen again, but Kalli beats him to the punch.

"No," she says, standing up. "He's not doing it. He promised he'd listen to you, which he did. The listening part is done. Now it's your turn to hear him. He says no. That means you need to take your Tiffany and Delilah and go away. Leave our town and our state. If I see you again, I'll find some way to hurt you."

If Kalli's little speech hadn't caused Soren's mouth to fall open in shock, the way she grabs his hand and pulls him to his feet would have.

Quinn gets up and crowds close to his back, guarding him from behind. Together, the three of them walk out of the bar. Soren feels overwhelmed by the care and protectiveness his wolves are displaying.

Once they're outside, Kalli drags him to where they parked the car. Even if they worked together, Kalli and Quinn wouldn't be able to force him to do anything. Two wolf shifters are hardly a match for a vampire as powerful as he is. While he would happily let her drag him anywhere that she wants to, guilt makes him stop moving and pulls her up short.

"You two don't have to come home with me," he tells them softly, his heart breaking in two as he says the words. "I could get you a room here in town. I could visit and keep courting the two of you if you would let me."

"Is that what it's called, courting?" Quinn asks, his tone gentle.

"Sometimes," Soren admits. "The relationship between a vampire and his flock is close, intimate, and profound. It's more than dating or marriage. It's a sharing of a soul. It's the ultimate act of trust for a vampire."

"Now I feel like we should be courting you," Kalli teases him, and he feels a weight lift off his shoulders at the lightness of her tone.

"And I feel like we've been having all the fun so far," Quinn adds with a grin.

"Your pleasure is my pleasure," Soren assures them both.

Kalli's expression softens. "We're coming home with you. We aren't sure if we want to be a flock yet, but there's no way we're going to let you be unguarded with that Stephen guy around."

"We don't trust him," Quinn explains, his eyes sliding over to the bar where Stephen and Tiffany are still probably seated. "He's not done yet. We know his type. They're ruthless."

Soren doesn't have the heart to tell the two young wolves that there's little they could do against Stephen, but that doesn't matter. What's important is that they're willing to stay. Willing to give him a chance.

With no kind of signal that he can perceive, the two wolves step in close and clasp hands around him, trapping him between their smaller bodies. He lets out a bone-deep sigh and basks in their warmth.

"Yes," he says, even though they haven't asked anything of him. He's willing to agree to everything if it means they come home with him. It's all that simple. "Yes."

"We want to see your room," Kalli says the moment he steps into the main area of the house from the basement stairs. She and Quinn are standing shoulder to shoulder only a few feet from his door, expressions unreadable.

After they got back to the house the night before, she and Quinn retreated to their room. They didn't come back out.

He spent the night pacing at the bottom of the stairs, looking up at their closed door. His vampire hearing meant he could tell they were talking until the early hours of the morning, but he couldn't tell what they were saying.

He half expected to find them gone the next day, and even with the power of the sun flowing across the sky, he had a difficult time succumbing to sleep. He lay there, worry making his chest tight as images of them running away filled his mind.

But here they are, visible the moment he flings open the heavy, reinforced top door to his basement lair. He gives himself a few seconds to take them in, drinking in the sight of his beloved wolves.

Kalli with her shoulder-length, black hair pulled into a high ponytail. Her dark eyes are gleaming with an emotion he can't identify. Her lush, curvy body isn't tense, but she's not relaxed either. Her arms are crossed under her voluptuous breasts, pushing them high against her worn shirt. He's struck again at how beautiful she is.

Quinn stands next to her, tall and lean, the picture of shifter grace. His arms are held loosely at his sides, his shoulders back and his spine straight. While Kalli's stance looks impatient, he looks protective. Ready to spring into action to protect his mate.

Soren understands. Vampires have a reputation for being soulless monsters. Bloodthirsty, savage beasts who enjoy hurting others. It pains Soren to admit that many of his brethren are that bad, including the one that turned him. His maker, Matthew De Chambre, kidnapped him and thoroughly enjoyed the slow and torturous process of turning Soren into a vampire. Years have faded the memories, but not enough.

He tries very hard not to dwell on his rebirth, because over the course of only a few days, he lost everything. His family. His identity. His very life. And then he ended up as the property of a monster for decades.

Quinn and Kalli might have been mostly relaxed when they got home last time, but not any longer. Their long talk must have unearthed many concerns and fears. That would explain why they both have such severe expressions.

"You want to come downstairs?" he verifies, glancing over his shoulder at the dark staircase behind him and then back to his wolves.

Both of them nod their heads. He's not sure why they're so interested in his sleeping chambers, but if fulfilling this simple request would make them happy, he has no reason to hesitate. Turning on his heels, he flips the light switch on the wall and beckons them to follow.

They let him get half a dozen steps ahead before they start their descent. He hurries to flip on every light in his bedroom, trying to make it as bright and welcoming as he can. They file in behind him, both coming to a halt only a step past the bottom door. He sees surprise on their faces and looks around, trying to see the space through their eyes.

The room is large, almost the size of the house. Because of the long days during the summer months he spends a great deal of time down here. That means he tried to make the space as comfortable and hospitable as possible.

At the far end of the room, his enormous bed dominates, drawing the eye. Although he felt extravagant for buying it, the big four-poster bed is pleasing with its elaborate, carved wood and soft, off-white, gauze curtains gathered at the four corners. He never draws the curtains closed, but he likes how they look in contrast to the dark wood of the bed.

A little farther down the wall from his bed area is his office with shelves, desk, computer, and other electronics. That space is visually separated from the rest of the room by two waist-high credenzas. One credenza is covered in potted plants. Grow lights hang from the ceiling to light that area up and keep his little green space alive.

Then there's a sitting area with furniture picked for feel rather than style. An overstuffed couch along with a few reclining chairs circle a low, round table. One of his tablets is on the low table, along with some napkins, stained red. Embarrassed, he hurries over to clean up the small mess he left after consuming his last meal.

"Where's your, uh . . . food?" Kalli asks as she examines the room.

"I keep my stores over here," he explains and tosses the napkins into a small trash can on his way to the far end of the room where a small, nondescript refrigerator is nestled into a built-in shelving unit. He hesitates before he opens it, wondering how the two of them will react when he reveals his blood supply.

But they need to see it. They need to see all of him, even the ugly parts.

With a heavy heart, he opens the door and steps away so they can see the dozen blood bags sitting inside.

"That's it?" Quinn asks, looking confused.

"I'm keeping more on hand than usual," he explains. "I want to make sure I'm always well fed around the two of you. I don't want to let my instincts get any kind of foothold because I waited too long between feedings."

"But," Kalli says and then looks over at Quinn. They have one of their wordless conversations, and suddenly Soren understands.

"I don't keep humans down here to drain when I get hungry," he tells them dryly. "This blood comes from one of several donation sites I own."

"Don't donors think the blood is going to human hospitals to help people?" Quinn asks. His tone is curious, not accusatory.

"Most of it does," Soren explains. "But if the blood is tested and found to be impure, I have it sent here. The donation site thinks it's being disposed of, but I use it to feed. Human diseases don't affect me, so it's an excellent use of blood that might otherwise have gone to waste. Sometimes the blood tastes odd, but it still nourishes me just the same. I can't consume it all, so I sell what I don't need to other vampires."

Both of them seem to relax at his explanation, and he realizes they were genuinely worried he kept prisoners down here to feed on. Again, he can't fault them. He knows vampires who do that very thing.

Kalli and Quinn examine his room, wandering off in different directions. They must both be comfortable now if they don't feel the need to stick close together. Kalli walks over to his plants, leaning over to get a good look at them, even running her fingers through one of the leafier ones.

Quinn goes to his office to look over his set up, grinning at the old school fax machine and then taking in his sleek, state-of-the-art laptop with envy.

"I can get you one like it," he offers, and Quinn looks over at him. "Or you can use that one any time you like. The password is Winter."

Quinn tilts his head. "Winter?"

"It's my favorite season," Soren expounds.

"That makes sense since the days are shorter. That means more outside time for you," Kalli comments.

"And I like the snow. It feels cleansing somehow." When Soren was human, he hated the winters. The season was often deadly to humans like him, poor and struggling to make a living on a small farm with few resources. But once he was reborn, winter took on a much different context for him.

His master stole him in summer and after that, he forever associated the warm, sunny months with pain and loss. But it was winter when he killed De Chambre. That means that along with long nights to mark winter as a vampire's favorite time of year, winter became even more significant for him personally. The season of darkness and cold is now linked with gaining his freedom and destroying one of the vilest men to ever have drawn breath.

"Before we . . . back when we lived in houses instead of tents, we liked winter too," Quinn comments as he steps closer to Soren. Kalli joins him.

They stand shoulder to shoulder, but it's different now than when he first emerged at the top of the stairs. Earlier, they looked like a united front, ready to defend against him if necessary. Now they look like a couple, softer and inviting. It makes him smile.

"Even if you decide you don't want to be my flock, or even sleep with me again, you can stay," Soren offers and knows he sounds pleading, but he's unable to help it. "Stay for winter and early spring. Please don't leave until the weather is warmer. Or don't leave at all. You can stay. Just stay. Forever. I can leave if you want. I have other houses, other estates I can go to. You can have this one. Live here. Be safe . . ." He trails off, not sure what else to say.

The idea of them leaving breaks him, but above his own desire to have them bound to him, he wants them to be secure. Sheltered from both the elements and whoever might be hunting them.

"You would move?" Kalli asks, her tone gentle. "You would give us this house even if we don't want to be your flock?"

"Of course," he answers with a helpless shrug. How can he explain that the only thing worse than them not agreeing to be with him is the thought that they are out in the world, exposed and vulnerable?

To his frustration, they turn to each other and have an entire conversation with a few meaningful looks. He wants to demand they talk out loud, so he knows what they're thinking, but keeps his mouth firmly shut.

After what feels like an eternity but was probably less than a minute, they turn back to him. He waits, his heart racing and his chest feeling too tight to breathe.

Kalli is the one who speaks. "We're going to stay, for a while at least. We can't promise anything, but we both feel something for you. We're not sure we want to be a flock yet, but whatever's going on between the three of us is real and deserves to be nurtured."

The breath whooshes out of Soren, and his knees nearly give out from relief. He's forced to grab the back of a chair for support.

They're staying. They're going to give him a chance. "You won't regret this, I promise."

Then they're both on him, each taking a side and hugging him tightly. They feel incredibly warm, and he sinks into their embrace, hope for a future with them flowering in his chest.

"She's not just Volk," Memphis tells him over the phone. "She's the daughter of Dimitri Volk, the lider of the Volk Pack."

"That means nothing to me," Soren says, feeling annoyed at Memphis. "Who are the Volk? What's a lider?"

"That's the title for their leader, but king is more accurate. In the Volk pack, it's a hereditary position. Kalli would be the next in line."

"Do you know what happened? Is the pack still looking for them?"

"Not sure what happened. That pack is tightlipped. But they're still looking for them, well, for Kalli anyway. There's no one looking for Quinn. The fact sheet I got when I inquired about the job only mentioned a companion that could be disposed of if necessary."

That makes Soren hiss out a breath. He doesn't care how rich or powerful this Volk pack is. They're not taking Kalli or "disposing" of Quinn. "How concerned should I be?"

"The Volk pack might be strong, but they're all the way up in Alaska. I'd be cautious, but not too worried. And it's obvious they do not know where she is. The last location they have for her was over two years ago in eastern Canada. But I'd keep her name off any official documents if I were you. If they want to do something, like go to college, get them some aliases to be on the safe side."

"Of course," Soren agrees. "That goes without saying. Thank you for the research."

"You'll get my bill in the mail," Memphis teases and then hangs up.

Tucking the phone in his pocket, Soren listens to Kalli and Quinn in the kitchen making themselves dinner. Twilight gave way to full night while the three of them were downstairs.

They emerged from his room to a dark house, and his eager wolves headed straight for the kitchen to fix a meal. He got the impression that neither ate much during the day while they waited for him to emerge.

Making his way into the kitchen, he finds Quinn cooking and Kalli sitting at the kitchen island, watching her mate move with a contented expression on her face. The scene is so domestic and happy it makes Soren freeze in the open doorway, fearful if he moves it will all disappear.

"Does it bother you to watch us eat?" Quinn asks without looking at Soren. His focus is on the skillet as he scoops something from a skillet into a dish with a wide spatula.

Kalli turns to look at him, her expression telling him she's interested in the answer.

"Absolutely not, but I'd much rather not partake again," he tells them. The face he makes causes Kalli to giggle.

"I thought you were depressed," she announces, and Quinn raises an eyebrow at her. She gives her mate a little shrug. "We might as well tell him. It's funny now that we know the truth."

A small smile plays on Quinn's mouth as he nods. "We thought that was the reason you didn't eat much. And why you lived such an isolated life."

Soren chuckles. "I can see how you might have drawn that conclusion. I guess the reality is more disturbing. A depressed person is an ordinary thing to deal with; a vampire is much more troublesome."

Kalli's eyebrows furrow. "That's not what we think. You're not troublesome or scary. But you are powerful, and that makes us cautious."

"You don't think I'm frightening?" Soren asks carefully.

"We think you're scary as fuck," Quinn states with a calm, thoughtful expression that belies his words. "But not dangerous. At least not to us. No one has ever treated us like you do."

Soren tries to keep his excitement in check. "What do you mean?"

"You seem to care for us equally. Kalli's not more important to you than I am. And your first thought is always about our safety and comfort. I mean, come on, Soren, you offered to leave your house so we would have a comfortable place to stay for the winter. Who does that?"

Soren sees his point but feels obligated to explain something to him. "I'm rich. I have other estates."

"We know, but this is obviously your fave," Kalli states. "Anyway, we know that you've got our back. Like a pack member. And we'll do the same."

The expressions of trust on both their faces gives Soren the courage to make his next request. "I want to see your wolves."

Far from looking upset, both shifters' expressions turn to ones of delight.

"We would like that too," Kalli says, and he gets the feeling that's something the two of them were discussing as he tossed and turned the daylight hours away.

"But dinner first," Quinn demands with a grin. "And then into the forest."

Brimming over with impatience, Kalli practically drags Quinn out of the kitchen even though there are still a few dirty dishes to clean up.

Soren follows the two through the mudroom and out the back door. In the last few days, his garden has withered at a rapid pace, and now there are only a few evergreens with leaves. He can feel that the snow will fall early this year and more than ever, he looks forward to it.

Pulling Quinn to a halt in the middle of the dormant garden, Kalli grabs Quinn's waistband and unbuttons his pants. Laughing, he pushes her hands away.

"I can get my own clothes off. You strip with me." He casts a glance up at Soren, and that's when the vampire realizes the two of them are seducing him.

Blood flows to his cock, and he winces as his pants get uncomfortably tight.

"You're only allowed to watch," Kalli declares as she grasps the hem of her shirt and slowly starts teasing it up, revealing her belly in slow degrees. Finally, it comes off over her head, displaying her lacey bra. "No grabbing us up tonight. You watch us, understand? If there's going to be touching, we will do it first."

Soren curls his hands into fists, fighting the urge to touch her. "I'll only watch," he gets out.

His self-control is further tested as Quinn tugs his shirt off and hangs it on the bare branch of a nearby potted tree. Then he toes off his shoes, pulls off his socks, and glances up to gauge Soren's reaction with every movement.

Kalli is right behind her mate as she hangs both shirt and bra on the tree next to his. They both start wiggling out of their pants.

Soren nearly swallows his tongue when they finally stand before him naked, tan bodies gleaming in the light of the half-moon.

If he thought they were beautiful when lit by the fireplace, he was mistaken. This version of them is exquisite. The moonlight makes their dark skin shine and their black hair highlight blue. They stand still in front of him, and he finally understands they're waiting for him to say something.

"You're both magnificent," he whispers, and they beam at him.

"We were worried," Kalli explains. "We were worried that maybe you were caught up in the moment. You didn't join in with us in the library. You didn't strip or let me put my mouth on you. We were worried that maybe we didn't . . . we weren't . . ."

Feeling all kinds of upset that he made his wolves doubt their appeal, he shakes his head.

"No, *annwyl*. No, *cariad*. I didn't want to push. I didn't want to overwhelm you. I promise it has nothing to do with a lack of desire." He rubs his hand over the front of his pants, making the bulge there strain obscenely against the fabric.

There's a beat of silence as the wolves take in the evidence of his desire.

"I wish I'd done more that night in front of the fire," Soren admits. "I was told to leave you wanting. Not to give you everything."

Now he feels sheepish for taking Memphis's advice. The chimera is good at many things, but seduction and relationships have never been his forte. Why did Soren think the man had any wisdom in that area?

Quinn licks his lips, eyes firmly set on Soren's swelling cock. "Then you would be willing later?"

With a soft, desperate sound, Soren nods his head. That reaction makes both wolves laugh. A breeze ruffles his hair, and although cold doesn't affect him, he notices gooseflesh rise on his wolves' skin. "Shift, my loves. Show me your wolves."

Without another word, they flow into their wolf forms. They drop to four legs, their outlines blurring for a moment as the beasts they hold inside themselves rise to the surface.

Once the shift is over, two beautiful white and gray wolves are standing, staring up at him. He sinks to his knees so the two creatures can approach him if they want to. They're both much bigger than their wild brethren, but that's common among shifters. It also doesn't surprise him that they have very similar fur patterns. That's common within packs.

Their fur is almost white at their feet and gets darker as it hits the top of their legs until it's dark gray, intermixed with russet brown on their heads and down their backs. Kalli is slightly smaller than Quinn, with more brown in her fur. Quinn's not only larger, but his fur appears thicker and longer than his smaller mate.

"You're both stunning," Soren breathes out.

Those words seem to release the wolves from whatever kept them standing stock still. They pad over to him, snuffling his hair and rubbing their faces against his face, neck, and shoulders. Quinn licks a long tongue across the seam of Soren's lips, and Kalli pokes her long snout into his crotch.

Laughing, he gently pushes the two of them away and then stands. Concentrating, he takes the form of a raven. He isn't a shifter, so it took him many years to learn this form and then learn how to use wings instead of arms.

His wolves give yips of excitement as he spreads his shiny black wings and launches into the sky with a loud *caw*. When he looks down, he sees them both lope to the boundary of the yard and down a narrow path.

He's forced to fly low as the path leads them into the woods. The trees are mostly evergreens, so there are branches full of leaves and needles to navigate. But if he flies high enough to have open sky, he won't be able to see them through the canopy. Going higher and losing sight of them is not an option, so he keeps lower and does his best to traverse the forest.

He's not the best flyer. No vampire is. They have no animal side to guide them, no instincts. Without it, they're only pale copies of the animals they impersonate. That means it takes a great deal of concentration, even after so many decades of practice, to fly the forest and not hit anything.

After the second time he misses a tree by only a feather's width, he swoops low to the ground and takes his human form as he lands. He's practiced this maneuver so many times that he only takes a few steps before he's able to stop his momentum from the landing. It's the most graceful thing he does with his shifted form.

His wolves appear next to him, coalescing from the dark. They're both panting, tongues lolling out and sides heaving.

"Keep running," he urges them. "I'm in no rush. Find me when you're ready to return home."

With twin barks of excitement, they dash off into the night, the pads of their feet making almost no sound. He wonders if all wolves are this silent or if his two are special.

He walks back toward the house. He can see it in the distance, one high peaked roof peeking over the trees. He loses track of time as he walks, his mind whirling with possibilities for his wolves. Things he wants to give them. Experiences he wants to share. He's so preoccupied he doesn't realize he's being stalked until it's too late.

Suddenly, his wolves are there, wearing their human skin and crowding around him.

"Missed you," Kalli sings out as her hands tug his shirt out from his pants and her clever little fingers find his bare skin. She moves her hands up, exploring his chest while her mate gets Soren's belt and pants undone. Quinn wiggles a warm hand down, grasping and stroking Soren's hardening flesh.

Standing perfectly still, Soren lets his wolves explore him as much as they are able. He should tell them to strip him of clothing if they want. The cold won't bother him. He wants to be to touch them back. Wants to promise he'll do anything they ask.

But he can't get words to form in his head, let alone verbalize them. The sounds he's making are closer to moans than words.

Kalli finds his small nipple and gives it a little pinch. At the same time, Quinn grabs a handful of his balls and rolls them gently with skilled fingers. Lust consumes him, and he tips his head down, desperate to taste one of them.

Kalli tilts her head back and invites a kiss. Greedily, he takes her mouth with his, moaning into her as their hands keep finding places that he never thought could cause him to be sexually aroused.

Who knew the skin of his lower back was so sensitive?

How is it possible that a nip to his earlobe could make blood flush to his skin?

Never would he have thought that blunt nails scratching gently along his semi-engorged shaft would cause him to shudder violently.

But of course, it's the fact that all this is being done by his wolves that makes the difference. The most important sex organ in a person is their brain, and his gray matter is screaming with desire for these two shifters.

Then, as suddenly as they started, both wolves pull away with matching smirks. "We'll see you back at the house," Kalli says as she shifts.

"Don't hurry on our account," Quinn tells him with an evil little smile, and then shifts as well. They dash off, yipping and baying as they go.

Soren stands stunned for almost an entire minute. Breath heaving, shirt half off, pants undone and hanging low on his hips and a throbbing erection thrusting out.

Dazed, he stares at the patch of forest they disappeared into. Then he shakes himself out of his lustful haze.

"You heathen mongrels!" he shouts out with a laugh, then shifts and pushes hard to beat them home.

Quinn barrels into the kitchen through the mudroom, ready to tackle Soren, or at least try to tackle the big vampire, only to find powerful arms grabbing him up and lifting him off his feet. Kalli shrieks with surprise behind him.

Soren growls low in his throat and takes advantage of the fact that Quinn's too stunned to fight. Lifting his smaller form onto his shoulder, Soren frees up one arm to snatch up Kalli and throw her on his opposite shoulder.

Straightening up, he gives a roar of triumph, making the hair on the back of Quinn's neck rise.

Fuck! That roar is terrifying and sexy at the same time. As his cock fills, Quinn considers he might be a bit broken to find this so erotic.

"The tables have turned, my pups," Soren growls out as he carries them out of the kitchen. Quinn watches the floor as Soren covers the distance from the kitchen to his downstairs bedroom in no time flat. Before he knows it, Soren is sending him flying.

He lands on Soren's bed, and he's still bouncing when Kalli lands right next to him. Looking over, he catches the gleam in Kalli's eyes and gives a curt nod of agreement. They're both on their knees and rushing at Soren at the same time.

But their vampire must have been ready for that because he catches them both in mid-leap and crashes the three of them back down onto the bed.

Kalli is laughing hard enough to make herself tear up, and Quinn's face hurts from the size of his grin.

"Do you yield yet?" Soren demands as he gets his legs under him and sits back, towering over the two of them.

"Yield?" Quinn asks. The only time he's heard that word used is regarding cars and driving. "As in giving you the right of way at a four-way stop?" Then he pretends to hit a horn on a steering wheel and makes a *beep-beep* sound that sends Kalli off into another gale of laughter.

Soren tries to keep his face stern, but a smile cracks his attempt at an austere expression.

Then the vampire does something Quinn isn't expecting; he pulls a set of leather restraints out from behind his back.

"Yield as in give up. Give in. Surrender. Capitulate." Soren leans in close, his eyes half-lidded with sensual promise, and whispers, "Submit."

"Like 50 Shades submitting?" Kalli asks, her eyes alight with lust.

"Something similar, but with more warning and consent," Soren says. "I'm not some untried youth who thinks he's a dominant just because he can shove a plug up a submissive's ass. I know that true submission starts here." Soren taps his head. "And here." He taps his heart.

Quinn's intrigued. "What do you mean?"

Soren leans in close and Quinn can see a hint of fang. His normally ice-gray eyes are darker now, and growing ink black as Quinn watches.

"It means pup, that you agree to be at my mercy. That I'll take you in hand. Torment you with my hands and mouth. Make you rage with desire until you don't think you can take it any more. And I'll keep doing that because you'll be trapped be me. Bound by me. Under my control." Soren voice takes on a power all its own, caressing Quinn's skin as he says the next few words. "You'll be my plaything."

Soren's words flip a switch in Quinn's head. It's hard to think as his body flushes with heat and wanting. He can feel Kalli practically vibrating next to him. She wants this too. She's offered to dominate him a couple of times, but he never took her up on it. He knew she wouldn't enjoy it, and that meant he couldn't relax and enjoy.

But now Soren is here. And by the look on his face, he wants this.

Licking his lips, Quinn nods his head. "Do, uh, do we get a safeword?"

An evil smile plays across Soren's face. "No."

That one word makes Quinn startle a little. "No?"

"No," Soren repeats. "A safeword lets you escape." If it's possible, his voice lowers until Quinn swears he's being stroked by Soren's next words. "You're in my bed, little wolf. That means you've given up your right to a safeword."

"But . . ." Quinn tries to protest. He knows he should insist. Everything he read included safewords. But Soren's dark promise is so tantalizing.

Give up control. Let him take charge. It's a temptation he never thought to face.

It doesn't help that he can't take his eyes off the damn cuffs in Soren's hand.

Does he want this?

Instinct has him looking over to check in with Kalli. She's regarding him with both encouragement and desire.

"I don't mind," she murmurs. "And Soren looks like he wants to be in charge. We could try it, and if you don't like it, we can go back to you and Soren both being in command. Besides, you and I never had a safeword."

That's true. They've known each other so long that they never bothered with one when they started to explore their sexuality. Soren doesn't know either of them that well, but he is perceptive.

Quinn knows in his heart that Soren will die before he caused them distress.

Tentatively, Quinn reaches out to take the leather restraints from Soren. Soren flashes a hint of fang as he lets Quinn take them.

They feel solid in his hands, and he can smell the leather. These cuffs are either brand new or have never been used before.

He wouldn't be surprised to find out that Soren ordered all kinds of sex toys specifically for the three of them. The thought makes him salivate.

"Maybe this one time," he finally whispers, and before he can even look up from the cuffs, Kalli pounces.

With more eagerness than skill, she buckles the cuffs on his wrists, then looks up at Soren for more instructions. Soren smiles and wraps a broad hand around the back of her neck. Her expression relaxes, and her eyes half close.

"I believe I'm in charge," Soren intones with an authority that makes both Kalli and Quinn shiver.

He reaches around her with his free hand and drags Quinn's bound wrists over his head and hooks them to a bolt in the headboard Quinn never noticed before.

Later, when everything is over and they've recovered, he might need to do a thorough examination of the bed for other hidden treasures. Maybe he and Kalli could tie Soren down one of these days and exact a little revenge. The thought makes him smile.

"Enjoying yourself, pup?" Soren asks, as Quinn tugs at his cuffs a little to get a feel for them.

The fact that he can't easily pull free makes him feel strangely calm. The bed is solidly built, the bolt is sunk deep into the wood, and the cuffs are sturdy. He could easily get loose by unbuckling the cuffs. There's no lock on the buckle to keep him from removing them. It would be a little awkward and a bit of a struggle, but he could do it.

But getting himself free isn't what he wants. The restraints simply mean he's not in charge. He doesn't get to call the shots. His only job is to do what he's told.

His mind goes to a place where all worry and fear evaporate, and he gets to live in the moment. Relaxing his head on the pillow, he meets Soren's eyes. The vampire smiles gently down at him.

"Yes, I'd say you like it." Leaning over, Soren brushes a soft kiss on Quinn's lips. "All you need to do is whatever I say."

Quinn nods and then feels disappointed when Soren straightens up and gets off the bed.

"You two teased me back in the garden," He comments as he stands tall and strong in front of them. "Don't think I didn't notice the way you both undressed for me in the garden. Then snuck up and played with me, only to run off and leave me unfulfilled. Well, the tables have turned. I'm going to strip, and neither of you are allowed to touch me until I say you can. And no touching each other either."

Kalli makes an impatient sound, but one look from Soren has her quieting down. Quinn licks his lips in anticipation.

Like Kalli, he was disappointed that Soren didn't take any of his clothes off in the den that first time they played. Now Soren's going to strip for them as if putting on a show, and Quinn couldn't be happier. Sometimes getting to the naked part is as much fun as being naked.

Without taking his eyes off the bed, Soren shrugs out of his suit jacket. He isn't wearing a vest and his shirt is haphazardly tucked in at the waist. With slow, deliberate movements, Soren unbuttons his shirt and pulls it free of his pants.

Entranced, Quinn watches as Soren's powerful chest is revealed. Broad shoulders, round muscled pecs, then sleek abdomen with a muscled V leading down to disappear into his pants. His alabaster skin glows in the soft bedside light. Muscles flex as long fingers unbutton the waistband of his pants and drag the zipper down.

When he stops, Quinn's eyes fly up to find that Soren's intense gaze is fixed on him.

"Are you still sure, my wolf?" Soren asks, a sensual smile playing around his lips. "I could stop now and leave you in Kalli's care."

A low whine sounds.

Quinn's a little shocked to realize it came out of his throat. He's never made a needy sound like that before. Next to him on the bed, Kalli stifles a giggle. He would glare at her, but he can't seem to tear his eyes away from the vampire.

"I take that as affirmation that you want me to continue," Soren comments as he toes out of his shoes and then gracefully bends over to tug his socks off. Every movement the man makes feels like a ritual or dance, elegant and captivating.

Straightening up, he lets his pants drop to the floor and steps out. He wasn't wearing anything under his pants, so now he stands gloriously naked before them. He holds his hands out to his side and waits, letting them take their fill of him.

As with his upper half, his lower body is heavily muscled. Quinn finds himself captivated by all the pale hair. He's never seen someone so fair naked, and the fact that Soren's pubic hair is as pale as the rest of him fascinates Quinn.

"Am I acceptable?" he asks, and although the words sound confident, Quinn can hear a slight note of insecurity.

Kalli ends up speaking at the same time as he does. "You're beautiful."

They look at each other and grin.

Making an amused sound, Soren stalks to the bed. Quinn is stretched out, and Kalli is kneeling next to him. Soren puts himself on the opposite side of Quinn and reaches across to grab Kalli. Tangling his fingers in her hair, Soren forces her face down until her warm breath ghosts over Quinn's straining erection. "Lick," he orders.

Taking him at his word, Kalli strokes her tongue up Quinn's length, making him moan and buck his hips up. Soren gives a little disapproving growl.

"Be still," he orders, and Quinn realizes why Kalli goes so crazy when he makes her stay still. This is torture. Real and true torture.

Kalli keeps licking his throbbing cock, and even pulls the tip into her mouth for a quick suck, but none of it is enough. All the touches are too brief, too light, and much too frustrating.

"Goddess, Kalli!" Quinn calls out when she nips at his balls.

"Ha!" Kalli crows out. Her sound of triumph is followed quickly by a whimper.

Quinn opens his eyes to find that Soren has a hand cupping her jaw, holding her head tightly against his chest. His other hand is brutally rolling her nipple between thumb and forefinger.

"Did I give you permission to taunt Quinn?" Soren asks her.

"N-n-no," Kalli whines.

"You do what I say, and only what I say. Understand?"

Watching Soren dominate Kalli is a treat. Her skin flushes, and her nipples tighten. He can smell her arousal and see it glistening on the insides of her thighs.

It's awkward, but he manages to move his thigh between her legs. Bending his knee, he puts pressure on her needy sex, loving the silky feel of her wet flesh on his skin. She jerks, then moans and grinds herself down on his leg.

"Naughty wolves," Soren reprimands them both as he lets go of Kalli's head to bodily pick her up and move her away from Quinn's leg. Sitting down on the bed, he easily puts Kalli across his lap. Then delivers several strong slaps to her ass. Quinn can clearly see her face go from surprised to aroused.

"Soren!" she gasps.

"Bad wolves get punished," he intones, his voice deep and aroused. He slips a hand between her legs and strokes the flesh there. Kalli whimpers and tries to move against his hand by bracing her forearms on the bed.

"None of that," Soren admonishes. "Be still or the punishment will continue."

Quinn can't see what Soren is doing between Kalli's legs, but he can clearly see the reaction on Kalli's face. Her eyes are tightly shut, but her mouth opens in a moan.

"Please," she begs.

"What do you want, little wolf?" he asks, his voice dripping with dark intent. Soren's eyes have gone from black to dark red. Under normal circumstances that color change would probably freak Quinn out. But this obvious display of vampirism only makes a bolt of lust go through Quinn.

"Kalli can come multiple times," Quinn offers. "You don't have to make her wait." When Soren raises those blood read eyes, Quinn feels a shudder go through him.

"It appears both of you need a lesson in obedience," Soren murmurs.

"I . . . no?" Quinn fumbles for a response. He doesn't know if he wants to be spanked like Kalli. She always likes a little bite of pain with her pleasure, but what if pain turns him off? And it's not like he could hide a deflating erection from Soren.

All those rapid thoughts must have shown on his face because Soren leans over Kalli's body to bring his pale face and glowing red eyes close to Quinn.

"Shhhh, my wolf," he murmurs. "Stop thinking. Stop worrying."

Reaching out, Soren wraps his other hand around the back of Quinn's neck and gives a firm squeeze. That triggers the submissive part of Quinn that he didn't know was there. His body goes lax and his world narrows to Soren's commanding presence.

Soren leans a little closer and kisses Quinn. When he pulls back, his eyes have gone from dark red to blood red. It's a shocking contrast to Soren's pale skin.

"Good wolf," he praises Quinn. "That's what I'm looking for. Let me be in charge. I'll worry about Kalli's orgasms. I'll decide who gets to come when. None of this is your concern. All I want you to focus on is being a good wolf for me."

"Yes Soren," Quinn whispers.

Giving him one last squeeze before he lets go, Soren straightens back up. Kalli remained still in his lap through that whole thing. When he meets her eyes, she gives him a little smile.

Then Soren is lifting her up again and placing her on the bed. He arranges her so she's kneeling over Quinn's erection then he roughly pushes Kalli's head down.

"Swallow him down, Kalli," he orders. "I want to see his entire length disappear down that throat. When you're finished with him, I'm going to hold your head steady and fuck that mouth myself."

A needy whine comes out of her as she parts her lips and delicately works her mouth over Quinn's cock. She knows what he likes it, so she swirls her tongue around the tip a few times before taking him deeper.

Closing his eyes and letting his head fall back, Quinn concentrates on not to moving his hips. Kalli makes him feel so good, but he knows Soren won't approve.

"Such good wolves," Soren coos. "My wolves."

Quinn feels Kalli's reaction to Soren calling them his wolves when she shudders a little and her movements stutter. Then she recovers and is more enthusiastic than ever, wringing a strangled moan from Quinn.

He's not sure how long he'll last.

The bed shifts a little and Quinn opens his eyes in time to watch Soren part his legs and settle on his knees between them. One hand is tangled in Kalli's hair, holding her head on Quinn's cock. The other one slides between her legs, and she moans around Quinn's hard flesh and Soren pumps his fingers into her.

"So wet," Soren murmurs. "Are you dying for a good fuck, little wolf? When I'm done with Quinn, maybe I'll bend you over the table. Pin you down and take you hard from behind. I'll save your throat by ravaging your sweet pussy."

One thing Quinn would always be reluctant to admit is that he never got the hang of dirty talk. He simply loved and respected Kalli too much to ever be able to bring himself to say nasty, crude, or demeaning things to her, even though they both knew it was true.

But it's clear Soren has no problem with being foul during sex. The words flow out of him, and Kalli's twitching and quivering clearly demonstrates their effectiveness.

"Has Quinn fucked that pretty back hole of yours?" Soren questions, then licks his lips. "Do you think you could handle my beast?"

"No," Kalli moaned, but Quinn could tell she liked the idea of being fucked in any hole by Soren. Just like she liked it with Quinn.

All kinds of delicious possibilities flood Quinn's mind, making him feel a little dizzy.

Or is he dizzy because all the blood in his body might be in his dick right now. Fuck, has he ever been this hard before?

"Quinn, don't you dare come before I give you permission," Soren warns him.

"Yes, Soren," Quinn manages to wheeze out. Quinn watches Soren's hand withdraw from Kalli, glistening with slick. He expects Soren to lick it off because that's what he likes to do. But instead, Soren takes those fingers and dives between Quinn's ass cheeks.

"Soren?" Quinn whimpers out, fearful that he's about to be ripped in two by Soren's massive cock.

"Easy wolf," Soren coos as he rubs those fingers gently across Quinn's pucker. With light pressure, Soren tries to slip his fingers into Quinn. His muscles tense and Soren goes back to rubbing. Every time he tries and doesn't slide easily in, he backs off.

Realizing he's not going to be hurt, Quinn starts relaxing and the next time Soren presses, his finger slide past that ring of muscles.

Quinn tenses, but all Soren does is work that one finger in and out a little. When Quinn's body has accepted that foreign presences, Soren slides a second finger in.

Now it no longer feels like an intrusion. It still feels odd, but not unpleasant. Then Soren crooks his fingers and brushes over something inside of him. Lightning sparks and he cries out.

"Ah, there is it," Soren murmurs. "That's your prostate, my little wolf. And I'm going to make you see stars."

Soren's touch combined with Kalli's mouth means Quinn is sure he can't keep his orgasm at bay.

"I'm . . . can't . . .," Quinn tries to tell him that, but his brain is buzzing with pleasure, not words. Straining against the cuffs securing his wrists to the bed, Quinn tries to hold back his climax.

Then Kalli starts moaning around his cock. Slitting his eyes open, he sees Soren now has a hand buried in each of them.

"My pretty matching set of wolves," he says as he pumps his fingers in both of them. "Do you think I can make you orgasm at the same time?"

"Yes, please," Quinn begs. It's taking all his concentration to keep from coming, and he's not sure how much longer he can keep that up.

Then he feels that same heat and pressure he felt back when they were first intimate on the floor in front of the fireplace.

Soren was pulsing raw desire into both of them. From the sounds Kalli was making, she had to feel what he was feeling. Heat building where Soren was touching. Indescribable pressure and need makes his skin feel tight and his mind fog with lust.

"Soren, I can't . . . I can't . . . I . . .!" he tries to tell Soren he can't hold back any longer, but his tongue is clumsy, and his mind refuses to work right.

"Come for me, my wolves," Soren growls. He pushes more magic into them and sinks a third finger into Quinn, pushing those three fingertips on Quinn's prostate.

"Oh, fuck!" Quinn screams as he comes harder than he's ever climaxed before. His vision dims and even as he feels Kalli swallow, he feels her shudder and cry out around his cock.

The vampire keeps them riding their orgasms until Kalli starts making soft distressed mewling sounds and Quinn whimpers. Only then does Soren pull his fingers free of them.

Quinn watches Soren gently pull Kalli up. Cool air hits his erection, a startling contrast after the heat of Kalli's mouth. With all stimuli gone, Quinn's body sinks into the bed, boneless and sated. He watches Soren cup Kalli's jaw and hold her steady as he kisses her.

A pulse of desire comes from the vampire, making Quinn's softening cock try to harden again.

Pulling back, Soren licks his lips. "You taste like you and Quinn. Delectable."

Kalli isn't steady on her knees and with a gentle expression, Soren eases her down until she's lying on her side facing Quinn.

Although his wrists are still bound to the bed, Quinn languidly moves his head to kiss Kalli. With a little bit of a struggle, she manages to meet him.

He can taste his essence and Soren's kiss on Kalli's lips. All of them together taste like perfection.

Soren settles in behind Kalli. Lazily, he reaches over her and unclips Quinn's wrists. Quinn groans a little with relief as he brings his arms down. He hadn't realized how stiff his shoulders had gotten from straining against the cuffs.

He likes the feel of the leather around his wrists, so he leaves the cuff on as he turns on his side to face Kalli and Soren. Propping his head up on one hand, Quinn regards the two of them.

"What about you?" Quinn asks.

"Me?" Soren asks. "What about me?"

"I want you to come too," Quinn insists. That statement rouses Kalli out of her daze.

She looks over her shoulder at Soren, her expression concerned. "You haven't come?"

"I don't mind waiting," Soren tells them with a gentle smile. But his eyes are still blood red and pulsing with need.

"It doesn't work that way with wolves," Quinn argues. He boldly reaches over Kalli's body and finds Soren, hard and throbbing. Soren hisses as Quinn pumps his hand up and down Soren's shaft a few times.

"You can't tell me you don't want it," Quinn insists. Rising up on his elbow, he leans over Kalli. "Let me help you."

"You don't need to—" Soren's words end in a hiss of pleasure as Quinn sets Soren's hard cock against Kalli's dripping entrance.

"Don't you want to feel Kalli's hot, tight pussy?" Quinn asks as he removes his hand from between Kalli and Soren. His words affect both Soren and Kalli. The vampire shudders and Kalli lets out a soft moan.

"Please, Soren," she begs as she moves her hips back to force Soren inside her. Soren clamps a hand down on her hip, keeping her from moving any further. "I want to feel you pounding inside me. I'm empty and need to be filled. I want to come around your cock."

"*Annwyl*," Soren cries out, thrusting forward.

Kalli gasps, then moans. "So good."

Quinn settles back down, putting his face in front of Kalli's. "How does it feel, my mate?"

"Stretched," she breaths out. "Delicious. I'm close."

Shifting himself a little, Quinn cups one of Kalli's breasts. Then he pinches the beaded nipple, making Kalli writhe. She might have come once already, but his mate is so worked up that it won't take much to make her climax again.

Then Soren's hand is there, tangling fingers into Kalli's hair and pushing her face to Quinn's.

"Kiss," he demands. "I want you kissing when I come. I want all three of us connected."

Soren's movements are getting faster and a magic so powerful that it's almost stifling is building around them. Kalli whimpers at Soren's grip in her hair and Quinn brings his face to hers.

The moment their lips touch, it's as if the three of them have completed a circuit. Magic flows through them, making Soren roar. Then the vampire's aura flares, and a sharp, pleasurable wave of power hits them.

Kalli and Soren climax together. Soren's voice fills the room with his shout of pleasure. Kalli's softer cries are muffled by Quinn's mouth.

The magic is so strong that Quinn comes again. This orgasm is nowhere near as powerful as the first one, but it's enough to leave him gasping and dazed.

He's never done that before and it's such an intense sensation that it borders on painful.

After a few more shuddering thrusts, Soren stops. The air around them is saturated with the scent of their passion and the smell of strong magic. Quinn feels overwhelmed in a good way and a little teary-eyed.

Soren doesn't pull himself free of Kalli. Instead, he crowds in close and reaches one long arm around until he can touch Quinn's back. Then he squeezes them close.

Quinn thought he knew contentment with Kalli. But know he realizes there had always been something missing. He and his mate are good together, but with the addition of Soren, they're whole.

A perfect peacefulness settles over him as he snuggles down into Soren's embrace and gives Kalli a last kiss on her forehead.

As sleep drags him under, Quinn feels Kalli move and when she talks, he can tell she's lifted her head to say something to Soren.

"You fuck like a wolf," she tells the vampire, a smirk in her words.

Soren makes a sound that's both joyful and amused. "I don't think anyone has ever paid me a higher compliment."

Soren watches Kalli carefully. Unlike Quinn, who is generally easy to read, Kalli's much more practiced at hiding her thoughts and feelings. He doesn't think she does it on purpose. It strikes him as a survival technique she's learned while growing up. She's practiced it so much that now it's an unconscious part of her.

It's been over a month since Kalli and Quinn agreed to stay with him and see what develops between the three of them. If the incredible sex the three of them share every day is any indication, their triad is a success. His wolves have settled in nicely, making themselves at home.

But Kalli remains a bit of a mystery. As responsive as she is when he's dominating her and Quinn during sex, the rest of the time, her enigmatic expression gives him little to work this.

He's desperate to know more about how she feels about him even as he tries to content himself with the fact that she never mentions leaving.

He could ask her. But that option is terrifying. What if the answer is that she feels nothing but mild affection?

No, better to give her time and hope that love grows between them.

Waiting is no hardship. Each day has been a pleasure. Beyond being friendly and joyful, his wolves are kind and considerate. They always ask before using his things, even though he's repeatedly told them to treat his home as their own.

They've also taken it upon themselves to help him redecorate, and each day brings Kalli and Quinn to him with ideas pulled from various websites. When he told them he wants to do their room on the second floor first and that they should pick everything out for their own pleasure, they still consult with him and try to find the best deals on everything.

Items should start arriving soon, and they'll all throw themselves into the redecorating project. Soren can't wait. Tailoring the room to his wolves feels like a tangible symbol of their intent to stay with him.

As far as he's concerned, the only problem is that he wants to buy Kalli things just for her, but he can't figure out what she would like best. He doesn't want to give her things that aren't thoughtful. He wants his gifts to have meaning. Whatever he gives her should have an emotional context. Random baubles won't do.

He's tried questioning Quinn about Kalli's glass and crystal collection. After some halting conversation, Quinn admitted that Kalli wouldn't like it if he said anything, so Soren stopped asking. The last thing he wants to do is cause strife between the couple. Not that he thinks it would be that easy, but better to keep Quinn from feeling pressured by either him or Kalli.

It's finally December, and because it's the season to shop for gifts, they're visiting the yearly winter bazaar. It's only a few weeks until Christmas and people are happily bustling around looking at the various booths for the perfect gift for friends and family. The hot food vendors are doing good business as the smell of roasting meat, fried potatoes, and funnel cakes fills the air.

With the days so short now, many activities going on in the town continue until well after dark, allowing Soren to take his wolves into town. They never complain about staying home, but he can tell they enjoy some time among the humans and experiencing new things.

Right now, Kalli is sipping mulled wine, still deciding if she likes it or not. Quinn is enjoying a bottle of local craft beer, uncaring about drinking a cold beverage in the chilly weather. The three of them are strolling from booth to booth, most filled with handmade items by local craftsmen and artists.

Kalli examines a few items but never touches or picks anything up. It's slowly driving Soren insane that he can't tell if she's interested in anything or not. His frustration must show on his face because Quinn grins at him.

Placing a hand on his shoulder, Quinn goes on his toes to whisper in Soren's ear. "I can tell you if she likes something she looks at."

"Please do," Soren agrees readily. "You're easy to buy for. Books, video games, and socks."

"Not just any old socks," Quinn huffs out.

"Oh no, I remember. Only that one type of wool mixed with alpaca fiber," Soren states with teasing solemnity. He never put much thought into socks, so he finds Quinn's mild obsession with finding the perfect socks vastly amusing.

"Don't knock it until you try it," Quinn comments, then finishes his beer and pitches the bottle into a nearby recycling bin.

"Soren?" Kalli calls to get his attention. "I think this would look good in your bedroom." The two of them crowd in on either side of her to see what she's holding. It's a woven wall hanging. The colors are dark-hued greens and blues, the pattern abstract, but pleasing.

Soren feels hope rise. "Do you like it?" He sees Quinn shake his head where Kalli can't see.

She bites her lip and shrugs. "It's nice, but I was thinking of it for you. You have that bare space, and the colors make me think of you. Dark, but not sinister, you know? Maybe it could go on the wall near the credenza with all the plants?"

Now he understands why Quinn shook his head. Kalli is picking things out for him, not herself. He looks at the woman watching them with a hopeful expression. He recognizes her as a local. With a smile, he purchases the weaving without haggling.

"My card is in the bag. I do commissions all the time so if you want anything specific, don't hesitate to contact me," she offers with a wide smile as she hands over the purchase tucked neatly in a decorative paper bag.

"Thanks," Kalli says with a smile. "Your stuff is gorgeous."

While Soren's happy to support this woman, he's still frustrated. They're halfway through the bazaar, and he's no closer to finding something for Kalli than when they started. It isn't just about giving a gift for winter solstice, a traditional wolf shifter holiday, but being able to help cement her place with him. If she starts collecting things, it's an indication that she feels safe and secure. It's a sign that neither wolf needs to be ready to run at a moment's notice.

Then he sees it, and even without Quinn's input, Soren knows it's perfect. Normally, he'd walk right by this booth without a second glance. Nothing there is in a style he's fond of. But now he steps closer, giving himself time to examine the items with Kalli in mind as Quinn and Kalli move a little ahead of him.

The tables of the booth are covered in handcrafted miniature trees. They are styled to look like bonsai trees but are made of wire with leaves made of semi-precious stones and set in rectangular, black glazed pots filled with glass beads. Each tree is unique and without even needing to ask Quinn, Soren knows exactly which one Kalli would want. It's one of the smaller creations, with a pot full of cerulean blue beads and peridot leaves at the end of copper wire. It's perfect. He can just see her opening the box now. Her eyes will light up, and she'll pull it out reverently, holding it up so she can examine every facet of it.

But first he needs to buy it without her noticing.

Quinn unwittingly distracts her by demanding a sip of her mulled wine and then making a face that doubles her over with laughter.

"I need something to get that taste out of my mouth," Quinn pronounces as he smacks his lips a few times. "Ugh, how can you drink that stuff?"

Seizing on the perfect opportunity, Soren points to the area where most of the food trucks and booths are located. "Why don't the two of you go over there and grab a bite? I see someone I need to speak to for a moment."

"Sure, I guess," Quinn says hesitantly. He looks up at Soren, then rushes to say, "I was kidding. I don't need to eat. I'm not that hungry. We don't need to split up if being around so much food will make you uncomfortable."

The rumble of Quinn's stomach disproves his previous statement.

The boy is sweet to stay hungry because Soren might be uncomfortable. At the same time, Soren wants to snatch up the wolf in a big hug for being so caring, he also wants to growl at him for disrupting his plans.

He lets his affection for Quinn show on his face. "Being around food doesn't bother me, I promise. But I thought I saw Kingston, one of Memphis's brothers, and I wanted to talk to him about doing some work at the house. He's a general contractor."

The only part Soren's lying about is having seen Kingston. The rest is true. Thankfully, the wolves are too drawn to the smell of food to bother on insisting to meet Kingston. They take the cash he thrusts at them and wander off to the food area hand in hand.

Soren hurries back to the booth, relieved to find the tree he wants is still there. He's quick to arrange it to be gift-wrapped and delivered to the house. Feeling buoyed, Soren heads out to search for his wolves.

Jealousy burns through him when he finds the two of them chatting with a bear shifter almost as big as Soren himself. Unlike wolves, bears don't form groups. They'll pair off, but they don't do packs or slithers like wolves and nagas. Normally, Soren wouldn't be worried, but this bear shifter has a reputation that is well deserved.

The next thing Soren knows, he's pushing himself between Quinn and Kalli. He doesn't remember covering the distance, only the intense need to guard his wolves.

"Bayard," Soren grits out between clenched teeth. "You can walk away now."

"Bowen," Bayard acknowledges with lazy unconcern. "I'm having a delightful time with Kalli and Quinn. I saw the three of you walk by my booth earlier. I was busy then, but I'm not anymore."

Envy floods Soren as he takes in Bayard. The man isn't just big like Soren, but he's far more handsome, with classical features and lightly tanned skin. As a bear shifter, the man isn't anywhere near as powerful as Soren, but he's strong enough to take on almost any other shifter and win, perhaps even a small pack of wolves. He could offer protection to Kalli and Quinn, along with having some shifter culture in common.

Bayard is a temptation for his wolves that he didn't think about before now. The man is hardly the only shifter in town, but he is the only one that would be interested in the two wolves in the same way as Soren.

"Soren?" Quinn's questioning tone brings Soren's eyes to the wolf's concerned face. "What's going on?"

"Is this guy a threat?" Kalli asks, casting a suspicious look at Bayard.

"I'm not a threat, not like that," Bayard protests quickly. He gives them one of his charming smiles, his dark eyes twinkling with humor. "I'm Sebastian Bayard. I'm a CPA here in town, but I carve chess sets for fun. That's my booth over there. My nephew's manning it at the moment." Then he leans in a little closer and uses a stage whisper. "Don't mind Soren. He's a little sore after a certain Megan Henderson picked me instead of him a few years back."

"I was not upset then or now," Soren grumbles out. "I'm merely still appalled by her lack of taste."

That makes both his wolves laugh and hug him tightly. "You don't need to worry about that," Quinn assures him. "We aren't picking anyone over you."

Bayard's eyes widen a little, and the charming grin slides into something softer, more real. "It's like that, is it?"

"It is," Soren confirms. "Mine."

"Huh, didn't think it would happen for you," Bayard comments.

"You mean you didn't think he would ever pick someone to be his flock?" Quinn asks, interest sparking. "Because we aren't official yet."

"Maybe not right at this moment, but you will be soon," Bayard says with confidence as his eyes travel over the three of them. "Now that I can see you all together, it's obvious this is a good match-up."

"What did you mean you didn't think he'd pick anyone?" Kalli presses.

"For as long as my family's known Soren, and we go back generations in this town, he's been alone. Most vampires are picky about their flock, but they usually form one, eventually. Except for Soren. You two must be damn special for him to decide he's ready."

"They are special," Soren agrees, giving Bayard and his perfect hair and charming smile a little growl. "And you'll stay far away from them."

"Easy there," Quinn soothes. "We aren't ones to be fooled by a pretty face or friendly smile."

Feeling mildly ashamed for his overbearing attitude, Soren tries to rein in his possessiveness. "No, of course not. You're both far too smart to be taken in by a smooth-talking bear."

"I am pretty, and I am smooth-talking," Bayard says as he strikes a silly pose like he's a bodybuilder on stage. Then he pretends to smooth back his hair, gives them a big, toothy grin, and winks. "And I should have a perfect smile. I paid a pretty penny for it!"

His silliness makes Soren relax. Bayard might have stolen a lover almost literally out from under him, but neither he nor Megan were anything but casual. It was more about a feeling of competitiveness than anything else. And now that he thinks about it, Megan probably manufactured the competition between him and Bayard to begin with.

"Uncle Sebastian, help!" a youthful voice calls out, and they all turn to see Bayard's nephew surrounded by patrons and looking a little panicked.

"Got to go," Bayard calls out as he hurries to rescue his nephew.

"He's a character," Quinn comments as they watch him slide up to his booth and start charming the patrons.

Unable to help himself, Soren pulls Kalli in for a kiss, taking his time and feeling her relax into him. He hears a few whispers of people as they walk by, but nothing to bother him. When he eventually ends the kiss, Kalli sways and looks a little dazed. She clings to Soren as if she's not feeling quite steady on her feet.

Quinn is right there grinning, and with his typical patience, waiting for his turn. When Soren grabs the young man by the back of his head and draws him in, Quinn doesn't resist at all. He accepts Soren's kiss, pressing his body close so Kalli is sandwiched between them. She murmurs appreciatively and snuggles down while Quinn lets him stake his claim. He floods the area a little with his scent and pushes his aura out so both Kalli and Quinn take on some of his magic.

By the time he's done, no one could possibly think these wolves are available. They smell of him to the point where humans might even scent something. And they both have a thin layer of his magic over their auras.

When he looks up, he finds Bayard staring at him, and the bear shifter is no longer smiling. He looks turned on, flustered, and covetous.

Soren lets a big, satisfied grin stretch across his face. The smile is so wide that his fangs are peeking out. Something he was usually very conscious of, but at the moment, he can't help himself.

"Feel better?" Quinn asks with a small smile. The expressions on his and Kalli's face tell Soren they know exactly what he's doing.

"Much," Soren agrees with no guilt at all. "Now let's keep exploring. We still have half a bazaar to look through."

Because Soren spent well over a hundred years of his life forced to use open flame as the only way to heat a home or cook food, he was never particularly entranced by fire until his wolves arrived. But Kalli and Quinn love fires.

To his wolves, winter means a roaring fire every evening with the two of them often stretched out in front of it. The young couple likes to read or watch something on the devices he gave them, chat, or occasionally drift off to sleep. They enjoy it so much that he ordered the plushest rug he could find and large soft pillows for the area around the hearth.

Except for the times where work forces him to sit on the couch with a laptop, he joins them on the floor. The three of them end up snuggled together in some kind of affectionate configuration. Kalli likes to rest her head on his leg while Quinn likes to lean against him while Soren uses the front of the couch for support. If Quinn's falling asleep, he'll curl his body around Soren with a hand tangled in Kalli's.

These two are all about touch and have included Soren in their tactile world.

Soren expects tonight to be like any other, as the three of them make their way to the den. Making himself comfortable on the rug, Soren leans his back against the couch, and watches Kalli and Quinn build a fire with practiced ease. It's once the fire is lit, and no longer needs to be tended, that the evening goes off script.

With no signal that Soren can discern, the two wolves pounce on him, dragging him to the floor. He doesn't fight them. Being under these two is no hardship. Kalli tugs at him until he's far enough away from the couch so she can straddle his chest. Quinn throws a leg over him too, hugging Kalli from behind and resting his weight on Soren's abdomen.

Both wolves are smiling, but there's an odd tension to the two of them that worries Soren. A frisson of fear goes through him and makes him blurt out the first thought that comes to mind.

"You're leaving. Please don't leave yet. Give me more time!"

Going by the startled expression on their faces, that's not what they expected him to say at all. Quinn's expression softens and turns reassuring, while Kalli takes on a more serious visage, and her smile disappears altogether.

"We've come to a decision," she pronounces. "But before we go any further, Quinn and I have something we need to tell you."

"Anything," Soren assures them, feeling less panicked. If they were going to leave, Kalli would have said it right off. "You can tell me anything, and it won't make a difference."

That makes Quinn's smile disappear. "Hear us out before you promise stuff. Kalli and I aren't, um, we aren't exactly what you think."

Confused, Soren shifts a little under their combined weight. He's not uncomfortable, except in so far as they're still wearing clothes. This position would be much better if all three of them were naked.

"How could you be anything else but what you are, right here and now, with me?" Soren asks carefully.

Something's bothering both of them, and he has a strong hunch it has to do with the Volk pack. He wishes he'd broached the subject much earlier, but now he can't confess anything, or they'll know he investigated them. The last thing he wants is for them to believe he doesn't trust them. Nothing could be farther from the truth.

Perhaps it's better this way. They can confess their falling out with the Volk pack, and they can put it all behind them.

He gives them a reassuring smile. "Tell me what you need to confess so I can explain that it's not a big deal at all."

That cracks Kalli's composure. A smile flashes across her features before her stern expression is back.

"We're being serious here, Soren. There are things you don't know about us that might make you change your mind."

"Change my mind about what?"

Quinn's smile turns sad. "About you wanting us to be part of your flock. Or hell, you might not even want us to stay here any longer."

"No, *cariad*, there's nothing you can say to me that would make me change your mind, except that in your hearts you don't want me as much as I want you." He knows his words are falling on partially deaf ears. There's too much anxiety built up in Kalli and Quinn to believe him yet. How long have the two of them been talking and stewing over this? "Come now, tell me this deep, dark, horrible secret. Unburden yourself."

Kalli takes a deep breath and begins. "We had to run away from our pack. It's the Volk pack, and they're powerful. Maybe one of the biggest and most influential packs in North America."

Ah, now he might find out what drove Kalli and Quinn to live on their own. "What happened that made the two of you decide to run?"

Kalli and Quinn exchange a quick look before Kalli frowns down at him and continues their story. "They were going to make me mate with someone else. My father is Dimitri Volk, lider of the Volk pack."

Soren pretends ignorance. "Lider?"

"Uh, our word for Alpha. Every pack has a different term. Anyway, Dimitri contracted with another pack to match me up with a guy. I never even met him before he showed up. Poor Ryan, I got the feeling he didn't want to be there either. He's a third or fourth son of a leader from another powerful pack." She pauses and looks over at Quinn.

"It's okay," he urges, and she nods her head and continues.

"Anyway, I refused, and then Dimitri got nasty." That Kalli refers to her father by his first name tells Soren everything he needs to know about this man. Kalli is set up for loyalty. It's written into her very DNA. If Dimitri turned her against her own family, he did it through a lifetime of neglect and probably abuse.

"How bad was it?" Soren asks gently.

"Dimitri threatened to have Quinn executed if I didn't do what he wanted," Kalli tells him with no change of inflection. A betrayed look crosses Quinn's face, but it's gone quickly, replaced by affection. He places a gentle kiss on Kalli's cheek.

"He probably wouldn't have done it," Quinn whispers. "He was my lider too. My family has been with the pack since the beginning. He was just trying to get you to obey."

"You know that's not true," Kalli states, bitterness making her tone harsh. "Dimitri is a bastard and will stop at nothing to get what he wants. He hurt you in the past to get to me. There is no question in my mind that he would hurt or kill you. Even if it's only to prove he can."

"I can keep you safe from this man," Soren offers, as if he didn't already plan to keep Kalli and Quinn safe from anything that threatens them.

"It's not just Dimitri. If we were only running away from my father, that would be one thing. But we're wolves. We ran away from an entire pack," Kalli explains. "I'm sure he's still looking for us. As long as he's alive, he'll keep looking for us. Even if he can't mate me off, he'll want to drag us home and make an example out of us."

Quinn's expression is resigned. "We're dangerous to have around. Dimitri would hurt or kill others to get to us."

Kalli nods her head. "We've survived so far because we've gotten good at hiding. Part of that is not staying in one place for long. If we settle here, if we become part of your flock, then we put you in danger too."

Soren goes silent for a moment, trying to think of the best way to answer. The best way to assuage his wolves' fears. He decides the most beneficial thing to do at this point is to be honest.

"The growls and yips of a bunch of mongrels, no matter how rich, don't frighten me in the least. But if they threaten you, if they come anywhere near you, I will eliminate them. All of them. The Volk pack will cease to exist. Their name will become nothing but a word, spoken in hushed tones by people fearful I will come for them next."

That vicious diatribe doesn't scare his wolves. Far from it. The tension eases out of both of them, and genuine smiles appear on their faces. They've been afraid for so long, running and looking over their shoulders, that his offer of protection must mean everything to them.

A depressing thought occurs to Soren. "Is this why you're willing to think about becoming my flock, for protection? Because you're fearful of Dimitri Volk?"

Complicated emotions flow across the faces of both wolves, and Soren can't even begin to sort them out. Sitting up, he effortlessly shifts Kalli and Quinn's weight to his lap and hugs the two of them, Kalli tucked close to his chest and Quinn snuggled in behind her. They relax into his embrace, eagerly accepting his comfort.

"Dimitri is a scary guy," Kalli admits. "And now you know everything."

"We want to be your flock if you still want us," Quinn adds. His tone is anxious and fills Soren with sorrow. His poor wolves. Too young to be forced to make such harsh decisions. Forced to choose between safety and love. Between the Volk and each other.

Considering the threat looming over them, are they free to choose him? He can't pretend their choice is being made without undue influence. Even Quinn, with his easy optimism, must know that a pack with the resources of the Volk will find them, even living in the woods as they did before moving in with him. It's only a matter of time before a bit of bad luck means someone sympathetic to the Volk or looking to win favor with them stumbles across Kalli and Quinn's location. Even a general location would be enough for the Volk to rain down hunters and sniff the two out.

"I can't," Soren vocalizes his realization. Both wolves stiffen and try to pull away from him. "No, I mean I can't yet," he amends. "You two think you don't have a choice. Or that I'm the lesser of two evils. That's not a good foundation for a flock. You need to come to me out of love, joy, and devotion, not fear."

"We're not afraid of you," Kalli protests.

"We love you," Quinn adds, and Soren can hear the truth of both statements. But that's not enough.

"And you both hold my heart in your hands," Soren pledges. "I'm heartened by your assurances that neither of you views me as terrifying. But I can't let fear from others be the reason you're willing to join me. That's the two of you still being coerced into being my flock. Let me look into neutralizing the threat of the Volk. Then we can join together with no doubts about motivations."

He hears their hearts beat wildly. The strong scent of fear comes off both of them.

"Don't go near them!" Kalli states sternly. "Don't even search for them on a web browser. They'll find out. I don't know how, but they'll find out!"

"Easy," he murmurs. He puts more power in his aura and lets his calming scent fill the room. It works. Heartbeats slow and agitated movements subside.

"I'll be subtle," he promises. "I have a lot of resources of my own. I can hire some people so no attention will be drawn here. I'll have them go over that pack with a fine-tooth comb. There's got to be something I can leverage. Give me a chance to find the key to bargaining with the Volk. To get Dimitri to give up on you two. And I promise to warn both of you before I make contact."

"There isn't and he won't," Kalli proclaims morosely. "We'll be stuck in limbo forever waiting for you to figure that out."

"Give me six months," Soren negotiates. "If I can't find something in six months, I'll make you my flock even if I can't force the Volk to do as I want them to do."

That makes both of them brighten. "Six months isn't too long," Quinn agrees.

"You'll make sure they don't find out where we are, right?" Kalli checks.

"If it would make you two feel more comfortable, we can move around a little. As I've said before, I have estates in other places.

Both of them nod their heads as Kalli voices their opinion. "That sounds like a good idea. But let's finish out winter here."

"Of course," Soren says with a smile. He rests his cheek on top of Kalli's head and strokes a hand down Quinn's back. Content, the three of them watch the crackling fire as companionable silence fills the room.

It took him centuries, but he's finally found the loves of his life.

There's something Quinn can't get out of his head and for the first time in his entire life, he's scared to tell Kalli. She probably won't judge him, but the idea feels so forbidden that he's still worried about her reaction.

It's been a week since the evening in the den when Soren refused to accept them as flock until he is sure they aren't doing it out of fear.

For the first few days, they tried to make him understand that fear had very little to do with their adoration of him, but it didn't work. That's fine. Six months isn't long in the grand scheme of things, and Kalli and him have had plenty of practice being patient.

He's not so thrilled with the idea of Soren poking around the Volk, but they've decided to trust the vampire. If the man has survived for over two hundred years, he must be clever.

Absently, Quinn drains the pot full of boiling water and pasta into a colander. Steam fills his vision as he listens to Kalli and Soren talk behind him. They're sitting at the kitchen table, discussing one of Soren's businesses. Quinn only listens with half an ear; he's not intrigued by Soren's companies. Not like Kalli.

The moment he could, Soren started giving Kalli minor tasks to do. Answering a few emails, putting together spreadsheets, and getting quotes from vendors. Quinn can see that Soren's training Kalli. It's obvious that the vampire fully expects Kalli to take over a lot of the day-to-day running of several, if not most, of Soren's enterprises.

From what Quinn has witnessed so far, Soren's an excellent teacher. Patient and methodically building up the complexity of the tasks he gives Kalli, so she doesn't get overwhelmed. While Quinn admires Kalli's enthusiasm, he shudders at the idea of having to take on even one of the projects Soren's handed her.

No, he'd much rather spend his days playing video games and cooking for his mate.

And reading.

The luxury of getting to spend hours each day reading is amazing, and it's pure joy to have access to so many books again.

He plays with the idea of trying to write something himself. Maybe a short story to start with. He's got plenty of ideas in his head, but he hasn't had the courage to organize them yet.

Creativity wasn't encouraged by the Volk pack. Quinn can perfectly remember the day his parents found his first attempt at creative writing. He was only ten, and it was nothing but badly drawn pictures and chicken scratch on a dozen rough-cut pages of butcher paper all held together with a few staples. It might have been amateurish in the extreme, but it was obviously a fictional story. They deliberately tore the pages up while calling him lazy and useless.

If the story ended there it would have been a tale of woe, but there's a Kalli in this story so it has at least a satisfactory ending.

Unbeknownst to him, his future mate dug in the trash until she found every scrap of his story. Then she painstakingly pieced it all back together and used so much tape on it that the entire thing was glossy by the time she was done.

She gave it back to him and then they clung together as he cried happy, relieved tears. It wasn't that she rescued his story. It was that she didn't denigrate him for creating it. She loved him even if he wasn't interested in the blood sports that got all the other pups excited. She loved him, even if he liked to make up stories in his head.

She simply loves him for him.

And Soren loves him the same way.

If he wanted to try writing again, this would be a safe place to do it. But maybe he should read some books on the subject first?

"I don't remember what it was like," Soren admits, his tone drawing Quinn out of his thoughts. "It was so long ago and only that once. I remember the pain, but that's it."

"Does it have to hurt?" Kalli asks. "I've heard it's erotic, but that could be from all the human books about vampires, so I don't know if it's true."

"Sometimes the humans get it right, but more often they are very wrong. We don't sparkle in the sun. We combust, and it's not pretty." His dry humor makes both Quinn and Kalli laugh.

"What are we talking about?" Quinn queries, even though he's already pretty sure he knows.

"Vampire bites," Kalli answers, unaware that her simple statement has sent blood rushing to Quinn's cock. "He's never even tried to bite either of us, and I was wondering if biting is only about food or if there's a sensual element to it like in the books and movies."

Goddess bless Kalli for the question, but damn her for the timing. She just voiced something Quinn's been wondering about for . . . well, ever since he found out Soren is a vampire. His imagination went haywire, and he's had a couple of reoccurring wet dreams that included Soren biting him.

But why did they need to have this conversation right now? He's got sauce bubbling on the stove and hot pasta in the sink to deal with.

"Well?" Kalli presses when Soren's silent a beat too long.

Quinn tries to make himself look busy while he waits for Soren's answer. But when he looks up, he finds Soren regarding him with a knowing expression. Damn perceptive vampire.

"Quinn, I'm sure dinner can keep for a few minutes. Why don't you join us for a bit?" Soren's tone is neutral, but there's an undercurrent to his words that makes lust pool in Quinn's belly.

"I really should, uh, you know, finish here," Quinn says even as he shuts off the burner under the sauce and nearly drops the empty pot on the counter in his haste to put it down.

"Quinn?" Kalli's voice is amused, and her expression can only be labeled as anticipatory. "I'm not all that hungry. Dinner can be late."

As if drawn by invisible strings, Quinn stumbles over to where Soren has pushed his chair away from the table. Lust sparks on the vampire's face when he sees the evidence of Quinn's arousal straining the front of his pants.

"Have you been thinking about it?" Soren's voice is soft and seductive, making a strange shiver go through Quinn. "Maybe you've been daydreaming about me. About these teeth." He grins widely, showing Quinn his descended vampire fangs.

Licking his lips, Quinn tries to deny it, but no words come out. Embarrassment makes his face flush at the same time arousal is making him feel a little dizzy.

He's a wolf. He's a predator. He shouldn't want to know what it would feel like to have sharp fangs slide into his hot flesh. He's not food.

Quinn doesn't resist when Soren pulls him down to sit sideways on his lap. He half expects Soren to tangle his fingers into Quinn's hair and wrench his head to the side, baring his throat to those long vampire teeth. He sits, tense and waiting, unsure what to expect and uncertain how to feel about it.

No, that's not true. He knows exactly how he should feel about it. Ashamed.

He braces for Soren to be rough. Waiting for Soren to do something painful and humiliating.

But he should know better.

Soren takes one of Quinn's hands in his own and brings the back of it up to his lips, pressing a gentle kiss to the skin there. The unexpected action makes Quinn melt a little and some of his shame dissipates. They're just talking. And Soren would do nothing without permission.

Quinn is relieved that he doesn't have to worry about having a vampire bite forced on him. He's relieved. Completely reassured. Totally relaxed. No, he isn't longing for it. Or pondering how it would feel. He's not like that.

Except those stupid dreams keep popping up in his mind.

"It's true that we need blood to survive," Soren explains. "But biting isn't always about food. Just like eating isn't always about getting nutrients into the body. Sometimes food is about pleasure. Biting can be like that too."

"Dessert," Kalli interjects. Quinn slides his gaze over to her, surprised to find she isn't looking at Soren. She's watching him, and there's lust in her eyes. "Biting for pleasure, it's like dessert."

"Yes, exactly," Soren agrees. He places a gentle hand on the back of Quinn's neck and urges him closer. Quinn gives to the pressure of Soren's hand, and soon he feels the Vampire's hot breath across the side of his neck.

"The first bite is always the hardest. You don't know what to expect. You think it will hurt, and you brace for that. I've had a lover look like she was about to faint even as she turned her head to give me access to her neck."

"Did she faint?" Kalli asks. Quinn is holding himself perfectly still. The vampire's gentle voice sends waves of desire through him. He's so hard that it's painful to have his cock trapped in his pants.

"I didn't bite her," Soren tells them. He runs his tongue along the edge of Quinn's ear and nips at the earlobe, making Quinn quiver.

Kalli asks the question that Quinn can't get his lips to form. "Why not?"

Soren doesn't take his mouth away from near Quinn's ear. When he speaks, Quinn can feel his breath on the shell of his ear.

"She was only willing to do it because she thought to appease me. But bites between lovers shouldn't be like that. One shouldn't feel the need to brace or to fear. It should be something you relax into. Something that makes your pulse leap from the anticipation of pleasure, not pain. It should be all about seduction, not duty or force."

Quinn doesn't even realize he's moved his head to the side until he feels Soren's hand move up from the back of his neck to cup the back of his head. The hold is still soft, and Quinn knows he could easily pull away if he wanted to.

Soren leans his face close to Quinn's exposed neck. It's the same side as the old scars Kalli gave him when they mated. When Soren runs one long canine over the upper mark, Quinn can't hold himself still. It feels like a live wire just touched his skin. Goddess, is this what it feels like for Kalli when he bites at her mating scar? Soren has only scraped the skin, not even pressed down, and it feels intensely pleasurable.

Soren draws back a bit, and Quinn makes a needy sound. "Shhh, my sweet wolf, I'd never leave you unfulfilled," Soren whispers. "But you're going to have to be patient."

He lays a butterfly kiss on Quinn's skin, then brings his head up to address Kalli. "Would you care to join us?"

"Oh hell, yes," Kalli breathes out, and when she draws close, Quinn can smell her arousal.

The world spins slightly as Soren rearranges Quinn on his lap. Now his legs are dangling on either side of Soren's, his turgid cock uncomfortably confined in his too-tight pants. "If you would be so kind as to free him," Soren tells her, rubbing a palm over Quinn's erection. "Then you could put your mouth on him."

"You get the top half. I get the bottom half," Kalli declares with a grin. Her pupils are blown with desire as she sinks to her knees between Soren and Quinn's legs. "Seems like a fair deal to me."

Quinn can't help the low moan that comes out of him after Kalli gets his pants unzipped and pulls his throbbing dick free. He jerks when she wraps her hands around him and strokes his length a few times, murmuring about how beautiful he is.

Soren's hand moves around to cup under Quinn's chin, applying a little pressure until Quinn tilts his head so the back is resting on Soren's shoulder. Even after Quinn's head is where

Soren wants it, he doesn't remove his hand. He slides it down a little so he's petting the front of Quinn's neck with his fingers. Quinn knows he can move away, but there's something intoxicating about having the vampire's big hand wrapped around his vulnerable throat.

"There now, isn't that comfortable?" Soren whispers as he rubs a small circle with his thumb over the pulse point of Quinn's neck, just below Quinn's ear. More than anything, Quinn wants Soren to replace that thumb with his mouth.

"Soren," Quinn whines, feeling all kinds of overwhelmed. Between Soren's hot breath on the skin of his neck and Kalli teasing his cock, he feels ready to combust. She gives him a playful nip. "Oh please, Kalli!"

He's not sure what he's begging for, but when Kalli slips the head of his cock into her hot, wet mouth, he jerks and almost comes right there. Long familiar with the signs of his orgasm, she deftly wraps her small hand around the base, stopping him from being able to come.

"It seems our little Kalli knows you well," Soren comments with a light, almost soundless chuckle. "Everything feels so much more intense when you're on edge, doesn't it? Now, where was I before Kalli joined us? I believe I was explaining about bites."

As he talks, he keeps his thumb on Quinn's pulse point, but also brings his mouth there too, licking the skin below his thumb, making Quinn moan. Between what Soren is doing to his neck and Kalli's mouth on his cock, this is the sweetest torture he's ever endured.

"As I was saying, what many don't understand is that allowing a vampire you love to sink his fangs into you doesn't make you weak or prey. It shows trust and devotion. Think of it like a blow job. Right now, Kalli's soft lips are wrapped around your cock, her tongue stroking you. She's making little moaning sounds because you taste so good. But you're also trusting her to not use her teeth on your vulnerable manhood. A vampire bite is like oral sex. It can be a show of affection and adoration, a way for one partner to give the other pleasure. If done wrong or unkindly, it can be painful and humiliating."

Quinn is panting now, and Kalli pulls her mouth off him, raining little kisses down on his groin. Soren moves his thumb out of the way and scrapes a fang over the unmarred flesh of Quinn's neck.

For a moment, Quinn fantasizes about having two marks on him. Kalli's on one side and Soren's on the other. The image is so real in his mind that he knows he doesn't only *want* Soren to bite him, he *needs* the vampire to mark him.

"Soren, you have to," he demands, his voice so soft it's barely audible. "I need it. I need your mark."

"I won't scar you," Soren tells him, his soft words leaving a heated trail down his neck. "But I'll sink myself into you in a way no one ever has before. Later, I can leave a mark, but not this time. Never the first time."

His skin feels overheated. His heartbeat is roaring in his ears, and his erection is throbbing in time with his pulse. He doesn't think he can last another moment, sitting on the edge of this precipice. The sensations are so intense that his eyes are watering, and even the mellow light from the small chandelier over the kitchen table is too much for him.

Soren slides his fangs against Quinn's skin, laying the points gently with only a hint of pressure. Then they're sliding in, his flesh offering no resistance, flooding Quinn with power and sensation. Kalli sucks him back into her mouth and down her throat, making him come with a strangled scream.

Pleasure explodes in him, and he can see starbursts behind his closed eyes. He sobs because he feels like he's being consumed by his orgasm. He's experienced nothing this intense. All he can do is let it wash over him like a powerful wave and hope he can breathe when it's all over.

Seconds or hours later, Soren withdraws his teeth and Kalli gives him one last lick, then lets him pop out of her mouth. She stands up and somehow fits herself on Soren's lap as well.

Much like he does every night, Soren wrap those long, powerful arms around both of them, drawing them close and holding them tight.

If the orgasm was the most intense thing he's ever experienced, this afterglow is the most beautiful. He sits between Kalli and Soren, feeling protected, loved, and cherished.

They're silent as they embrace. Quinn can feel contentment radiating off both Kalli and Soren.

He feels mildly guilty that he took everything for himself, but knows he'll get the chance to return the favor later. He'll make sure Soren and Kalli are thoroughly pleasured to thank them for this moment.

When Soren speaks, Quinn feels like he's saying something that all three of them are experiencing. "I never thought I'd feel the sun again. Then you two entered my life, and I get to bathe in warmth."

It's true. The warmth surrounds them, their love adding together until it's greater than the sum of its parts.

After a while, Kalli wiggles out of the embrace and sits up, giving both of them a wide grin. The scent of her unfulfilled arousal perfumes the air, and Quinn thinks he should get up and focus on pleasing his mate, but his body feels drained at the moment.

"Me next!" she announces, making both Soren and Quinn chuckle. She cranes her neck to the side and offers up the unscarred side to Soren.

If he wasn't feeling so boneless and content, Quinn might have done more than laugh. As it is, he's lucky the big vampire is holding him steady because, otherwise, he would have wobbled off the man's lap and landed in a heap on the floor.

The fact that Kalli wants Soren to bite her evaporates the last vestiges of doubt Quinn was feeling.

"After dinner," Soren promises.

That makes Kalli nod her head and settle back down and murmur, "I can't wait to be dessert."

Snow blankets the ground as Kalli jogs back from checking the nearby pond. Soren told her that if the winter is cold enough, the pond will freeze, but it doesn't happen every year.

Then he offered to take her to the skating rink in town if she wanted. But she doesn't want some manmade rink. She wants to skate on a pond just like she did as a child.

That gives her pause and makes her come to an abrupt halt within sight of the house. Why is she so eager to relive her childhood? The best of it is sitting in the house waiting for her.

If it wasn't for Quinn, she would never know what it's like to be happy or to feel love. If it wasn't for Quinn, she might have done something she would have regretted before she hit twelve.

The eagerness to ice skate dims. Forget ice skating. It's a dumb activity anyway. Besides, Quinn isn't a fan, and that's enough of a reason as any to put the idea aside. Maybe she'll get back into skiing. She and Quinn skied regularly as teenagers. That's a hobby they could do together and enjoy.

It's funny. She hasn't thought about those things in the years they've been on their own, but now they have the time and space to indulge. And if she's honest with herself, she gets a little bored during the day while Soren sleeps. Even with the days shorter and his time confined to the basement reduced, she and Quinn aren't good at sleeping in or staying confined in the house while the sun's up, no matter how late they stay up the night before.

The two of them read, play video games, watch movies and TV shows. Quinn cooks meals, and Kalli helps Soren with projects. But none of that is enough movement for either of them. Shifters are athletic and aren't good at remaining still for long periods of time.

They've been with Soren for almost two months now, and both of them are mentally and sexually fulfilled, but physically restless.

So that means finding hobbies is their new pastime. Maybe they should look into online classes. Nothing too serious, but Quinn might like to learn more about cooking. Or maybe psychology because he's so good at judging emotions and helping people talk through things. He might like to study it for real. And she could do a few classes on business or economics. Maybe she could learn enough to be a bigger help to Soren. That would be fun.

A twig snaps loudly in the quiet, snow-filled silence around her. That sharp sound draws Kalli out of her thoughts and makes her look around. It's the middle of the day, and she's only fifty feet from the house, but a sense of danger invades her. She freezes in place, trying to figure out where the danger is coming from. Is it her imagination or is there something out there?

She searches the area carefully, looking for anything out of place. Her human eyes see nothing, but that doesn't make her relax. Her human eyes like to see colors, not patterns. Unlike most other shifters, she can change a single part of herself, so switching to her animal vision only takes a moment of concentration.

The colors of the world become muted. Greens and reds disappear altogether, and patterns jump out at her, making it easy to spot the three men crouched in the woods wearing winter camouflage.

Fear and rage fill her body in equal measures. Who are these men that think they can invade their territory? How dare they!

They haven't noticed her yet. She's wearing the new coat Soren bought her, and it's a soft sage color that blends in well with the evergreens behind her. The men are all focused on the house, creeping through the forest with rifles and shotguns in their hands.

Silently ducking back behind a nearby tree, she strips off her clothes, leaving them in a pile in the snow. The moment she's naked, she shifts and sprints through the forest to get behind the hunters. They've gotten to the east side of the house now, and they've stopped to argue.

"Why the fuck aren't there any windows?" the biggest of the three grumbles, looking around nervously. All three smell human, but that could be misleading. Some spells can make even the most powerful magic creature look and smell human. Hell, Soren is a perfect example. He's so strong that he could completely mask both his scent and magic from them.

"There are windows, Ted," the man to his right argues, pointing up to the second-story balcony that leads to her and Quinn's room.

"I mean windows we can climb through, you dumbass," Ted snarls. "Windows on the first floor."

The second man cowers a little. "Sorry," he says quickly. "Maybe there's a back door or something."

"We could go through the front," the third man suggests. "Ring the fucking doorbell and wait for someone to answer and then take them prisoner."

Ted smacks the man on the back of the head. "What if they look through the peephole and see us? They run off, and then we have to break down the door to get to them."

"If there aren't any windows, then they can't get very far," the second man reasons. "We bust down the front door and trap them in the house."

"Yeah, you have a point, Lenny," Ted says, and Lenny smiles in relief. "Go around back, and if there's a back door, keep it covered. George and I will come in through the front door. Remember, we're after that girl. The delivery guy said that she and two guys live here. If you have to shoot her, make it non-lethal. But fuck the guys. Take 'em out if they try to stop you."

"I've never shot anyone before," Lenny whines, looking nervous.

"If we do this right, you won't have to this time," George assures him. "We've got the guns. That will make them afraid. We tell them that we're only here to collect the girl, and they'll probably let us leave with her. I mean, if some fucker came into my house and demanded Linda, I'd hand her over. No bitch is worth getting shot over."

Lenny perks up. "Yeah, you're right! This will be easy."

They talk a little more as Kalli debates with herself. She could sprint around the building and get inside before any of these jokers get to the door. That would allow her to warn Quinn, but that would also trap them in the house. As much as she hates to admit it, those guns intimidate her.

Growing up in Alaska, she's hunted in both her human and wolf form. She's shot moose and caribou with a rifle to provide fresh meat for the pack. She knows what one well-placed bullet can do to a body. Wolf shifters are tough, but not even they can survive a round to the head or the heart.

The other issue is that Soren is in his basement room, probably sound asleep. He's vulnerable. Even if these men can't get past the reinforced door leading down, they could decide to set fire to the house to flush her and Quinn out. No, going in is a bad idea.

But getting Quinn out might be a good bet.

Loping away from the men, she finds a suitable spot on a nearby rise and starts howling, loud and insistent, over and over again. The men are ignoring her as they part ways, Lenny heading to the back, George and Ted going to the front.

Before Lenny can get in place, Quinn's wolf bursts out the back door. She hears Lenny's cry of surprise as her mate bolts past him and through the garden. The man doesn't even have time to bring his rifle up before Quinn has disappeared into the woods.

She howls again to help Quinn find her. Soon he's skidding to a halt next to her. He shifts and grabs her in a tight hug. She shifts in his arms, and they shiver in the cold as they hold each other.

"What's going on?" Quinn asks. "Who was that guy at the back door? He had a gun!"

"I don't know, but I'm pretty sure they're here for me," Kalli admits.

"How the hell did they find us?" Quinn spits out.

She shrugs helplessly. "No idea. But they sound like they don't know what's going on. They definitely don't know a vampire lives here."

That makes Quinn laugh humorlessly. "If they did, they wouldn't dare walk into that house. Soren can come up to the first floor if he has to."

"I know, but he's probably dead asleep."

No sooner are those words out of her mouth than the two of them hear a blood-curdling roar, then gunfire.

Soren's not asleep any longer.

Without a word, both Kalli and Quinn shift back into their animal forms and sprint back to the house, both of them coming to an abrupt stop in the doorway to take in the chaos.

"What the fuck is that!" Lenny screams. He's cowering near the front door, reloading his shotgun with shaking hands. "What the hell is he doing to George?"

"Keeping firing!" Ted orders as he pulls the trigger on his rifle. Kalli's sensitive wolf ears fill with pain at the sound of the guns being fired indoors. Looking over, she sees Soren holding the third man, his fangs sunk into the man's neck. The hunter's shirt is saturated with blood and one arm is hanging at an odd angle. George's head hangs limply, and his eyes are staring off, unfocused. He's still alive, but barely.

With horror, Kalli sees one of Ted's shots hit Soren in the chest. Her vampire brings his head up from where he was draining George dry, mouth and chin covered in blood. He roars again at the men who invaded his home. How powerful is Soren? Will a round to the heart kill him? Fearful that she's about to watch one of the men she loves die, she lunges for Ted. Quinn goes for Lenny.

Lenny is closer, and Quinn takes him down in a tangle of limbs. But that gives Ted enough warning to bring his gun around. He fires at Kalli. She feels something burn a trail along her flank. The pain doesn't even register. She's too focused on her prey.

Ted doesn't have time to fire again before she's on him, driving him to the ground. She opens up her jaw and goes for his throat, but he gets his arm up to shield himself. Her teeth sink into the thick sleeve of his coat, allowing him the time to wrench his body to the side and fling her off.

She impacts hard against the nearby wall and falls to the floor, stunned for a moment.

"Wolves! I told you I saw a wolf!" Lenny screams. She watches helplessly as Lenny hits Quinn in the head with the butt of his shotgun repeatedly. Quinn has a good hold on the man's belly. He's thrashing his head, trying to rip the flesh off. Lenny is crying out in agony when Ted stumbles to his feet and swings his rifle like a baseball bat to knock Quinn off.

The round to the chest had driven Soren to his knees, but now he's getting back up. His eyes are blood red and glowing. The room fills with magic as he hisses at the men, showing off his lengthening vampire teeth.

The men forget about Kalli and Quinn as they stumble out the front door. Soren flies across the room at them, but he's too late. He roars in anger when the bright sunlight stops him from pursuing the humans.

Kalli gets to her feet and checks on her mate, nosing him with her snout and whining softly. Quinn shifts into his human skin and moans. There's a rapidly swelling lump on his head.

Swallowing back her wolf, Kalli hurries to cradle her mate's head with her human hands.

"I'm okay, Kalli," he tells her, his skin pale from the pain.

"No, you're not okay," she answers, tears welling up in her eyes. "We'll make them pay. They came into our home. Hurt us. We'll hunt them down. We'll make them the prey."

"I like that idea, but let's wait until my head stops pounding," Quinn says and tries to smile at her, but ends up wincing instead.

Soren is still on his knees at the front door, roaring and raging as the men disappear down the snow-covered driveway. When he can no longer see them, he turns to face her and Quinn.

If his expression isn't enough to clue her in, the way he shuffles up to them without saying a word would be a dead giveaway.

His thinking mind has retreated, leaving only emotions and instincts. His hands tremble a little as he reaches for them. He moves slowly, as if scared he'll either spook them or hurt them by accident. The worry in his eyes breaks Kalli's heart.

Grabbing one of his hands, she brings it to her lips to give him a kiss. George's blood covers his thumb and palm, but she ignores that. Blood is nothing new to her, and all three men deserve to die.

Glancing over, she sees George is staring back at her with blank, dead eyes. Good. One down, two more to go.

Soren edges closer to her, and soon he's picking up Quinn with gentleness usually reserved for infants. Quinn's eyes are shut tight, and he whimpers a little. Soren still says nothing, but he brings his head down and kisses Quinn gently on the mouth, then walks to the door that leads down to the basement.

Kalli gets to her feet and trails after him, startled to find she's slightly unsteady on her feet. Her chest hurts, and there's an ache in her head along with a long, throbbing wound down her side where the bullet scored her skin.

She's been hurt worse. She got cornered by a moose once and flung ten feet. She hit a tree so hard she doesn't remember anything until she woke back up in her bed, covered in bandages and looking up into her father's disapproving face.

The level of pain she's feeling now tells her that she's hurt, but nothing's broken, and she'll probably feel much better after a few hours of sleep.

By the time she makes it down into Soren's room, the big vampire has placed Quinn in the bed and is halfway across the room, probably coming back for her. He hurries up to her and picks her up the same way he did with Quinn. She sighs out a breath and lets him carry her to the bed and lay her next to her mate.

She closes her eyes for a moment. When she opens them again, Soren is gently licking the blood off Quinn's head wound. It's such a wolf shifter thing to do that it makes Kalli smile, despite her pain.

Quinn's eyes are shut and by the time Soren's done, the wolf is fast asleep. With the blood gone, Kalli can see the swelling is already going down. If it had been a serious injury, it wouldn't be healing so rapidly. Kalli lets out a sigh of relief and then closes her own eyes as Soren shifts over to begin cleaning her off.

She should get up and at least bar the bottom door. She should see if Soren has any guns and bring them down to the basement. She should get some high-protein food for Quinn to eat when he wakes up.

But she doesn't have the energy to do any of that. She falls asleep to the sound of Soren's wordless cooing and the feel of Soren's tongue laving her skin.

Soren comes back to himself slowly. Being woken in the middle of the day and forced to face a deadly situation where his wolves were under threat caused him to succumb to blood lust for the second time in his vampiric life.

He became nothing more than a raging beast. He'd wanted to tear the house apart when he was denied the second and third man. Even under the influence of blood lust, he didn't go into the sun and certain death. But that didn't stop him from roaring at the sun that kept him from chasing down his prey.

That was until he heard Quinn whimper in pain.

All the violence drained away, leaving him full of concern and fear for his wolves. He couldn't speak yet; couldn't explain to his wolves that those men will pay. Couldn't assure them that even though he drained that other man dry, that he would never do that to them. His thinking and talking brain weren't ready to come back to him. He was stuck with body language and sounds.

But his wolves understood. They didn't run. They didn't fight. They accepted his ministrations without complaint, even though he should have done so much more than merely cleaned.

As they sleep, he stands at the foot of the bed, holding vigil over his wolves.

The lead rounds in his body slowly emerge, forced out by his healing. He took six bullets during the fight, one of them even nicked his heart. It's good that he fed before going to sleep that morning or he might have succumbed to the injuries.

Bad luck for the hunters that a well-fed vampire is hard to kill. He absently notes the rounds making plinking sounds as they emerge from his body and drop to the floor. He's unconcerned. They don't matter, only his wolves matter.

As intellect returns, Soren watches his wolves, feeling deep relief every time their chests rise and fall. Fearful of accidentally hurting either of them but no longer able to maintain his distance, Soren kneels next to the bed. He takes Kalli's small, dark-skinned hand in his own much bigger and paler one. Both wolves look small and fragile to him at the moment.

When his reasoning skills finally fully return, he curses himself for being a fool. His wolves have been hurt, and he's done nothing helpful!

It's hard to let go of Kalli's hand, but he has to so he can find his phone. Looking through his contacts, he finds a doctor he knows who treats shifters. The man answers, and it only takes the promise of a hefty fee to get the doctor to cancel all his appointments for the day and agree to be at Soren's house within the hour.

Then he calls Memphis.

"Men hurt Kalli and Quinn," he tells the chimera as soon as he answers his phone. There's a beat of silence, and then Memphis lets a long string of cuss words loose. Soren waits for him to take a breath before continuing. "I need you to find these men."

"Of course I'll find those motherfuckers!" Memphis agrees. "I'll hunt their sorry asses down. They won't know what hit them."

"No!" Soren says quickly. "They're mine! I need you to find them, but don't touch them. The moment it's dark, I'm going after them.

"Shit, Soren, are you sure?" Memphis says, his voice full of concern. "Don't you want to stay with Kalli and Quinn? Vampires don't like to leave when someone in their flock in injured."

"They aren't my flock yet," Soren states grimly. "If they were, they'd probably be up and moving by now instead of still healing."

Memphis sucks in a breath. "How hurt are they?"

"I'm not sure. Dr. Seaward is on his way over. He's going to make sure my wolves are going to be fine," Soren says, his chest tightening with worry.

"Seaward knows his shit. If anyone can help them out, it'll be him. But you could bind them to you while you wait for them to get there. Make them your flock now."

Soren already thought of that and dismissed it. "You know I can't. Consent must be absolute, or the flock will wither and fail"

"I never thought I'd meet a vampire with such a strict moral code," Memphis mutters. "I'd wager that you're more honorable than the average human."

Under different circumstances, Soren would laugh. Leave it to some disreputable humans to give a vampire the moral high ground.

"It's hours until nightfall," Soren notes. "I'll be with them until it's dark. Dr. Seaward will tell me how badly my wolves are hurt, and then I'll take action."

The implication is clear. The two men that invaded his home are dead men. The only question is how much they'll suffer before they die.

"What info can you give me on the guys that attacked you?" Memphis asks, getting down to business. "Names? Descriptions?"

"I can do even better," Soren says. "Give me a minute." He hangs up and forces himself to leave Kalli and Quinn and troop upstairs.

Sneering down at the human that dared to invade his home, he takes a picture of the man's face to send to Memphis. Then he searches the dead man's pockets until he finds a wallet. He sends a picture of the driver's license. Memphis texts him back right away.

Memphis: *Looks like he's local. That'll make it easy.*

Soren: *Two got away. I think one was named Ned or Ted and the other one was Lenny.*

Memphis: *These guys sound like amateurs and idiots. It shouldn't take long to track them down. I'll text you when I find them.*

Soren: *They're mine.*

Memphis: *Yeah, I heard you the first time, fang face. I'll just babysit the dumb fucks until you're ready for vengeance and a snack.*

Normally, Soren would find Memphis amusing, but right now he has no ability to see the humor in anything, so he ignores the chimera's comment. Looking around, he notes the state of the living room. Furniture is overturned, there are holes in the wall from the men's weapons, and the human's body is dead center with blood spattered all around.

Soren decides that even the good Dr. Seaward, who treats all kinds of magical creatures, might have an issue with seeing a dead human. It's probably best to clean up a little before the physician arrives.

Grimacing with distaste, he picks up George's body and carries it to the mudroom off the kitchen. Unable to get close enough to the back door to open it and fling the body out, he contents himself with dumping it on the floor of the mudroom and leaving it there in an undignified heap.

He picks up the weapon George was carrying and a few broken bits of furniture and shoves them in a nearby storage closet. Then he pulls a rug over to cover the bloodstains. The room still looks a mess, but at least it looks like a wrestling match took place. Not a gruesome murder.

"Hello?" the familiar voice of Dr. Seaward calls out from the open front door. With light streaming through it, Soren couldn't get close enough to close it.

"Come in," Soren calls out, hurrying over as Dr. Seaward and a woman come through the door carrying several bags. "Dr. Seaward, who's this?" Soren questions the doctor with a glance at the unfamiliar face.

"This is my wife, Natalie," Seaward explains with a dip of his head at Natalie. She's a pleasant-looking woman with a soft, round face, light brown hair, and a kind smile.

"Hello, Mr. Bowen," she murmurs. "Would it be okay if I assisted my husband?"

"She helps me all the time when there are, uh, special patients," Seaward elaborates. "And just call me Seaward, you know that."

"Of course. Sorry, Seaward. I forgot you're not fond of your title or first name." Although what's wrong with Edwin as a first name, Soren can't guess.

Seaward gives his wife a warm smile as he talks. "Natalie is a trained Medical Assistant and good with other non-humans."

Turning his attention to Natalie, he gives her a small nod. Soren couldn't care less if the good doctor brings his wife to help, as long as he sees to Quinn and Kalli.

"Whatever help you need is fine, Seaward. But both of you hurry, they're down here." Soren leads them to his room. The wolves haven't moved from where he placed them on the bed.

All three of them hurry over, Natalie making soft, comforting noises as she opens bags and getting out items.

"We should put both of them on IV drips, get some . . ."

Soren doesn't pay attention to what Seaward and his wife discuss as they get to work on his wolves. He can't stop gazing down at them. Worry for their health and safety, along with a longing to murder their assailants, compete for space in his thoughts.

"Anyway, all that means is that they'll be fine," Seaward says, making Soren realize the man's been talking to him.

"Repeat that," Soren demands.

Seaward gives him an impatient look and seems like he's about to say something rude when he stops himself, probably remembering that Soren's a vampire and paying him an obscene amount of money to be there.

"This kind of sleep is normal for healing wolf shifters. There's nothing here to signify that there's any permanent damage, although we won't know for sure until they wake up. I'm giving them IV fluids, steroids, and a few other things that will help their natural healing. We should see results within the hour."

"Good," Soren says with a nod.

"I could examine and treat you too," Seaward offers, his eyes on Soren's chest.

That's when Soren realizes his own bloody state. He sleeps in soft pajama pants, but no shirt, so when danger entered his house, he attacked bare-chested. There is blood all over him, from both the wounds he sustained and the human he killed. The bullet holes are mostly closed, but one large one in his abdomen is still weeping blood. That must have been the least life-threatening, so it's the last one his body will bother healing.

All this healing means he needs to feed, even after draining one of the intruders. And he needs to clean up. He doesn't want his wolves to see him like this.

"I'm going to shower and change. You will not leave my wolves," he orders.

Seaward's expression looks mildly irritated at Soren's imperious tone, but Natalie looks misty-eyed, and her smile widens.

"We'll take good care of your beloved flock," she promises.

Soren gives her a brief nod, then gathers clothes and shuts himself in the bathroom to clean up. He showers quickly and then dresses with none of his usual attention to detail. He wants nothing more than to be with his wolves again. He doesn't even realize he put on one of his three-piece suits out of habit until he exits the bathroom and glimpses himself in a mirror on the wall.

His eyes are still a bright red.

Before he goes to his wolves, he feeds. He drinks down three bags of blood without tasting anything. It's more than he probably needs, but he feels that it's important his eyes shift back to their normal pale gray. The last thing he wants to do is cause his wolves any more distress and seeing a vampire with glowing, red eyes when they wake might do just that.

Tossing the last empty bag into a trash can, he hears Quinn groan. He hurries to the bed in time to watch Quinn open his eyes and look around in confusion.

"You're safe," Soren tells him quickly. "You and Kalli."

"Kalli," Quinn breathes out and turns his head to see Kalli lying next to him. Then his nostrils flare. His eyes lock on Natalie who's standing next to the bed, and he growls out a warning.

Scowling at Natalie, Quinn struggles to sit up. "Get away from her!"

Natalie jerks in surprise, a hurt expression on her face.

"Honey, you're a naga, remember?" Seaward says with a little huffed laugh.

Natalie colors and quickly takes a few steps back and holds up her hands, palm out. "You're in no danger from me. I'm not part of a slither, and I have no territory to protect. I'm living by human rules now." She points to Seaward. "He's my bitten and bonded mate. I'd never do anything that would make him unhappy."

"Except for swallowing live rats whole while I'm watching," he mutters under his breath.

"That was one time," she counters with a roll of her eyes.

Quinn looks back and forth between the two of them, confusion on his face, and Soren realizes that his poor wolf isn't truly awake and processing yet.

When Soren smelled naga on Natalie, it didn't occur to him that she might scare his wolves. Nagas pose no threat to a pack, but two lone wolves would be easy and tasty prey for a slither of naga.

"She can't hurt you while I'm here," Soren assures Quinn, although now he feels bad for leaving his wolves alone with the naga. She wouldn't harm them, but the fact Quinn felt unnecessary fear bothers him.

Seaward taps his arm as he pointedly stares at his wife. "Darling, maybe you could do that thing?"

Nodding, Natalie pulls up the sleeve of her shirt. She concentrates for a moment and scales form on her arm. Then she clenches her fist and flexes, causing the scales to bristle. She plucks two off as if pulling a bit of bark from a tree. There's no blood on her arm and no pain registers on her face. Soren's never seen a naga do that before, so he watches with avid curiosity as she offers one of the scales to Quinn.

"Accept my flesh as a Promise Token that no harm will come to either of you."

With wary eyes, Quinn accepts the token and watches as Natalie tucks the second scale in Kalli's limp hand, murmuring the words again.

Natalie's gesture must mean something important because Quinn closes his empty hand around Kalli's, trapping the scale there as if fearful it will fall out.

Then he slumps back down and closes his eyes, clutching his scale to his chest. Within seconds, his breathing is even, and his body has relaxed back into sleep.

Natalie straightens up and looks over at him with a soft smile. "The giving of a scale is sacred. It's a binding, magical promise. If I deliberately try to hurt either of them while they're holding my Promise Token, the pain would be redirected back on me."

"Not that you would ever hurt a soul," Seaward declares. "You're the most wonderful person I know."

"I am now that I have you as a mate," the naga declares. They lean over the bed to kiss, and Soren feels both impatient and enamored of the two.

They're obviously in love and are making their relationship work, although the good doctor is human. To be with him, Natalie must have left the protection of her slither. It's a romantic pairing and normally he might ask them questions about how they met. But he has more pressing concerns.

"My wolves?" he reminds them. Seaward breaks off the kiss to give Soren a frown, then straightens up to look down at Quinn.

"As I said earlier, the male should be fine with the medications we're giving him. I expect he'll make a full recovery by the end of the day tomorrow. I'll need to apply some bonding agent to the area on the female's side. That's a pretty bad gouge where the bullet removed dermis and a little muscle tissue. I'm afraid it's going to leave a scar; the furrow is too wide for me to prevent that. But we can make sure it heals clean. She'll probably be up and moving around before he is. We'll stay for another three hours to monitor and administer meds. After that, you really shouldn't need us any longer."

Soren nods and fights his need to touch his wolves as the doctor works. He knows he needs to stay out of the way for the moment, but it's impossibly difficult to stand by and not even hold either wolf.

Seaward is tending to Kalli, and Natalie is handing him things or searching through the bags for other items. Hoping he won't be in the way; he goes to Quinn's side of the bed and carefully sits down. Leaning his back against the headboard, he clasps his hand around Quinn's hand. The wolf's fist is still clenched around the naga scale and Soren finds it reassuring to feel those tense muscles. It's evidence of life and strength in his wolf.

But holding Quinn's hand isn't enough. He needs to be touching both of his wolves, but he's not sure how to do that without disturbing either of them or bothering Seaward.

And then Natalie is there, leaning over him to lift Quinn off the bed with her impressive naga strength.

"Scoot over," she urges. "So you can be between them. Your flock will heal better if you're close."

He doesn't bother explaining that they aren't his flock yet as he moves over. Once he's in place, Natalie lays Quinn back down. Even unconscious and hurt, Quinn rolls to his side and throws a leg over Soren. On his left, Kalli sniffs, whispers something unintelligible, then snuggles up to him as well.

With his wolves healing and tucked in on either side of his big body, Soren feels himself relax enough to let his head thump back on the pillow and close his eyes. He dozes off as Seaward and Natalie talk in quiet tones while they care for his wolves.

The minute the sun goes down, his eyes pop open and his fangs descend.

It's time to hunt.

With the setting of the sun, the doctor and the naga depart, leaving several bottles of pills to administer to the wolves over the next twenty-four hours and detailed instructions for wound care. Soren watches the couple leave with mixed feelings.

He wants them gone so he can lock up his wolves in the underground room and go hunt for those humans. But he worries that there might be unforeseen complications and his wolves will need the doctor again.

No sooner does the doctor's small SUV disappear down the drive than a loud, ancient, rusty truck comes barreling up. It skids to a stop in an unplowed patch of snow and a familiar, grinning face opens the door to hop out.

"Knoxville, what are you doing here?" Soren asks.

"Now come on there, Soren. You know it's just Knox. Don't Knoxville me. Mama is the only one that calls me that, and she is a damn sight prettier than you," Knox says with a chuckle as he crosses the short distance from his truck to Soren. "Memphis asked me to come over. He said you've gotten yourself a flock and might need someone to look after them for a bit."

Leave it to Memphis to think of this. Knox is the youngest of the Granger brothers, but also the one most eager to help his siblings. He makes a modest living as a roofer, earning enough in the spring, summer, and early fall to spend his winter dedicating himself to his music.

It always amused Soren that the brother named Nashville has no musical talent. All the musical aptitude went to Knox.

The other thing he finds amusing about the Granger family is that not a single one of the sons has ever been to Tennessee, despite all of them being named after the cities of that state.

Their mother grew up there and pays homage to her home state with the names of her sons but refuses to return. Soren's never gotten the story of what happened, but it sounds like there might have been a major family dispute over her choice of husband.

All that aside, after Soren rescued Memphis from Darius's fledgling, the whole Granger family adopted him. The Granger matriarch, a human woman named Lizzie, even visits him occasionally. She declared him her seventh favorite son.

The fact that she has eight sons in total led to an argument over which sons Soren replaced in her favor. It all would have been more entertaining if Soren hadn't been in danger of losing furniture and maybe even walls during the resulting quarrel and tussle among the siblings.

As much as he adores the family, Knox is the only brother Soren would trust besides Memphis to look after his flock. "They're in my room."

"Still out cold?" Knox asks as he glances into the house through the broken front door.

"They'll probably sleep through the night," Soren explains, and leads him inside. Knox only glances at the door to the basement as he heads straight for the kitchen. All the Granger brothers are always hungry. He hosted the whole family for a single four-day weekend once a year ago. He ended up ordering the equivalent of three cows in an attempt to keep the family sated.

"Try not to eat all the food. Quinn and Kalli will need to eat when they wake."

Laughing, Knox glances over at him and gives a brief nod before ducking his head into the fridge. "I'll cook up a feast for the three of us while you're out teaching some dumb humans a permanent lesson in manners."

"I take it Memphis told you everything?"

"He sure did. Don't you worry. He's there now, still making sure those boys stay put. He said they're busy calling back and forth with some important muckety-mucks trying to get more money out of 'em." Knox gives Soren a feral grin. "They got no clue. Go make them understand the error of their ways then send them off to meet their maker."

Knox digs his phone out of his back pocket. After a few taps, he turns it to show Soren. A map is on display showing a pulsing dot. "That's Memphis," Knox explains. "Head to him and he'll take you to your next meal."

Soren takes a few seconds to memorize the map, then dips his head in a sharp nod, turns on his heels, and strides out the front door. He's shifting into his raven form the moment he's out from under the porch roof.

He wings his way to Bend, easily spotting the familiar landmarks that will lead him to the part of town housing the men. He circles until he spots Memphis's Jeep, then swoops down, shifting in the shadows behind the vehicle.

Memphis is already getting out, his expression grim. "It's about damn time you got here."

"Thank you for sending Knox," Soren growls out without looking at Memphis. His eyes are locked on a house across the street. A war movie is being played so loud that Soren can hear the dialog of two soldiers along with the sound effect of bullets being fired continuously in the background.

"These two are loud, annoying, and they stink," Memphis mutters as he follows Soren's gaze across the street. "I think we're about to do the entire neighborhood a favor."

Soren ignores the chimera as he walks down the driveway to the back of the house. There are several windows, one broken and half covered by a piece of wood, and a back door sagging on its hinges. The house is in a sad state of disrepair, unlike the neighbors' modest but well-tended homes.

Without pause or hesitation, Soren rams through the back door. The door might as well have been made of cardboard for all the resistance it offers.

The house is small with an open floor plan, so he sees the two men sitting on the couch, watching TV, and surrounded by empty beer cans and full ashtrays. Splinters from the door don't even have a chance to land before Soren is charging at the men.

The larger of the two of them tries to scramble off the couch, crying out in fear. The smaller, wiry one with a straggly beard, fumbles for something tucked into the waistband of his pants.

"Ted! It's the monster! You said you killed him! You said he was dead!" The man in the corner is quaking with fear. Memphis flashes past Soren to grab the cowering man, allowing Soren to focus on Ted. The human pulls a gun out from his pants and fires one wild shot before Soren is on him.

With ruthless efficiency, Soren cracks the man's head to the side and sinks fangs in, making the feeding as painful as possible. Ted cries out and struggles weakly, but agony is rapidly overwhelming his body.

It doesn't take long for Ted's heart to start laboring as his body is deprived of blood. Soren unhooks his fangs and pulls away from Ted's neck. He holds the man up, forcing the human to meet his gaze.

"Can you feel it?" he asks. "Can you feel death coming for you? This was the last day of your life. I hope you enjoyed it."

"Please," Ted begs, but then seems to realize that Soren has no mercy in him. "Fuck you." His curse is whispered because he's having a hard time forming words. His lungs are laboring to get oxygen to his system, but with no blood to carry it, his brain is dying. "Fucking devil. Fucking burn in hell."

Soren grins, showing off long fangs and bloody teeth. Ted whimpers out a "no," before Soren drops him to the ground. He lets the man lie there, his breathing becoming more erratic as he dies.

Ted is scared and in pain. He'll die on the filthy floor of his house and, judging by the lack of pictures on the walls, without family or friends to mourn him. Soren briefly considers this death too kind. Unlike other vampires, it wasn't in him to draw out Ted's suffering any further. At least the man's death will bring safety to his flock. That's more important than keeping the human alive for torture.

The second man, Lenny, is sobbing and begging Memphis to let him go. The chimera is unmoved by his pleas, but Lenny keeps trying anyway.

"I've got money. And you can have my car. It's paid off and everything. And I could get money from my mom. She's got some stashed away. I can get that. Don't kill me. I'll do anything, but don't kill me!"

That plea for his life is high-pitched and ends with snot flowing down his face. Memphis winces, both at the pitch of Lenny's voice and the sight of his face.

"Fuck, man. Have some dignity," Memphis admonishes him. "You wanted to play tough guy and kidnap a couple of people. Now you think you deserve compassion?"

"Not my idea! Ted wanted to do it. It was his idea. All of it. Swear to God, I didn't want to go. I didn't!"

Soren hisses, showing off fang, and Lenny squeals in terror and talks faster. "And we didn't get close to anyone. They had wolves in that house. Big, fucking wolves!"

"Those wolves are my people," Soren growls at him, and Lenny's body goes slack.

"No, no, no, no, no," he mumbles, eyes glazed with fear. "Not real. No, no, no, no. Can't be real."

"Tell us why," Memphis demands. The human doesn't respond right away, so Memphis shakes him. That gets Lenny's attention.

"T-t-t-ted found a bounty," Lenny stammers out, his wide, fearful eyes bouncing between Soren and Memphis. "He's on this site for uh . . . dark stuff? And he saw her picture. Kalliope something. Pretty thing. He was going to let me have a go. Bounty was for her alive, but nothing said she had to be whole. Bruises don't count, right?"

They need this information, or Lenny would already be ripped in two. As it is, Soren is barely keeping himself in check. This human is vile.

"But then we didn't get her, and there were those wolves and you . . . and . . . George died . . . and Ted wanted more money. I said to leave it. We got out alive, and we shouldn't go back. But he said that they wouldn't expect a second attack, and it would be easy. We could burn the house and smoke them out. Kill the wolves with a rifle and hit the girl with a tranq shot. Easy money." Lenny closes his eyes, tears flooding down his face. "Easy money. He said it would be easy money."

Memphis gives the man another shake. "I want to see the bounty notice."

Lenny points to an ancient laptop on a nearby table littered with old takeout containers. "There."

Memphis drags him over and dumps him into a chair. Lenny's hands are shaking so hard that Memphis is forced to help him type.

Soon Soren is looking down at an old picture of an unsmiling Kalli. There is text under it offering a large reward for knowledge about her location and a massive sum of money if she's handed over alive.

"Damn, that's fucked up," Memphis mutters. He points to a part of the post that says she can be *restrained in any way necessary for transport.*

There's no name of any kind, but there is a number. Soren notes it's an Alaska area code, then raises his gaze to Memphis.

"As long as this is out there, she'll never be safe. Neither of them will." Soren's words are quiet, but the chimera understands the level of rage and anxiety that simple statement is causing him.

"I know someone that might be helpful with the website," Memphis tells him. "She's into hacking and shit. Might be able to pull this bounty offer down for a while. They'll keep putting it up, but that might give us a little breathing room."

"They're coming," Lenny suddenly volunteers. Soren almost forgot he was present.

"Who's coming?" Soren asks.

"Whoever put that up . . . Ted's been talkin' to them. Said they'd give us more money and all we gotta do is tell them where she is. They said they'd come quick like." Lenny gives the two of them a hopeful look. "I can call them and could throw them off. Say you guys left or something like that."

"I need to get back," Soren growls out, fear making his heart thunder. He stalks to the back door, Memphis right behind him, dragging the crying Lenny.

"They can't have gotten here that fast," Memphis reasons. He grabs Soren's arm to keep the vampire from shifting into a raven.

"The Volk might have a demon on their payroll," Soren snarls.

"Then why would they need these two to show them where you live if they're going to portal there?"

Soren tugs his arm out of Memphis's grip and glares at the chimera. "They don't need these men! They wanted to make sure these idiots wouldn't go back there and mess things up more. They only need to get within a few miles of Kalli and they'll be able to track her aura."

Memphis gives Soren a puzzled look. "Track her aura?"

"She's an Alpha! She glows with it. The scent of their campfire told me they were in my woods that first night, but I didn't need to follow a mere fire after I took to the sky. I saw her within minutes of circling. She radiates power. How can you not see it?"

"No . . . I . . . chimeras don't have that kind of sight," Memphis says, and then his face turns fearful, and he shoves Soren into the backyard. "Fuck man, go! Get back there. My brother's strong, but he's only one guy, and he's not trained for heavy combat shit. Go!"

Soren leaps and shifts at the same time, frantically pumping his wings to gain altitude. In his haste, he almost hits a powerline, but he makes it into the open sky and wings his way home. He knows before he even lands that he's too late.

He can smell unfamiliar wolves have been and gone. There were many of them, and they were efficient. He finds Knox naked and groaning on the floor of his bedroom. There's blood everywhere. The chimera must have fought hard before being defeated. It looks like they impaled him with a silver-tipped weapon, probably originally meant for Soren.

The spear-like weapon buried in his chest isn't the only wound on Knox. He's covered in lacerations and puncture wounds. His handsome face is a swollen mess.

"They came out of nowhere," Knox whispers as Soren kneels next to him. "So many of them. I fucking bitch slapped the first two." He grins, then coughs and spits blood. "But they just kept coming. I'm sorry. They got Kalli and Quinn. I couldn't stop 'em. They hit me with silver. How the fuck did they know to hit me with silver?" He coughs again, his face pinched with pain.

Soren is frantic that his wolves have been taken, but that doesn't stop him from caring about Knox. The poor chimera needs help. "You did well, now hold still and close your eyes."

After spending so much time with Memphis, Soren is familiar with chimera physiology, so he takes hold of the shaft sticking out of Knox's chest and pulls.

Knox cries out in pain and then slumps back, unconscious. But with the silver tipped weapon no longer buried in his flesh, his whole body starts to rapidly heal. He watches Knox carefully for a moment. The gaping wound in the chimera's chest stops bleeding within a minute and his breathing never falters.

Sure that the man is on his way to healing, Soren does a swift check of the house. His suspicions are confirmed. His wolves are gone. By the look of it, they fought every inch of the way.

He finds a scorched circle in the backyard and the scent of magic heavy in the air. Remnants of a portal.

They haven't been gone long, but that's almost inconsequential. They could be anywhere. That portal could put them in Siberia or Florida. All he knows for sure is that they aren't here.

By the time he makes his way back into the house, Memphis's jeep is coming to a screeching halt out front. As the chimera comes barreling in, Soren points to his room. "He's down there, healing."

Memphis's expression is one of relief, but that doesn't stop him from galloping down the stairs to check on his brother with his own eyes. Soren follows at a slower place, worry for his wolves paramount.

"Here, talk to her," Memphis says the moment Soren steps into his bedroom. The chimera flings a phone at him. Soren catches it out of reflex and then stares dumbly at the screen that says Baby Doll Hacker.

"Hello? What the hell, Memphis! Hello out there!" a woman's voice calls out from the phone.

Soren puts the phone to his ear. "Who is this?"

"Be nice, asshole, or I won't bother helping," the woman responds without hesitation. "Memphis is important. You're just another dick demanding shit."

This must be the woman Memphis talked about earlier, the one who might be able to track the creators of Kalli's wanted poster.

Soren works hard on keeping his tone even. "I apologize. I'm scared for my friends, Kalli and Quinn. They're young, and they've been kidnapped by ruthless people."

"Yeah, the Volk pack isn't anyone to mess with," the woman agrees. Either she's part of the magical community or one of the rare humans who knows about them.

"I can help. I'm already working on it. Their firewalls are a joke. I'll call you back." She hangs up before he can say anything else, and Soren brings the phone down to stare at the blank screen dumbly.

"She'll find 'em," Memphis assures him as he helps his brother sit up.

"Crap, that hurts," Knox whines. He's pale and shaking but healing well.

"Toughen up, buttercup," Memphis smirks. His taunt is half-hearted, and his hands are gentle on his wounded brother.

"Does he—" Soren's words are cut off when Memphis's phone rings in his hand. Baby Doll Hacker. He answers it, and she talks right away.

"This is the fastest hack I've ever done," she tells him. "It's like they were begging to get hacked. Asking for it. If I didn't have you and Memphis going ape-shit over this, I'd think it was some kind of joke."

Soren tries to keep his impatience in check. "What do you know?"

"Everything," she says, and he can hear the satisfaction in her voice. "Their poster on the website gave me a backdoor to the servers at the Volk packhouse. They have a big compound a few miles north of Fairbanks. I can see them on Google Earth and everything. Say hi, motherfuckers." She cackles with glee before continuing. "Looks like they make most of their money from oil. They've got some drilling sites that pay out a good amount. But they also live pretty cheap. No fancy-ass anything except for a few small planes. But it's Alaska, so I think small, four-seater planes are kinda their version of a car."

"I need their address," Soren demands.

"No," she argues. "You need a demon. Put me on speaker. Memphis needs to hear this."

Soren walks over to his ripped apart bed where Memphis has laid out his brother. Tapping the speaker option, he sets it on the bed. "We can all hear you now."

"What you got, Baby Doll?" Memphis asks.

"Is this vampire a good friend? Like, you'd rather he didn't end up dead, right?" she asks.

"He's the only person who isn't blood related that I'd die for," Memphis tells her. And then Soren watches with fascination as Memphis blushes. "Except you. I'd die to protect you, Baby Doll. You should know that by now."

"You're a sweet talker, Memphis," the woman says with a light laugh. Soren can tell that she doesn't take Memphis's words seriously, but she should. The chimera would never announce something like that if it wasn't true. Whoever this woman is, she's important to him.

"All you need to do is tell me where you are, beautiful. I'll be there in a hot second," Memphis promises, expression hopeful.

She laughs again. "Trust me, sweet stuff, it's better we don't meet face-to-face. Your imagination is much better than reality."

"I fucking doubt that," Memphis mutters; then he must catch the expression on Soren's face. Soren mutes the call.

"After I get my wolves back, I'll help you find her," Soren promises. "I'll help you buy flowers and gifts and tell you all kinds of things to whisper to her in the dark. But for now, I need you two focused on Quinn and Kalli."

"Yeah, sorry about that," Memphis says, looking embarrassed.

"Who is the chick on the phone?" Knox asks, sitting up without help now.

"No one yet," Memphis says quickly, and Knox gets a devilish grin on his face.

"Oh man, I can't wait to tell Mom you found your female. She's going to freak out!" Knox crows. Memphis smacks him, careful to hit a bit of bare flesh on his chest that isn't healing. Knox grunts in pain, but the grin doesn't go away.

"Fuck off, we need to help Soren," Memphis growls. Soren unmutes the call, and Memphis addresses the phone. "What's going on Baby Doll?"

"These Volk guys have some serious protection spells going on," she warns them. "The perimeter around their compound is so heavy with magic that humans might even see the glow. I can't see much past that, but I have a buddy who did a job for them, and he says they're paranoid as fuck."

"Who's this buddy?" Memphis growls out.

"Later," Soren barks. His sharp tone makes Memphis stop growling with a chagrined expression.

Baby Doll Hacker misses the interplay entirely. "I can get you the basic layout of the place. But other than that, you're on your own. The Volk have a reputation for getting nasty with anyone who crosses them. I hope the people you want to get back are worth it. Because they might hunt you down and fry your ass, vampire."

"If I can't get them back, then I don't care if I live," Soren states simply, and Baby Doll Hacker makes an *awww* sound.

"Damn, that's romantic shit right there. Fine, I might be able to do a bit more. I'm going to see if I can find you a couple of demons to get you in there and out again. Those guys take days to recover from a portal jump, so you'll need two, one to get you in and one to get you out. And this is going to be as expensive as shit, so I hope your checking accounts can take the hit. I know waiting is hard but give me an hour to help set things up. Do nothing until I call you back."

Then she's gone, and Soren has no choice but to wait.

Coming awake in a rush, Kalli bolts up with a growl on her lips. She sees her father sitting in a chair at the foot of the bed and lunges for him. She doesn't get far. A chain around her neck pulls her up short. Coughing, she kneels on the bed, glaring at the calm face of her father.

"You brought this on yourself," Dimitri tells her, his expression pitying. She doesn't answer, and he sighs, shifting forward in the chair. "You were born special, Kalliope. You were supposed to be my successor. You were supposed to be the next lider."

Ignoring him, she pulls hard at the chain. It's attached to a bolt in the floor. It's unlikely she'll be able to pull it from the concrete, but that doesn't stop her. Common sense has no place in her mind right now.

Dimitri watches her struggle without expression. "I hope you enjoyed those three years with Quinn because you've doomed that poor boy."

That makes her stop pulling at the chain. Pivoting, she faces her father with a sneer on her face.

"No, you have!" she snarls. "Don't act like you had no choice. I could have been lider with Quinn at my side. I'm strong enough for the both of us."

"That boy isn't fit to be the mate of any alpha, let alone the lider of the Volk Pack," Dimitri argues with clear disgust. "He's too soft. He'd make you weak."

"He's kind, not weak, you fucking bastard," Kalli shoots back. "We need to be strong, not brutal. There's a difference. Quinn would have made sure I never crossed that line. He would have made sure every member of our pack was cared for. He would have—"

Dimitri's harsh laugh interprets her. "He'd let anyone join who had a sob story. He wouldn't have the heart to dispose of inferior stock. That boy would have been the end of us as a dominant pack in North America. He's already caused a rift between us and the Otosa pack. They were our closest allies before you two ran off."

"We ran off because I refused to mate with Ryan Otosa. That rift is because you wouldn't listen to me. Quinn and I are meant to be mates. Fated to be. You know what happens to anyone who impedes fated mates!"

Dimitri dismisses her words with a wave of his hand. "Fairy tales. Fated mates aren't a real thing, Kalli. You're just being stubborn. I thought I taught you better than this. I thought you understood what it means to be lider."

"You'd have me kill babies that aren't considered 'perfect' by some random standard? You'd have me control our pack with fear and violence? You'd have me go to war with any pack that dares to disagree with us? How can you possibly think that makes someone a good lider?"

That finally gets a rise out of Dimitri. His face darkens with anger, and his eyes narrow. But when he talks, his voice is still calm and controlled.

"I'd have you keep our people safe no matter what unpleasant task needs to be done. It's unfortunate that execution is part of being lider, but that's a harsh reality of our world."

"But it doesn't have to be!" Kalli practically screams at him. "We can be strong and kind. Those two traits aren't mutually exclusive."

It's an argument they often had when Kalli thought she might be able to persuade her father to change his draconian leadership methods. In the end, all her words fell on deaf ears, and she and Quinn were forced into taking drastic action.

Standing up, Dimitri shoves the chair away. "Enough of this. You will be mated to Ryan. You will provide pups. And I'll make sure they don't go soft like you. I'll make sure they're the lider our pack needs."

"I'm mated already," she taunts him, pulling her loose hair away from her neck to show him the mark Quinn made the first night they were on their own.

Dimitri's anger disappears, and his eyes go cold and distant. "And that will be undone soon."

Dread fills Kalli. "You can't. That could kill me too," she whispers. Dimitri's next words tell her the dread is justified.

"I've got a powerful ved'ma here now."

Kalli hisses out a breath. "You let one of those hags in the pack?"

His expression is accusatory now. "You forced me to take extreme measures. The ved'ma will make sure you don't die when I execute Quinn. Then Ryan will mate you. By then, the drugs I've given you will put you into heat. I've been told the drugs often result in twins or triplets. If that's the case, you'll only have to go through this unpleasantness once."

"Unpleasantness?" she sneers. "Say the word Father. Say it: rape. I'll only have to go through a forced mating mark and rape once if I get pregnant with more than one baby. Is this what a good lider does? Kills his daughter's fated mate and then turns her over to another wolf to be used?"

"That's an ugly word," Dimitri says, but he doesn't argue with her. He can't. "And this is what a lider does when his daughter forces his hand. It didn't need to be this way. You brought this on yourself and Quinn."

That makes her scream at him. The raw pain in her cry causes him to flinch. Then anger crosses his face. He doesn't like that he flinched. In his world, liders never flinch away from any duty.

And that's all she's ever been to him, a duty.

"I can see you are as unreasonable now as you were three years ago." With that, he leaves. Leaves her to scream and rage in the dim basement room.

She pulls and shrieks at the chain around her neck until she's worn out and her voice is hoarse. Feeling helpless, she falls back on the bed and lets a few tears slide out of her eyes. That's how her mother finds her, flat on her back, crying. How fucking perfect.

"Tears?" Angelina Volk asks, her voice dripping with disappointment. "I don't see how you have the audacity to be crying when you aren't the one who was betrayed."

Kalli sits up and keeps a wary eye on her mother. Her father might enjoy verbally reprimanding her, but Angelina has never been one to spare the rod. She spent a good deal of her childhood with bruises because Angelina found something to punish her for. By the time she was six, she learned to give her mother a wide berth. When they had to interact, she kept it to the bare minimum.

Dimitri hurt her because he thought that was how to make her strong. Angelina hurt her because she could. Or at least she did until Kalli hit puberty and became stronger than her mother.

Nothing stops a bully like strength and the willingness to use it when provoked.

"Hello, Mother. If I'd known you were going to drop in for a visit, I would have cleaned."

The look of disgust on Angelina's face doesn't change. "Sarcasm is the lowest form of wit. Although I shouldn't be surprised. You've proven how witless you are with your actions. Witless, cowardly, and selfish."

Angelina comes from a highly esteemed pack in Greece. Despite living in Alaska with her politically matched mate, Dimitri Volk, for almost twenty-four years, she still has a hint of an accent. She also never acclimatized to living in the middle of nowhere in rough country. She's always dressed as if she's about to head to the country club to attend a high-scale luncheon with other social elites.

Although she never verbally complained about her arranged mating, she showed her displeasure in a thousand little ways. She made sure everyone in the Volk pack knew she married beneath her station for the good of Lykos, her birth pack.

After Kalli was born and showed the potential to be a powerful alpha, Angelina never had to share a bed with Dimitri again. She threw herself into the Volk investments, making the pack even more rich and powerful. She left the Kalli's upbringing to others, only interacting with her child when necessary or if she was irritated and wanted to take it out on someone smaller and weaker.

The fact that Angelina wasn't interested in raising her child worked out to Kalli's benefit because, until she was a teenager, she was mostly raised by the more maternal and kinder women of the pack. They folded her in with their own pups, and she got to be surrounded by love and caring.

And she got to be with Quinn.

Then it all started going wrong when Dimitri decided it was time that she started training to become the next lider. At first, she worked hard. She trained with the warriors. She memorized both wolf shifter law and Volk pack history. She shadowed her father at every meeting and event. But she came to understand that the women that raised her had shielded her from a lot of the crueler aspects of pack life.

She watched Dimitri punish others for daring to ask for even the smallest of changes. She watched him maim some and execute others. All the while claiming it was for the good of the pack.

The day he was presented with a one-day old infant and declared it unfit was the day her world shattered. It had been developing cracks, but that was the moment her faith in Dimitri as both a fit father and a good lider ended.

She always told herself he had to be hard on her and the rest of the pack for their own good. But that day opened her eyes. The second she could get away without drawing attention to herself, she searched out Quinn and cried on his shoulder. It was the first time she'd cried in years.

After she was done crying, she and Quinn talked. They made grand plans to change everything once she became lider. It made all the horrible things happening at the moment easier to bear.

That night they made love, hiding in the back of a storage building with the scent of dust and diesel in their noses. They promised to be faithful and true to each other, both knowing they had to keep their love a secret until Kalli was officially made lider.

The next day her father declared she would mate with Ryan Otosa and presented the scowling young man to the pack.

Two days later, she and Quinn ran.

The entire time they'd been running, Kalli knew they were on borrowed time. Always the optimist, Quinn believed they'd find a safe place to settle and raise a few pups. But Kalli knew better.

But she's not going down without a fight. Kalli stares at her mother, trying to figure out if there is any way she can manipulate the woman and gain her freedom.

Pasting a smile on her face, she meets her mother's gaze unflinchingly. "Did you miss me?"

Angelina looks momentarily confused by the question. "You ran away from your duty and obligation."

"Yes, but did you miss me?" Kalli asks. "As a mother might miss a daughter."

Comprehension dawns on Angelina's face, quickly replaced by disgust. "You've made yourself into a worthless daughter."

Right, no sympathy there. No maternal instincts to tug at. Angelina's heart is nothing but cold obligation and archaic tradition.

"Let's make a deal," Kalli says, flopping back to sit on the bed and drawing up her legs to sit cross-legged.

"Deal?"

"Get me out of this." She taps the chain around her neck. "And I'll disappear. You'll never see me again. Never have to hear my name. Never have to listen to my voice. I'll be gone, and you get to go back to your perfect world of compulsory duty and an empty bed."

"If I could, I'd end you right now," Angelina says with relish.

That shocks Kalli. She knows her mother has no love for her, but that level of vitriol is unexpected. Smiling cruelly at Kalli's wide, surprised eyes, Angelina leans over to bring her face close to Kalli's.

"I should have smothered you as a baby the moment I realized I'd borne a girl. But that would have meant letting Dimitri rut into me again, and I couldn't stomach it. So, I let you live. And then your aura blossomed within a few days, and Dimitri had a party to celebrate your alpha status. But I knew you'd disappoint us. I knew you'd never measure up. A mother knows these things. But we'll get the next lider out of you, and then I'll personally slit your throat."

Angelina put herself within striking range, a mistake Dimitri didn't make. Kalli doesn't even blink when she smashes her fist into her mother's face.

The woman goes down with a cry of pain. The force of the blow sends her into a nearby wall and Kalli has the satisfaction of seeing that she might have broken her mother's jaw before a dozen wolves rush into the room, drawn by the noise.

They hurry to pick up the lider's mate and carry her out of the room, none of them making eye contact with Kalli. She recognizes all of them. Some are even pack members she thought of as friends. But now they're going to stand by and let Dimitri do as he pleases.

She can't blame them; how many years did she stand by as he did reprehensible things?

The answer is too long. Much too long.

Soon the room is empty again with the door shut. She flops back on the bed, staring up at the ductwork and piping on the ceiling. Punching Angelina probably wasn't the smartest thing she's ever done, but it has to be one of the most satisfying. She only wishes she could do the same to her father.

The door creaks open and she turns her head to see Ryan easing himself inside. She scrambles to crouch on the bed as he shuts the door.

"I'll fight you to my last breath," she warns him the moment he turns to face her.

Goddess, he got big. When she left, he was still on the scrawny side. That's all changed. In the last few years, not only did he gain a few inches of height but also a lot of brawn. He leans his wide shoulders back against a far wall and tucks large hands into his pockets. Black hair flops over his eyes as he ducks his head to stare at his worn boots.

He glances up at her, his expression woeful and scared. Then he ducks his head again, hiding from her intense, alpha eyes. She knows they must be alive with power. He's a brave soul to come into the room with her alone. She's powerful enough that she might compel him to get closer. She might not be the official lider of the pack, but she's a powerful alpha in her own right.

"I don't want to do this," he finally whispers. He shivers and wraps his muscled arms around his chest, hugging himself. "I was okay mating you back when I first got here because I thought you wanted it too. I thought after you had a kid, you'd leave me alone."

"I probably would have if I didn't love Quinn," she tells him, keeping her voice gentle.

He nods his head but keeps his eyes locked on his boots. Then he drops a bombshell. "I'm in love with Alex. If I . . . uh . . . do anything with you, he said he won't come anywhere near me ever again."

Kalli wants to say something, but she is too stunned by this news to speak. When he looks up, there are tears swimming in his eyes.

He pleads with her. "If I get you free, will you take us with you? We can't live like this anymore. We have to hide everything. We're afraid to even look at each other when anyone is around. And Dimitri's talking about pairing Alex off with Odessa."

Outrage helps Kalli find her voice. "Odessa? But she's ten or eleven, right?"

"She's only fourteen!" A little sob escapes him before he can stop it. "He says he's going to give her the same drugs he gives you. The ones that make you go into heat. She's too young!" Now the tears fall, cascading down his face. "I didn't think anything could be worse than my old pack, but the Volk is just as bad."

"Come here," Kalli demands, her face rigid and her eyes dry. Ryan walks to her slowly, dragging his feet, tears flowing unchecked down his face. When he's within reach, she grabs him by the back of the neck and pulls him close until their foreheads are touching.

"I'm your lider now," she tells him. She feels her power flare, and he shudders.

"Yes," he breathes out and his shoulders sag a little as if a weight has been lifted off him. His eyes close and his melts a little into her grip.

"If we can get me out of these chains and all of us away from the compound, I know where we can go." She thinks of Soren and how worried he must be. She knows he'll agree to help Alex and Ryan, if only because he wants her to be happy. "There's a place down south where we can form our own pack. And if my father tries to follow us, then I'll declare him vrag and kill him. Do you believe me?"

"Yes, Lider."

"We could all end up dead. Do you still want to follow me?"

Ryan opens his eyes, his expression determined. "Yes, Lider."

She lets go of him with a satisfied expression. "Good. Find the key to this fucking thing and some clothes. We need to get out of here before my heat hits."

Ryan straightens up and hurries out of the room. She hears a rushed conversation in the hall and then silence. Several sets of footsteps walk away, and she relaxes. Looks like she's done with visitors for the moment.

Hold on, Quinn, she thinks. *I'm getting us out of here.*

Huddled in the corner of the steel cage, Quinn watches as a few men put together a temporary stage. He's freezing, thirsty, hungry, and he hurts. He doesn't even try to shift. He knows better. Dimitri had this cage commissioned when Quinn was only a few years old. Its metal bars are magically enhanced to not only keep shifters from using their strength to break out, but also to trap them in their human form.

He fought hard when the Volk wolves came to take them away. Kalli woke to the noise of battle and joined him, but he was already injured by that time, and Kalli was still out of it from the medications the doctor had given her. The fight was over embarrassingly fast. The next thing he knew, they were dragging him through a portal and tossing him into this cage while they carried an unconscious Kalli into the main house.

As he watches the stage being set up, he feels a strange calm come over him. He's going to die on that platform. His execution will be a show that Dimitri puts on to remind the Volk that disobedience means a death sentence.

He knew that getting to live happily-ever-after was a long shot. But he'd always been an optimist. Why bother wasting time contemplating everything that can go wrong when you can look forward to a future where things might go right?

Too bad it looks like the worst-case scenario has happened. Not only did Dimitri find them, but he captured them and is wasting no time organizing Quinn's punishment. Idly, he wonders how Dimitri will do it. Knife to the heart? Behead him? Both are options he's seen done in the past.

A shadow falls on him. Looking over, he sees a terrified face looking back at him. He doesn't say anything. His teeth are chattering too hard to talk. Even if they don't kill him soon, he'll die from exposure if left in this cage after the sun goes down. It's winter, so there are only a few hours of daylight to work with. They'll need to make it happen soon or they'll be trying to slit the throat of a pup-sicle.

Ha! Pup-sicle!

Then he sees the familiar face of Alex staring at him. "Why are you smiling?" Alex asks, his voice horrified. "Have you lost your mind?"

Quinn tries to shrug his shoulders, but the shivers probably make it look like he's having a seizure. Alex's expression turns concerned.

"You need to stay awake," he whispers urgently. "We're going to get out of here. You, me, Ryan, and Kalli. But you need to be ready to move. 'Kay?"

He nods his head as best he can, and Alex looks slightly relieved. Then someone shouts over by the stage, and Alex hurries away before he's caught talking to Quinn.

Hope, that fragile flower, unfurls in his chest. They're not done fighting yet.

Quinn knows it's bad that he isn't shivering anymore. His body should be quaking and shaking to keep him warm, but it isn't. And his eyes keep trying to close. He wants to curl up and sleep. That sounds perfect, but he forces his eyes open.

If he lets himself go to sleep, he might not wake up.

A commotion makes him turn his head to watch several sets of people running across the large, open, communal area of the compound. The stage looks like it's not quite finished, but men are throwing down their tools and sprinting off. Women with their young are dashing out of individual homes and rushing to the main house. He hears snowmachines starting as men shout instructions.

Putting all of that together leads him to one conclusion—they're under attack.

It must be the northwest corner of the property that's been breached. It's only happened one other time Quinn knows of and that was a bloodbath. The pack drove off a small group of encroaching atshen. The nasty creatures thought to kill and devour the pack, then claim their territory. The price of victory was high, and that made Dimitri invest in a magical protective barrier for the compound. The investment was sound, and those barriers have never been breached. This attack has to be the distraction.

As if to prove his logic correct, Ryan appears and shoves an oversized key into the lock of the cage. He gets it open, then reaches in for Quinn. When Quinn can't even take a step on his own, Ryan manhandles him into a fireman's carry.

"Hang on, Quinn," he whispers as he sprints off.

Quinn tries to help Ryan carry him by holding on, but his hands are useless, numb hunks of flesh. Soon he's being lowered, and Kalli is there, shoving his arms into sleeves and Alex bends over to work his legs into pants. Everything feels hot to his frozen skin, and he grits his teeth against the tingling pain registering from almost every inch of his skin.

They must have put the clothes next to a heating vent to warm them up before launching the rescue. By the time he's wrapped in a massive parka, the worst of the pain is over, but his brain still feels mushy.

"Kalli?" he whispers.

"On the snowmachine, Quinn," she orders and pushes him toward Ryan, who's already sitting on a running machine. Once he's on and has his arms wrapped around Ryan's muscular body, she hops on behind Alex, and the two wolves gun the motors, taking off in the opposite direction that everyone ran.

Soon they're confronted by a magical wall so intense Quinn's face feels hot from being close. He can't imagine how they're going to get through it. He expects Alex or Ryan to unveil some powerful charm or shield, but neither of them moves.

To his surprise, Kalli gets off the snowmachine and steps up to the barrier.

At first, nothing happens. She looks like she's standing there staring at the magic. Then she starts to glow. That's when Quinn realizes she was glowing when she walked up, but he couldn't discern her spreading aura from the magic shield until it got much brighter.

As he watches, her aura matches the barrier until he can't tell where her aura ends, and the magic wall begins. Then she steps forward. He makes a protesting sound that Ryan hushes.

Nothing happens to Kalli. The barrier bubbles around her and then bursts, making the snow around her feet sizzle and melt. Now there's a clear hole in the wall, big enough for several people to walk through side by side.

As if they discussed it earlier, Ryan eases his snowmachine forward. Kalli stands stock still, her eyes closed, and her brows furrowed in concentration.

After Ryan and he clear the barrier, Quinn smells smoke, and he looks behind him to see the corner of one building is on fire. They didn't just cause a distraction; they caused chaos.

Once he and Ryan are clear of the barrier, Alex slowly steers his machine through. The moment he's gone through, Kalli steps away from the wall. Her aura calms, rolling back into her. As her aura returns to its normal brightness, she takes a few steps then collapses to her knees, retching and coughing.

Quinn's instinct is to help Kalli, but even as he tries to swing a shaky leg over the back of the snowmachine, Ryan stops him. "You're useless right now. Let Alex get her."

Shame fills him as he watches Alex rush to Kalli's side and pull her to her feet. Her face is pale, but she's stopped throwing up.

"That was harder than I thought," she mutters as Alex gets her on the snowmachine.

She slumps forward the moment she's straddling it and almost falls off. Alex mounts up behind her and keeps her from sliding into the snow.

"We've got to go!" Ryan hisses out, anxiously looking behind him as if wolves are going to appear at any moment.

"Go. I'm right behind you," Alex says, wrapping one arm around Kalli and grabbing the right handlebar with his free hand.

Quinn almost falls off backward when Ryan hits the throttle and starts barreling into the nearby wilderness.

He does not know where they're headed, but he's sure there is a plan in place. All he can do is hold on tight and have faith in Kalli.

It takes all of Soren's willpower not to reach out and snap Delilah's scrawny neck. Lounging back in one of his chairs, she crosses her legs and smirks at him. "It's a simple deal, Soren. My demon's help for yours."

Stephen must be able to sense Soren's pending violence because he steps between Soren and Delilah.

"Easy, Soren. I know you don't want to do this, but we're desperate." He leans a little closer so he can talk in a lower tone. "You're Delilah's best chance to survive being turned. And remember, she knows the risks. She knows this could be her death."

"Her death isn't the only risk," Soren bites out, glaring at Stephen. "Have you thought about what this will mean for you?"

"Yes, that I get Tiffany."

Soren shakes his head with irritation. "No, I'm referring to afterward. After Delilah is a vampire, assuming she survives. Will you spend the next year keeping her under control? Will you spend however long it takes safeguarding her until you're positive she won't succumb to a blood lust and massacre an entire family? Will you be responsible for feeding her? Training her? What if she tries to drink from Tiffany? Do you know what will happen if a vampire tries to bite someone from another vampire's flock?"

For the first time, Stephen looks uncertain. His eyes find Tiffany, then bounce over to Delilah. The idea of being responsible for Delilah hadn't occurred to him. And it's obvious he never thought of the possibility that Delilah might try to take blood from Tiffany.

Stephen turns his gaze back to Soren. "Perhaps you could . . ."

Soren bares his fangs with a frustrated hiss. "No. There's a reason I've never turned anyone. It's an enormous responsibility unless you plan to abandon her like our ancestors used to do. But in this modern world, survival of the fittest isn't an option anymore. In the old days, slaying vampires was a story told to scare children. Today there are cell phone cameras capturing everything. What do you think will happen to you if Delilah gets away and kills someone on a busy street? What if a video of her flashing fangs and covered in blood goes viral?"

Fear flashes across Stephen's face. "That happened to Nicolas."

Soren had forgotten about Nicolas until that moment. It happened about ten years ago. Nicolas's recently turned vampire lover got loose and killed a child. The tail end of that killing was recorded. The lover looked demented, but his looks and actions were explained away by people assuming he was on some kind of drug.

Both the newly turned vampire and Nicolas were hunted down and executed. Vampires don't have any kind of governing body, but there are a few rules they all abide by, no matter how cruel or heartless their population might be. One of those unequivocal rules is to never let the public know they exist. To never leave evidence.

His kind might be apex predators, but no matter how powerful, they're still vulnerable during the daylight hours. They don't want to return to the days where they had to hide in graveyards and deep in forests to stay safe.

In this age of science, humans have decided that vampires don't exist. The vampires would like to keep it that way.

"She could die," Stephen mutters too quietly for the sisters to hear. Soren shakes his head at the man's hopeful tone.

"She might survive. And if she survives, she'll be your burden to carry. You said the sisters don't always get along? What will it be like for the year or two that Delilah has to be near you all the time?"

Stephen's expression becomes even more depressed. "This is a nightmare."

He's quiet for a moment. Then his eyes meet Tiffany's. His expression lightens, and he sighs. "But I can't say no to my flock." Straightening up, he meets Soren's gaze, his expression determined. "I accept the burden of a newly turned vampire. If you want access to a demon, then you turn Delilah."

"Fine," Soren barks out and then points to Delilah. "Get the demon here. Once I have my flock safely back, I'll turn you."

Delilah looks delighted until she sees his harsh face. He lets the darker side of his vampire slide forward. Letting his fang drop, he licks his lips and stares at the pulse point in her neck.

"I'll hold you down and drain you dry. I'll put you through more pain than you can imagine. When you can feel your heartbeat failing, I'll fill you with my blood and set your veins on fire. I'll watch you scream and writhe as your body comes back to life under my magic. When the agony finally fades, I'll let you sleep for a few hours. And then do it all over again. If you're lucky, it will take after the third try. If you're not lucky, well, it could be days."

She sits tall and tries to look brave. "I can take some pain."

"Turning won't be the end of the pain. New vampires are always hungry. It's a different pain that will constantly gnaw at you. Even moments after feasting, you will be hungry. You could drink until you vomit, but you will never feel sated. And when the sun is up, you won't be able to move. But there won't be any restful sleep. Hunger will keep you awake. Your body will demand blood you can't provide and every moment you're not feeding, you'll feel like you're slowly dying again. Do you think you can handle that?"

Pale, Delilah stares with fear on her face. "I didn't know," she whispers, then shakes herself and turns her attention to her phone. She taps for a bit, then looks back up. "The demon my family keeps on retainer will be here within the hour."

Soren turns away from her, disgusted at what he's being forced to promise to save his flock. At least now Delilah is realizing that becoming a vampire is far more involved than simply a change of diet.

"Soren?" Memphis is standing against a wall. He's been quiet until now. "If we're going up against the Volk pack, we should take four or five more people with us."

Delilah makes a negative sound. "You can only take one more person," she explains. She glances over at Sara for confirmation.

Sara is a tall, slim demon that Memphis's hacker contacted only minutes after she hung up with Soren.

Sara rushed over, then gave Soren the bad news that she's not the kind of demon that can transport people through a magical barrier. That's how Delilah ended up in Soren's house. She has a contract with one of the few demons that can punch a hole in a magic barrier. Once it's breached, Sara explained she has no issue transporting them all out again.

It's been Soren's experience that demons are rather insular. They rarely interact with other magical communities and infrequently marry outside their own kind. They aren't aloof or mean, but uninterested in anything outside the demon community.

Because their portals flash a brilliant orange when formed and leave a burnt ring, early humans believed them to be minions of the underworld. By the time the medieval world developed, demons were firmly classified as evil by humans, along with just about every magical creature out there.

Looking at this woman Sara, no one would guess she's the mythical beast of evil. Tall and slim, she wears an outfit of simple jeans, sweater, and jacket. Her boots are sturdy, and her hair is pulled up into a loose bun. Hazel eyes peer out from behind large glasses, and a smattering of freckles grace the skin of her nose and upper cheeks. She looks more like a grade school teacher than a medieval image of a dangerous minion of Lucifer.

"Some of us can transport seven people in total," Sara reminds him. "A lot of us can only do two or three at a time. You're in luck because I can do seven. And I know John, the demon Delilah's bringing in, can do up to five."

"Only five can go in? That's fine." Memphis holds up a hand and starts ticking off fingers as he talks. "Soren and I are only two. That means we can bring three more guys with us."

"You're forgetting to include me. And I have to bring back the other demon with us," she reminds him with a little smile. "I'm the returning demon, and I can transport seven. We'll have John with us. That means two spots are already filled."

Her smile makes Soren realize that this happens all the time to her. People count the travelers and forget to include the return passage of the demon who got them out there. "If we are bringing back two people, then you can take one more person with you, besides yourself and Mr. Granger. We don't leave demons behind. It takes us about a day to recover from a jump. There's no way we're going to leave John to fend for himself during that time."

If it wasn't so dangerous, Soren would ask if he could buy a plane ticket home for the sending demon, John. But they're going to walk through a portal into enemy territory past some heavy-duty barrier magic. Leaving anyone behind for the wolves to hurt isn't an option.

"That leaves us with one spot to fill. Who should it be?" Soren asks Memphis. Both of them glance over at Stephen.

The vampire catches their look and scoffs. "I'm not interested in battling a bunch of wolves far from home, in hostile territory, with daylight less than two hours away."

"Not surprised," Memphis mutters, then taps on his phone. "I'll ask Lex to join us."

Soren winces. "Are you sure that's wise?"

Out of all the brothers, Lexington is the most dangerous and mysterious. There's a darkness to him that's concerning. No one in the family talks about it, but they all worry.

When Memphis looks at him with a questioning expression, Soren elaborates. "If he's overcome by the hunt and runs off, we might lose track of him."

Memphis doesn't seem bothered by that idea. "He'll be fine. Might take him a few weeks to find his way home, but we could land him in the middle of a nest of cockatrice with young to protect and he'd probably come out unscathed."

Soren shakes his head at the description of Lex surrounded by a family of venomous, aggressive cockatrice. Although he knows Memphis loves his brother, he can feel that Memphis's disregard for Lex's safety is real. Of course, there's also the fact that no one knows what Lex does for a living. He disappears, sometimes for weeks at a time. He makes more money than all the other siblings combined and occasionally comes home with new scars.

They all speculate about what Lex could possibly be involved in that can scar rapidly healing chimera skin.

"If Lex is willing, I won't refuse," Soren finally says.

Memphis's phone dings and he reads, then types something out. After another ding, he grunts and looks up. "We're in luck. Lex is in town and on his way."

They talk a little about strategy as they wait for Lex. There isn't much to talk about. Baby Doll dug up everything she could on the Volk pack and sent it to them, including satellite images.

Soren doesn't know who this woman is, but she's an excellent asset. He'll have to keep in touch with her if he ever needs hard to get information in the future.

Baby Doll also found some basic numbers: the pack has over one hundred and fifty members. About sixty of them are warriors. There are also several smaller packs nearby that are subservient. If the Volk calls on them for assistance, there will be more warriors showing up.

The thing that worries Soren the most is the weapons. He knows from Kalli's stories that the Volk have guns and they actively use them for hunting. But in the heat of the moment, will they run for their firearms or attack with tooth and claw? Soren can't be sure.

At least both Memphis and Lex will be armed. In fact, Lex will probably be armed to the teeth. None of them are sure how many guns Lex owns, but they have their own room in his house.

The moment Lex and John, the second demon arrive, Soren practically drags them to the backyard. John and Sara have a quick, quiet conversation while standing in the burnt circle. Then they both nod and call everyone in.

"John and I aren't fighters," Sara warns them. "So we're going to look for cover the minute we arrive. We can defend ourselves, so don't worry about that." She grins and opens her hand to flash some demon fire on her palm. "When you've got your people, all you need to do is get to us and we'll get you out of there."

"Understood," Soren says, and steps into the circle. Memphis joins, but Lex pauses.

Memphis gives him a questioning look. "Lex?"

"These wolves, they're your flock, right?" Lex asks, his intense gaze focused on Soren.

"Yes."

"And that means you love 'em," he continues.

"I do," Soren agrees. "They're more important than my own life."

"Then you leave me behind if you gotta," Lex says, finally stepping into the circle. "You don't hesitate. You leave me and Memphis behind if you get those wolves."

"Hey, don't go sacrificing me," Memphis protests, but looks startled when Lex focuses his eyes on his brother.

"I won't let you die," he states in a monotone. His dark eyes making the promise feel like it has magic backing it. "But we stay behind if we have to. We're chimera. We're tougher than a couple of young wolf shifters. We are the shadows that go bump in the night. We are the things other creatures fear."

"Fuck it, fine," Memphis growls out. "We can stay if it comes to it."

With a sharp nod at Memphis, Lex slides his eyes over to Soren. "Let's retrieve your flock, vampire."

"Put your tray tables up and buckle your seatbelts," John says with a grin as he raises his open palms to the night sky. Power is gathering around him, making him glow and his hair stand up on end. "Time to take a trip."

This isn't the first time Soren's traveled by portal, so he knows what to expect. "Close your eyes," he orders the chimeras. "It will feel less disorienting."

His warning comes too late because John has already clapped his hands together and the world tilts on its axis.

Everything happens so fast it's hard to follow. One moment they're standing in his garden, surrounded by familiar woods. Then they're in the center of pandemonium.

"Oh, shit!" John curses.

Soren's eyes pop open to find at least a dozen men running at them brandishing weapons and shouting. Behind those men are snowmachines spraying up rooster tails of snow as they zoom off. Beyond the snowmachines there is a building on fire with dozens of people circling, trying to battle the blaze.

This chaos can't possibly be normal for the Volk pack. Something must have deliberately caused this level of confusion, forcing people to scramble in all directions.

A grin of admiration spreads across his face. This must be the work of his wolves. Kalli and Quinn aren't princesses waiting for their handsome prince to rescue them. They're courageous and resilient. They're going to do their damndest to organize their own escape! And he's seeing the results of their hard work.

"Holy shit," Memphis mutters, and he tackles Soren to the ground. Weapon fire fills his ears, and bullets whiz overhead. Thankfully, there are several mounds of hard packed snow between them and the wolves with the guns.

Soren looks over to see John and Sara rapidly belly crawling to a nearby outbuilding. Hopefully, they'll find shelter there until the fighting is over.

"That answers the question on weapons," Memphis growls out as Lex crawls up one of the snow embankments to return fire, then ducks back down.

"Two down," Lex reports. He waits for a moment, then pops up, fires two more rounds, and then ducks again. "One more down."

Even Soren, with his limited weapons experience, knows that Lex is making impossible shots with unbelievable ease. His expression is cool and calculated. No matter how close a bullet comes to hitting him, he never flinches or moves with anything but deliberate, fluid grace.

"We need intel," Lex declares, then looks at Memphis and points off to the right. "There's a guy over that way, running like hell. Catch him and bring him back here. I'll keep their focus away from you." Then he's gone, sliding over the top of a snowbank and disappearing.

Memphis stares at the spot where his brother had been a split second ago before cursing and running off in the direction Lex pointed.

It's not often that Soren is left to twiddle his thumbs during battle, but that's exactly what happens. He didn't bring a gun, fearful that his lack of experience would cause him to injure someone on his side instead of efficiently killing the enemy.

He gorged himself on bagged blood, so he could take a lot of hits and not feel a thing. He's faster, stronger, and can shift to his raven form if necessary. But for the time being, he stays put, waiting for the two chimeras to rejoin him. Lex and Memphis work well together. The last thing he wants to do is disrupt their plan.

Memphis gets back within a minute, dragging a round, middle-aged wolf behind him. The wolf is crying and begging, but he doesn't fight the chimera at all. By the time Memphis dumps him at Soren's feet, Lex is jumping over the snowbank, clearing it easily and landing in a crouch right next to the sobbing wolf.

Lex doesn't miss a beat. He puts his gun to the wolf's head and leans in close. "Where are Kalli and Quinn being held?"

The man doesn't even attempt to prevaricate. "Not here," he says through his tears. "Got away. They took off. Them and Alex and Ryan. Took off on snowmachines."

"Which direction?" Memphis growls before Lex can ask.

The man points, his hand shaking badly. Then he closes his eyes and goes limp.

Soren's aghast. Did this wolf faint? They haven't even done anything to him except drag him around and threaten him. That makes Soren realize Lex did an excellent job of picking out who Memphis needed to capture. There were probably men running around all over the place, and he honed in on one of the most cowardly members of the pack—a man easy to scare and unlikely to attempt giving false information.

"I'm thinking we need to follow those guys that left on the snowmachines," Lex says as he stands up. That's when Soren notices there's no more weapon fire. Lex strides off, forcing Soren and Memphis to scramble after him, leaving the unconscious wolf to recover in the snow alone.

There are two snowmachines not far away. One is lying on its side and the other is upright with a man's body half sprawled off it. There are two more dead men visible, and Soren guesses that if he looked around, he'd find more bodies due to Lex's efforts. What feels bizarre is the lack of opponents coming at them.

"The ones fighting the fire are too busy to notice what's going on over here. And I scared the rest of 'em good. They all ran into that building," Lex says with a nod of his head at one of the biggest buildings in the compound. "I'm guessing those guys were backup. Second string. I'm thinkin' the primary warriors are out hunting your wolves. We need to get moving and follow or we might be too late. I can't imagine anyone here is feeling too forgiving toward a couple of wolves that caused this much destruction."

Memphis rights the overturned snowmachine with ease and straddles it, his expression gleeful. Lex takes the other one after tossing the body away from it. He looks over at Soren and dips his head to direct the vampire to the seat behind him.

Soren shakes his head. "I'm going to take to the sky."

"Good," Lex says, then starts the engine and guns off, Memphis right behind him.

Shifting, Soren wings his way in the direction the captured man pointed. John warned them all that his portal might punch a hole in the magic guarding the Volk estate, making the barrier unstable. The demon wasn't wrong.

An extensive section of the wall is now missing, magic crackling and hissing around its uneven edges. He swoops down and leads the brothers through it, beating his wings hard to gain some altitude once he's free of the Volk estate shields.

It might be night, but the wilderness is well lit by a bright moon reflecting off the bright, white snow. It's easy for him to find the well-established trail left by so many snowmachines. Even as the path becomes more wooded, he's able to follow it.

Then he passes over a group of eight snowmachines, each one with two warriors mounted on them, traveling fast. They're following the path created by two earlier snow machines, probably driven by Kalli and Quinn. This group must be Volk warriors pursuing his flock.

He pushes hard to catch up with his wolves. It's a little harder to follow the path made by only one or two snowmachines, but soon he doesn't need to follow a path.

He can hear the horrific sound of a crash in the distance.

It takes all of Kalli's concentration to hold on to Alex as he follows the trail Ryan's making in front of them. She never tried that trick with her aura before and only knew about it in theory. She wasn't sure it would work.

Thankfully, it was successful, but it took a lot out of her. If not for the adrenaline flooding her system, she might have collapsed into unconsciousness the moment she stepped away from the barrier.

Thank the goddess for Alex and Ryan. The two of them arranged a plane and pilot, not easy during harsh winter months. The pilot will be waiting for them at a small runway a few hours away by snowmachine. From that small airstrip, they'll fly to Anchorage. From there, the four of them will get a commercial flight south. Back to Soren.

Back home.

It doesn't even occur to her to go anywhere else. Soren represents home now. The third member of their triad. She knows if she could talk to him, Quinn would feel the same way. She also knows in her heart that Soren will accept Ryan and Alex. Not only did she agree to be their lider, but they helped her and Quinn escape. After he hears how the two bravely assisted Quinn and Kalli, Soren will be more than happy to grant those two wolves anything.

But before any of that can happen, they need to make it to the airstrip. She's never felt the cold more than she does now. She's so depleted that it feels like her muscles are starting to freeze up. Her fingers cramp. She grits her teeth and focuses on their goal. Her job right now is to hang on. To let Alex and Ryan push the snowmachines as fast as possible.

She gets only a second of warning. The sound of another snowmachine pushing hard to her left. She doesn't even get a chance to turn her head before it T-bones them, sending her and Alex tumbling violently into the snow

It happens so fast that neither of them has time to react. She's trying to pull air into her lungs, desperate to breathe after the landing knocked the wind out of her. She hears shouts and growls. There's movement around her. Then a wolf is standing protectively over her, teeth bared and scruff up.

It's Quinn. She would recognize him anywhere. He's trying to present the image of a strong, fierce wolf, but she can see his legs shaking slightly. He couldn't even walk when they pulled him from that cage. He couldn't have recovered much in the short time they've been riding the snowmachines.

He might not have much left in him, but he'll fight to protect her with every last bit of energy he has. She can only try to do the same for him.

Slowly, painfully, she sits up. About fifteen or so men are surrounding them, weapons in hand. She can see the wrecked snowmachine she and Alex were riding. The other machine sits perfect and pristine, which tells her Ryan stopped to help instead of running. Turning her head, she sees Ryan in wolf form standing over Alex, the two of them almost a mirror image of her and Quinn. Alex is conscious and sitting up, but he looks dazed, and blood is running down his face and pooling in the snow.

A man steps up, his rifle pointed to the ground. Kalli recognizes him as the lider of a small pack subservient to the Volk. His expression is resigned.

"We don't plan to hurt any of you," he tells them. "But we are taking all four of you back."

Heat prickles along Kalli's skin. Like hell they're going back. Better to die here in battle and on their own terms than to meekly allow capture. She knows by the way he's standing that Quinn feels the same way.

She sinks her fingers into his ruff, feeling some of her strength returning just from being near her mate.

She whispers to him, "I love you, Quinn. I've never regretted what we did so we could be together. Never."

He doesn't take his eyes off the wolves surrounding them, but he huffs out a breath and briefly leans against her. *Me too*, he's saying.

"I wish Soren was here," she murmurs. "I would tell him the same thing."

"Enough," the man says. "Can you get up, or do we need to help you? Quinn, you're going to have to shift back. We can lend you some clothes, but we're traveling hard by snowmachine, so you need to be in your human form."

"Give me a minute," Kalli says to him, making herself appear extra clumsy as she gets to her feet. She pretends to stagger forward at the same time she pulls out the knife she had concealed in her coat.

Reflexively, the man reaches out to catch her, and she shoves the knife hard into his belly. It's not a killing blow, but it causes enough damage to let her snatch his rifle as he drops to his knees, blood pouring through his fingers. With practiced ease, she brings the gun up and puts the barrel to the man's head.

"Back off or he gets a wound he won't be able to recover from," she warns all of them. To her surprise, not a single one of them moves. Instead, they all bring their guns up and take aim at Quinn.

"I'm sorry Kalli. Even if you kill him, we're taking you in. Dimitri told us to kill anyone with you if we had to. He said that you are the only one he needs alive," another man explains. They're all much too calm about this. The man's next words are a revelation. "Manny would die to assure our pack's acceptance into the Volk."

Kalli brings the gun up and steps in front of Quinn, shielding him from the men. If she's the one they want alive, then it's up to her to protect her mate as best she can. Manny slumps sideways into the snow, groaning and clutching his bleeding stomach.

"I won't go back," Kalli warns the men as she edges sideways. Quinn moves with her, understanding that she wants to get closer to where Ryan is protecting Alex. The others let them move. It probably doesn't make much of a difference. They're so outnumbered that Kalli is only delaying the inevitable. But every moment seems precious. Soon she's standing with her back to Alex and Ryan, Quinn pressed in tight against her legs.

"Adrian?" Alex asks. Kalli spares a glance behind her. Alex looks like he's coming out of his daze. The graze on his head is still bleeding, but it's slowed to a trickle now.

"Hey there, Alex," Adrian says with no real emotional inflection. "Sorry to do this to you all, but our pack is struggling. Dimitri put a call out to all the local packs that whoever brings you in gets to join the Volk. We need that. This winter has been hard on us."

"No, I . . ." Alex trails off as he blinks and tries to figure out what he wants to say.

Adrian takes a small step closer, and both Ryan and Quinn start growling. Kalli can feel her strength waning. The tip of the rifle keeps trying to dip down, and she has to concentrate on keeping it up and pointed at Adrian.

Normally, her mind would buzz with calculations. She would have strategies flowing and plans forming in seconds. But her brain is failing her. There's nothing there. No clever tactics come to mind. No ideas on how to negotiate with these wolves.

The four of them are going to die in a hail of gunfire. Manny and Adrian might be cool and controlled, but all the wolves behind him are tense and twitchy. The moment she fires, they'll all start firing back. The rounds will rip through her first—then the wolves behind her.

It's not the death she would have picked, but then again, very few get to pick how they will die. At least dying this way means she's denying Dimitri.

Adrian moves forward, and her finger tightens on the trigger. Their reprieve is up.

But before a single shot is fired, a shape swoops down into the small, treeless spot near the wrecked snowmachines. Everyone, including Kalli, looks over as Soren effortlessly shifts from raven to human.

His blood red eyes start glowing as he roars. With effortless strength, he picks up one of the mangled snowmachines and tosses it at the wolves who are only now bringing their guns around to fire on him.

Three men go down under the snowmachine as the others empty their rifles and shotguns at Soren. Kalli can't be sure, but she thinks at least one round hit the vampire as he moves toward them with preternatural speed.

Kalli lets the muzzle of her weapon drop. She can't fire. Soren's moving too quickly among the enemy wolves. She could easily hit her beloved vampire instead of the men he's battling.

When a round hits the snow near Quinn, Kalli realizes that the wild firing could end up getting one or all four of them killed, even while Soren's trying to save them.

Looking around, her eyes land on a dead tree lying on its side nearby with snow piles on either side of it. Swinging the rifle over her shoulder, she tugs at the wounded and dazed Alex.

"Come on. We need to take cover."

Ryan shifts to human and helps her get Alex to his feet. Quinn stays in wolf form, probably too depleted to shift back to human yet.

No sooner do the four of them make it to the shelter than a few bullets go whizzing by. Goddess, that was close.

She slumps down in the snow, and the cold feels good on her face. Oddly, she feels overheated and has the strange impulse to take off her parka. Quinn settles down next to her. His warm wolf's body also feels too hot to be close to hers. Is she running a fever? Did she get hurt and not realize it?

Then it hits her. She's going into heat.

She's never experienced a heat before. Female wolf shifters only go into heat when they feel safe, secure, and loved. Female shifters need to know their pup will be born into an environment that will cherish them or their inner wolf will refuse to make them fertile

In all the years she's been with Quinn, both in the Volk pack and on the run, she's never felt secure enough to go into heat.

But there are drugs that can force females into heat, no matter how insecure her wolf might feel. Kalli knows a lot of the women in the Volk end up taking the drugs so they can conceive. And Dimitri told her that he gave her those same drugs.

It won't be long now before this drug-induced heat takes her over completely. She's heard the stories. She'll be needy, wonton, and will only want Quinn near her. And maybe Soren, if her wolf sees him as her mate too. She can't be sure. But if anyone else comes close, she'll attack, even if they are friends.

She grabs a handful of Quinn's scruff to get his attention. He brings his wolf face to her and whines.

"I'm in heat," she whispers to him. "Dimitri injected me with something."

He jerks a little in response, and his wolf eyes go wide with apprehension. Then, almost as if a switch has been flipped, a roaring fills Kalli's ears. Her body goes from being a little too warm to so hot that she's sweating profusely. And the scent of Alex and Ryan so close to her is unbearable.

With an angry scream, she rolls onto her belly. She gets her feet under her and attacks them.

Soren gazes around him, sweeping his blood-red eyes over the dead bodies littering the snow. The rest of the enemy has run off, and he has no interest in chasing them down. His focus is to eliminate the threat. His primitive, violent mind doesn't see fleeing wolves as a danger.

He stalks a large circle to verify that none of the wolves are playing possum. He leaves a trail of blood as he walks from the five bullets that hit him. Most of the rounds fired by the panicked wolves missed him, but even those that hit weren't silver coated, so his body is already pushing them out. If his mind wasn't clouded with blood lust, he would feel more pain and more remorse for the lives he ended.

But they shouldn't have endangered his wolves.

"Kalli, no!" Quinn's shout has him flying across the ground, leaping a fallen tree and landing in the middle of a confusing scene. He stops dead in his tracks, trying to work out what he's seeing.

He expected to find Quinn and Kalli under threat. But far from being terrorized, Kalli is growling ferociously and trying to attack two young male wolves who are cowering against a nearby tree. One of the two men is in wolf form and the other is bleeding from a head wound and still in his human skin.

"Why's she doing that?" the bleeding wolf cries out. "Has she gone feral?"

"She's in heat," Quinn grunts out. He's barely keeping Kalli restrained. "If you guys could move a little farther away, I think I can get her attention back on me."

Heat. Soren knows that word, but his brain won't cooperate. He wants to bang his head against something until his thinking mind comes back. He needs his reasoning skills. He needs to help Kalli. To do that, it would be useful for his cognition to return.

"Soren, get over here," Quinn calls out.

Something deep in Soren sends a warning, making him hesitate. What if Kalli doesn't recognize him? He could easily withstand a physical blow from her, but if she rejects him during her heat, then that means she doesn't see him as her lover. As someone on par in her heart with Quinn. Her rejection would gut him.

But he sets aside those concerns when Quinn calls out again. "Soren, please!"

As he moves to join Quinn, the two other wolves put more distance between them and Kalli. That combination of movements calms Kalli down considerably. The moment he's within arm's reach, she grabs him and pulls him close, throwing one last growl in the direction of the retreating duo.

"Mine," she states in a low, intense voice and slams her lips down on his. There must be blood on his face from draining several of the wolves dry and his eyes are still glowing red, but she doesn't seem to care.

With aggression he doesn't expect, she thrusts her tongue into his mouth. Her hand comes up to cup the back of his head, holding him still.

A body presses against his side. It's Quinn getting closer to the two of them, whining slightly because he feels left out. Kalli breaks off the kiss, then drags Quinn close so she can kiss him too. Some of the blood on Soren's face has rubbed off on Kalli, making her look positively primitive.

Soren likes it.

His world narrows down to Kalli and Quinn as the three of them take turns kissing. Quinn is naked, so when he shivers it causes Soren's humanity to return and his eyes to bleed back to their ice-gray color.

Pulling away from the two of them, he looks around, ignoring their vocal protests. He needs to find shelter for his wolves. They can't stay out in the open, not with Kalli in heat and Quinn suffering from the cold.

"Soren?"

His name, whispered so softly it might have been a sigh on the wind, makes him look to his right. Memphis and Lex are standing about fifteen feet away. Kalli and Quinn are distracted with each other and don't notice the chimeras.

He's forced to stare at Memphis for several minutes before he can talk.

"Kalli's in heat," he gets out.

Memphis's eyes go wide with concern, and Lex grunts in acknowledgment, then turns and hurries away.

"Lex and I took care of the wolves that were following you, but I don't know how long until they rally and come after us again," Memphis says.

"You can't leave us."

Soren and Memphis look over to find the two young wolves that Kalli was growling at walking toward Memphis, giving Kalli a wide berth.

"And who are you guys?" Memphis asks.

Quinn pulls his face away from Kalli long enough for an introduction. "That's Alex and Ryan. They helped us escape. They need to come back—"

With a growl, Kalli pulls him back and seals her lips over his, muffling whatever else he was going to say. The air is getting thick with the smell of her arousal. Soren's mind is no longer overwhelmed with blood lust, meaning he might be capable of logic again, but now it's hard to concentrate on anything except Kalli.

Lex returns, sliding to a halt next to Memphis, breathing hard and pointing off into the woods behind him. "I found an empty cabin not too far from here. There are some provisions and a bed for these three to ride out Kalli's heat. There's a large, cleared area around the cabin, good for defending."

"You think we should lock them in there, then hold off the wolves by ourselves?" Memphis asks. He doesn't sound worried. He sounds interested.

"Naw, you stay and guard. I need to go get those demons and bring 'em back too."

Soren would curse if he had the mind for it. He forgot about the demons, patiently hiding and waiting for them to get back. It would be nice if they could portal now, but in this state, Kalli won't let anyone near her. The portal won't be an option until Kalli's heat is over.

"How long do you think this will go on?" Memphis asks Soren with a nod at Kalli.

"About four hours total," Quinn tells them. "Most heats go about eight to ten, but the drugs make them shorter. More intense, but shorter."

"Right. Let's get you guys to the cabin. Lex and I will take care of everything else," Memphis instructs. Soren nods and stands up, cradling Kalli in his arms. He tries to pick up Quinn too, but the wolf bats his hands away.

"I can walk, damn it. I'm not some weak pup," Quinn growls out. His words are proven wrong when he stumbles on the first step, almost tumbling back down into a large snowbank.

"Fuck," he curses, and grabs hold of Soren to keep himself upright.

"He was beaten pretty good, drugged, then put in an outdoor cage with no clothing, food, or water for hours," Alex explains.

"I want to carry you," Soren tells him. Soren could easily shoulder the burden of both wolves, but Quinn shakes his head again, his expression stubborn. "Fine, then hold on to me," Soren orders.

That's a compromise Quinn's willing to make. With a relieved sigh, he leans heavily against Soren. With Quinn clinging to his side and Kalli in his arms, the three are able to follow the chimeras to the cabin Lex found.

The front door is wide open, and the lock is busted. Lex must have kicked it open. At the doorway, Quinn pauses and sniffs. "The owner's dead," he pronounces before stepping in.

Soren takes a sniff. He smells an unfamiliar wolf, old ash from a dead fire, and some bread made a few hours ago, but doesn't smell any death. "How do you know?"

"Because you killed him back there," Quinn says with a small, bloodthirsty grin. "I recognize the scent. Serves him right." Soren grunts in agreement at Quinn's proclamation.

They stumble through the small house, easily finding the only bedroom at the end of a short hall.

Memphis keeps his distance and calls out to Soren as he closes the bedroom door. "We'll keep you guys safe."

And then Lex slams the front door shut, leaving the three of them to ride out Kalli's heat together.

The moment Soren sets Kalli on the bed, she grumbles and tugs at her clothes. Her movements are frantic and uncoordinated. Quinn collapses into the queen-size bed next to her, naked and shivering. Soren gets to work helping Kalli out of her clothes while Quinn watches.

The smell of her arousal is making Quinn hard, despite the depleted state of his body. He can only be thankful Soren is here, or he'd worry about being able to take care of Kalli through the hours of her heat.

As if to prove his concerns valid, the moment she's naked, Kalli throws herself on Quinn and impales herself on his erection. He shouts out in surprise and pleasure while she arches her back and sounds a bone-deep moan of satisfaction. Instinct is driving her hard and the only thing that will appease it is his hard flesh inside of her.

Quinn's entire body is shaking from a combination of how good Kalli feels and fatigue.

"Easy, Kalli," Quinn begs, but she's in no mood to be told what to do. She moves over him, pounding down against him. Her moans, gasps, and whines tell both Soren and Quinn that she's close.

He lets go and allows her to use him. Pleasure makes him tighten exhausted muscles and his eyes roll back in his head as Kalli moves.

It only takes a few minutes before Kalli is screaming from orgasm. Her body tightening around his cock triggers his climax, and he shouts out with pleasure as his seed fills her.

After holding herself rigid for a few moments, Kalli collapses down on Quinn's chest, panting and petting him as if to tell him he did a good job.

"That was intense," Quinn mutters.

Soren is watching the two of them with an expression that is both envious and elated. Quinn doesn't like it that the vampire didn't get to be part of this first round.

He reaches his hand out, waving the vampire closer and keeping his hand extended. Soren takes his hand and lets Quinn tug him down beside him on the bed.

"She's going to need both of us to get through this," he warns Soren. "The stronger the wolf, the more extreme the heat, and Kalli is the most powerful female I've ever met. I don't think it's an accident we found you. I might not have been able to deal with her heat alone. I think the three of us were meant to be together."

"Even though I failed to keep you safe?" Soren asks. It's easy to see that he's afraid of the answer.

Quinn doesn't even hesitate. "You didn't fail. You were avenging us; you couldn't have known they would use demons to portal to your house and steal us."

"I should've—"

Quinn cuts him off with a growl. "Let it go. If we don't blame you, then you don't get to blame yourself. Besides, Kalli and I talked, and we decided we were done thinking about it. We were going to have a romantic evening and seduce you into finally making us your flock. But then those guys showed up and everything went to shit. That's still something we both want. You're making us your flock. Got it?"

Soren's expression reveals that the vampire is both overjoyed and astonished. "I can't believe you still want me."

"We do. We love you, Soren. Vampire. Lover. Friend. Protector. You're everything to us. I didn't think I could ever feel this way about anyone except Kalli, but I feel it for you. Take a piece of our souls and give us some of yours. We're ready."

"But are—"

"We are yours," Quinn interrupts him in a soft, but steely voice. "Still and always. We are yours, and you are ours."

The impulse to make them his flock right then is overwhelming. Soren almost does it. Almost acts without bothering to verify consent. But he can't. There must be absolute trust within a flock, or no one can be happy.

"I will as soon as Kalli is herself again. She has to tell me; you can't speak for her."

"Mine."

They both look over to find Kalli has her eyes open and is staring at Soren intensely. She still has a feral look to her, but he can tell there's some intelligent thought going on in her heat-addled mind.

"Mine," she states again, her voice firm and strong. Then she brings a hand up and slaps it down on Soren's chest. "Mine."

"I think that might be her way of saying that she wants to be in your flock too," Quinn says with a chuckle. Soren smiles and covers Kalli's hand with his own.

"I'm yours, *cariad*," he assures her. "And I'm not going anywhere. When this heat is over, I'll bind the three of us together. But let's focus on one thing at a time."

She sighs out a long breath, and her eyes close again. "Mine," she mumbles, and then her face scrunches and she whimpers. "More. Want you."

Soren can see that her heat is building again. Beads of sweat have formed on her skin, and her eyes are glazed with need.

Quinn casts Soren a pleading look, making him chuckle and maneuver himself behind Kalli. Making a soft, hopeful sound, she lifts her ass invitingly, pulling herself free of Quinn's softening cock. Soren grabs her hips, admires her glistening pink folds and forbidden dark pucker.

"Do you want me, *annwyl*?" he asks her.

Kalli makes a desperate, mewling sound as an answer. The heat is too strong again. She's lost her ability to talk.

Quinn huffs out a laugh under her. "I think want might be mild. Need is what's going on."

Kalli makes a sound of agreement and moves against Soren's fingers, pushing back and trying to get penetration.

"Patience, my heart," he murmurs. He continues to massage her tight hole with the fingers of one hand while he reaches around with his other. He dips two fingers of his free hand into her slick heat, rubbing and stroking. She bucks up against him as his thumb rubs her engorged clit.

A glance over her shoulder gives Soren a view of Quinn's face. The wolf is watching him through half-lidded eyes, stroking his semi-hard cock and smiling. He's enjoying the show.

"After I get you good and ready with my fingers, then I'm going to slip my big, fat dick in there and make you come from that alone."

His words are having a similar effect on both Kalli and Quinn. Warmth floods her pussy and starts dripping down the insides of her legs. Quinn's cock goes from only chubbing to fully erect and throbbing. Their reactions make Soren feel desired and powerful.

He keeps one hand in Kalli's channel, stroking and penetrating. Making a frustrated sound, she grinds against him, begging without words for more.

"Bad Wolf," he admonishes, pulling his hand away. "If you want me, you have to be still."

She whimpers and goes motionless, whining and looking over her shoulder at him with pleading eyes. Then Quinn shifts a little, and she turns her head down to see his throbbing cock waiting for her. With an aggressive growl, she tries to slam herself down on Quinn, but Soren catches her with an arm around her waist.

"You will wait for us," he orders her. She goes limp and looks longingly down at Quinn.

Grinning, Quinn makes a show of cupping his balls with one hand and running his other hand up and down his dick. "Come here," he demands. "Stick that ass up in the air for Soren and bring your head down here and kiss me."

Kalli doesn't even hesitate. This time when she moves, Soren lets her. Her legs are on either side of Quinn and when she leans over to take him into her mouth, she shoves that perfect, wet pussy in his face.

Soren can hear her moaning around Quinn's cock, all the while Quinn is murmuring dirty thoughts and descriptions.

Ignoring his throbbing cock, Soren runs his finger through her feminine folds. He finds that numb he knows will bring her pleasure.

He takes his time, teasing her with light touches. Getting to listen to her moans and watching her quiver is an absolute pleasure. The needy sounds she's making are probably pleas for more touching. For penetration. For orgasm.

For him.

His cock is rock hard and dripping pre-come as he pulls his fingers free of her heat. Standing at the foot of the bed, he holds her hips still and lines up his throbbing shaft with hot, welcoming pussy.

She makes mewling sounds around Quinn's cock but behaves by not trying to push back.

"Take her hard, Soren," Quinn growls out, his fingers tangled in her hair, holding her still with her mouth wrapped around his erection. "Make her scream around my dick."

His crude words make moisture gush from Kalli. They're also her undoing. She can't be still any longer. Crying out she tries to move her hips back, to force him in deeper, but Quinn's grip on her hair and Soren's hands on her hips hold her still.

He eases himself inside, going slowly to allow her body time to get used to his size. Quinn might be large, but Soren is even bigger. As much as he wants to thrust forward, he'd never do that.

Besides, the frustrating sounds she's making are perfect.

He works his way inside her inch by inch, until he's completely enveloped by her tight, wet heat. Her muscles flex and loosen slightly around him. Soren can't help but verbalize a moan of his own. She feels amazing. It takes all his considerable will power to keep his climax at bay.

"My sweet wolf," he grounds out. Then he looks up to see Quinn's expression, part pain, part awe.

"You're both perfect," Quinn breathes.

"No," Soren argues. "You and Kalli are the perfect ones. I'm the lucky one."

Quinn flashes a grin at him before Kalli does something that has his eyes rolling back and a moan coming out.

"Easy Kalli," Quinn orders, but his voice is too soft to have much command to it.

Soren gives her a light slap on the thigh. "Behave naughty wolf." He works himself out and then pushes back in, keeping the pace agonizingly slow. "Behave or I'll keep the pace so slow you'll never get to come."

She makes a sound that he thinks might be argumentative words if her mouth wasn't stuffed full of Quinn. Realizing she can't say anything, she focuses more on working Quinn into a frenzy. Soren only thrusts a few more times before Quinn is tugging Kalli's mouth away from his hard cock.

"I can't," Quinn pants. "I'm too close." He looks up at Soren with begging eyes. It seems Quinn wants him to take charge also.

Seeing Quinn's glistening cock gives him an idea.

He pulls out of Kalli, ignoring her whining, then tugs her free of Quinn's hold, forcing her to straighten up. Quinn watches with a combination of interest and lust.

"Hold yourself straight for me," Soren orders Quinn. The wolf eagerly grabs his dick so it's pointing straight up instead of resting heavily on his abdomen. With one hand, he holds Kalli steady as he situates her over Quinn. With his other hand, he parts Kalli's folds, then uses pressure on her hip to guide her down onto Quinn's throbbing shaft.

Both wolves moan as she sinks, taking Quinn in with ease. Once she's fully seated, Soren pushes her forward until Quinn can grab her head again and hold her still. "Neither of you move," he orders.

Quinn gives a short, sharp nod, his face tense as he controls both himself and Kalli.

Soren runs his fingers around where Quinn is deep inside Kalli, pulling her flesh taut. He gathers her natural lubricant on her fingers. There is so much that it's easy for him to coat his fingers. Then he eases a finger over Kalli's tight back hole.

"Have you ever had two men in you?" he asks her, pressing one finger gently against her pucker. "Two dicks working in and out of you? Two men using your two holes for their own pleasure?"

"Please," she begs, her voice right with need. "I want both you." She tries to look over her shoulder at Soren, but the angle is too awkward. Giving up, she gazes into Quinn's eyes. "Make us a true triad!"

"You want this, *annwyl*?" Soren says as he puts more pressure on that finger. His digit pushes past that first ring of muscle, making Kalli moan and Quinn gasp.

Both his wolves shudder when he presses a second digit inside Kalli. Scissoring his fingers, he loosens her back hole. He gathers more slick several times and by the time he's done, Kalli and Quinn are shaking with anticipation.

Soren's hands are trembling with need as he guides himself back into Kalli's tight hole. With her already full of Quinn, she feels unbelievably tight, and both Quinn and Kalli cry out as he seats himself fully.

"I can feel you, Soren," Quinn gasps out, his entire body tense with the effort to keep still. "I can feel you and Kalli and everything."

Soren moves in Kalli, slow and steady, at first. Then speeding up. He watches as his wolves come undone under him. Kalli comes first, thrashing and screaming, but thoroughly trapped in place between Soren and Quinn. As she finishes, Soren moves faster, taking her harder, unable to keep the pace slow with her muscles convulsing all around him.

Quinn moans and then goes stiff as he climaxes, and Soren is right behind him. The three of them are sweaty, panting, and momentarily sated.

Kalli collapses down on top of Quinn, and Soren carefully removes himself. Standing on shaky legs, he finds the bathroom and wets a cloth. Taking it back to his lovers, he cleans them as best he can before he settles next to Quinn on the small bed. With Kalli still on top of the young man, if Soren lies on his side, he can just fit into the bed with his wolves.

He knows Kalli will need to be satisfied again soon, but for now, they can rest.

Both Quinn and Soren are passed out. Quinn is softly snoring away, and Soren is so still that Kalli can't even hear his heart beating. The one window in the room is boarded up from the outside, probably Lex or Memphis, making sure Soren is safe. Between the gaps of the badly matched together boards, she can see a hint of sunlight. At this point in winter, daylight only lasts a few hours, so Soren won't be trapped inside for long.

Now that she's no longer suffering from her heat, she feels the urge to get up. The alpha in her is pushing her to be ready to defend her mates while they're both vulnerable.

She might only have vague memories after she and Alex got rammed by another snowmachine, but she knows they're all still in Alaska. That means they're all in peril. Hopefully, the fires they set before leaving kept the pack so disorganized that they couldn't chase them down yet.

But when Dimitri does come after them again, she needs to be ready.

That thought has her carefully rising from the bed. She needs to explore the small house, find food, clothing, and maybe even a weapon.

She manages not to disturb either of her lovers, probably due more to the fact that Quinn is clearly exhausted, and daylight is pushing Soren into one of his vampiric sleeps rather than any stealth on her part. In fact, when she practically lands on her butt on the floor next to the bed because one of her feet got tangled in a sheet, neither of her men even stirs.

She winces a little at the delicate places on her body that are sore. No wonder some wolves rave about going into heat and others abhor it. Kalli was so needy that her partners could have hurt her, and she would have let them. Even begged them for more.

She doesn't remember the hours she spent in heat perfectly, but she remembers enough to know that Quinn and Soren were careful and loving with her. Even with their preparations and drawing out the orgasms as much as possible, there was enough fucking going on to make her feel it today.

She catches a glimpse of herself in a cracked mirror on the wall and is startled by the wolf looking back. She looks sated. Happy. Fulfilled. She doesn't have the exhausted, hollow-eyed look she's seen on many wolves after their heat.

She expected to feel horrible after her heat was over, especially since it was drug induced. She thought she would look like the other women in the Volk after their heats. They always looked starved and abused when they emerged. None complained, but it was often several days before any of them smiled again.

Part of it is probably because she was with two men who love her and who took great pains to care for her, even when she was insatiable. Everyone knows that wolves that are cared for properly endure their heat with minimal issues.

Yawning big enough to make her jaw crack, she finds a pile of folded clothes left on the floor outside the bedroom door. The living room is empty, but she can smell food in the small kitchenette. Tugging on an oversized shirt, hoodie, thermal pants, and then insulated jeans, she yawns again as she makes her way over to see what food she can find. She's suddenly ravenous.

There's a pile of sandwiches, and she eats the first one in four bites, barely chewing before she swallows. She drinks straight out of the tap, then eats a second sandwich only slightly slower.

She doesn't recognize the cabin, but she's sure Soren will compensate the owner for letting them use it. The smell of a strange wolf is strong in the place, so it might even be owned by one of the men who attacked them as they were fleeing. Serves that enemy wolf right if they commandeered the cabin and used up the resources.

That reminds her that she needs to make sure Alex and Ryan are okay. She remembers both wolves were still alive when Soren showed up, but other than that, she has no clue what happened to them. That's concerning. They're her responsibility.

She makes plans in her head. Get them to Oregon. Get them some basic things like a few sets of clothes. Once they're settled, she can help them figure out what they might like to do with their lives.

She remembers a long-ago conversation with Alex about how much he liked math. Does he still? There are all kinds of math-heavy professions for him to pursue. She does not know what Ryan might like. The moment her father brought him into the Volk as her arranged mate, she all but ignored the man. She was civil but refused to engage him in any kind of meaningful conversation. She'll need to —

This line of thinking makes her heartbeat pick up. When did that happen? When did she go from only caring about Quinn and then Soren, to being concerned about two wolves who were never and will never be her lovers?

Then it hits her. She's acting like a lider. Didn't she even tell Ryan she was his lider now when she was chained in the basement?

That makes her smile. Dimitri wanted her to be his successor. Well, she'll be a lider, but not of the Volk. She'll start a new pack.

Hmmm, they'll need a pack name. She should ask Soren; he might know the names of packs that have dissolved over the years. Or she could come up with something unique. Eh, it's nothing she needs to figure out right away. She has time. It's not like she's planning on having anything incorporated under a pack name. At least not anytime soon.

She can hear voices outside. She can't make out what they're saying, but she thinks one of them is Memphis. Good, he can help her find Alex and Ryan. She can't find her boots but confidently walks to the front door anyway. Flinging it open, she steps out onto the covered porch, barely noticing the cold, rough wood under her bare feet.

It was Memphis she heard talking, but he's not talking to a single other person. Standing shoulder to shoulder with Memphis is a male she's never met but looks dangerous, as well as Alex and Ryan.

They're all standing with their backs to the house and facing down about twenty wolves. Everyone is tense, but no one is moving.

The area smells so strongly of a dangerous smell that she almost sneezes. It takes her a moment to realize that it's coming from Memphis and the man next to him. They're throwing off some intense scent as a warning to those around them.

It's that same frightening smell she and Quinn experienced the day they found Soren's house. She'll be talking to Memphis about that later.

For now, she watches the intimidation tactic work like a charm.

Most of the wolves are ignoring Alex and Ryan in favor of watching Memphis and the stranger with alarm.

None of them steps forward to engage, even though Dimitri is facing them down without a shred of fear.

That's when she realizes that Dimitri deliberately waited for the scant daylight hours to show up, hoping to neutralize Soren while he is vulnerable.

What father dearest doesn't realize is that the vampire isn't the only threat. She's strong too, something he rarely acknowledged, but a fact that she's ready to shove in his face. She was tough before she and Quinn ran. The last three years have only made her more resilient and determined.

"There you are," Dimitri calls out. "You're the cause of all this. Come back with me now and I'll spare the cur and the vampire. I'll even leave Ryan and Alex to their fate. But I need you back or I'll slaughter them all."

His threats don't touch her. Giving him an unconcerned smile, she saunters down the porch to stand next to Memphis. This position gives her a clear view of both her parents. The snow is freezing on her feet, but she doesn't even notice it. Her entire focus is on the two people who created her. "Hello, Dimitri, Angelina. Lovely day, isn't it?"

"If shit gets ugly, you need to get back into the house," Memphis tells her without taking his eyes off the wolves in front of him. "Lex and I can handle this, but not if we gotta worry about you."

Ah, Lex, probably short for Lexington, one of Memphis's many brothers. She remembers Soren mentioning them in passing. A glance at Lex has her seeing the family resemblance now.

"The only thing that's going to happen is that Kalli is coming back with me," Dimitri growls out. "As you can see, I have you outnumbered."

"By numbers, you have the greater force," Kalli announces nice and loud so everyone can hear her. "But as far as power goes, I think we have you outmatched."

Dimitri ignores her comment and sneers at her. "I don't see Quinn out here. Is he cowering in the house, afraid to face his lider? Afraid to face his pack? He should be. We have you outnumbered and surrounded. But this doesn't need to end in slaughter."

"I'm pretty sure Quinn's still asleep. After the fucking I gave him, he probably won't wake up for a few more hours yet," Kalli says to Dimitri with a taunting smile. "Those drugs you gave me sure were potent. Quinn and Soren thank you."

"You whore," Dimitri spits out.

"Considering you're the one who was so eager to drug me in the first place, what does that make you?" she asks, not intimidated at all by his angry expression. "Certainly not my father. A real father wouldn't do that to his child."

"If there's a pup growing in your belly, it can be gotten rid of," Dimitri mutters to himself, probably still plotting and planning around having Kalli bear the next generation of Volk leadership.

"If a child is growing inside me, it will be born to a family of love and kindness," Kalli retorts. "Two things you know nothing about."

His expression turns to one of genuine puzzlement. "What happened to you? You were always the perfect child. Doing as you were told. Working hard to please me. Then one day you left. Disappeared with that boy. Was it the boy? Did he do something to you? Is he the reason you're talking about stupid, inconsequential things like love?"

That makes Kalli laugh. "I convinced Quinn to leave with me, not the other way around."

Taking the last step, she stands slightly in front of Memphis to face down her father. "There's something I've been meaning to say to you for a long time. I never had the courage before, but I think now is finally the right time."

But Dimitri isn't done being puzzled by her actions. "But what happened? Three years ago, what happened to make you behave so badly? And why won't you do as I say now? You can't possibly think you're a match for this many wolves?"

Dimitri looks confused that she isn't begging for the lives of the men in the cabin behind her. At the very least, she should show fear. She almost feels sorry for him.

Almost.

She takes a moment to examine her father. He's aged considerably in the last three years. His hair used to be as dark as hers but is now liberally streaked with gray. His face has gotten leaner, and there are far more worry lines than before.

It's his eyes that catch Kalli's attention. They're still as hard as she remembers, but there's a new aspect to them now. They look desperate.

Locked on a course of action, Dimitri can't even contemplate how to change his own mind. He wants someone of his blood to be lider. Nothing else will do. Stubbornness and desperation have made this man act foolishly, and now he's about to pay the ultimate price for his actions.

Taking a deep breath, she calls out loud and clear so there will be no misunderstanding. This all ends today.

"Dimitri Volk, I declare *Unichtozheniye Vyzov* on you. Face me in one-on-one combat here and now or be labeled a coward. There are no words you can speak to appease this challenge. Nothing short of death will end this *Unichtozheniye Vyzov*."

Dimitri's expression goes from shock to rage in a split second. Her entire focus is on him, but she can see the surprise on everyone else's face in her peripheral vision. Everyone except Ryan who mutters, "It's about damn time."

"What the hell is this *Unichtozheniye Vyzov* bullshit?" Memphis asks.

"It's a challenge for dominance," Alex explains. "A duel to the death between Dimitri and Kalli in their wolf forms."

"Oh, shit," Memphis breathes out and moves so he can face Kalli, turning his back on Dimitri and his wolves. Lex moves a little closer to his brother to help guard as Memphis gives Kalli a beseeching look.

"Call this off, please? That man's a big fucking wolf right there, and you're just a slip of a girl. Don't do this, darling. If you die, it will destroy Soren and Quinn. Don't throw your life away for pride or some kind of misplaced sense of justice. That's all just bullshit. All that matters is family. Yours is in that cabin, asleep and vulnerable. Go back inside and guard over them. We'll keep you safe from out here."

She knows Memphis is talking from a place of sincere concern for her life, so when her aura spikes from annoyance, she manages to keep it from doing more than brushing up against him. Even that makes a few sparks fly as two powerful auras make brief contact. Memphis hisses out a breath and takes a step back, putting him even with his brother.

A slight smile plays at the corner of Lex's mouth as he glances over his shoulder and gives her a wink.

"She's more than you think," Lex states loudly enough for everyone to hear.

"The *Unichtozheniye Vyzov* has been declared and accepted," Dimitri shouts, making those closest to him jump in surprise. They skitter away from him as if he might strike out at one of them and within seconds, a large ring of people has formed around the red-faced, enraged lider.

Kalli leisurely ambles into the circle, finally drawing up across from Dimitri. To her surprise, she only feels anticipation. There's no fear in her. No dread at facing her father. No panic at the coming fight. Only eagerness and clarity.

Slowly they strip down, neither taking their eyes off the other as they toss discarded clothes to nearby wolves. Her world narrows down to Dimitri. When he shifts, she shifts too, watching him flow into his wolf and leap at her. Foolish man, there's no way he can shift faster than her.

No thought is necessary. Her wolf form sidesteps him with ease, and he crashes into the snow. She watches with interest as he gets back up and postures: his scruff is up and his tail tense and pointed straight out behind him. His ears are lying flat against his skull and his lips are pulled back in a snarl.

Kalli doesn't feel the need to do any of those things. A strange calmness has taken her over, and it almost feels like time has slowed. When Dimitri charges her again, he expects her to dodge, so when she does, he tries to change direction and ram his shoulder into her.

She could read his intent before he even stepped forward with the first paw. She takes two steps sideways instead of one, easily dancing out of range. Pirouetting on her hind legs, she swoops her head down and grabs one of his legs in her mouth and throws herself backward. She hears a snap, and he howls in pain. Her hold on his leg means he ends up partially buried nose-first in the snow.

She spits out his leg and backs up, curious to see what he'll do now. Somewhere in the back of her mind, she's thankful her father still fights the same way he always did. He's unintentionally making it easy for her.

His style is all about brute strength. Finesse and speed were never important to him. Why would he care about speed when the shifter can't flee the battle? Why care about finesse when he can barrel into them and break bones?

But here is where that particular battle philosophy stops working; when you have a smaller, faster, and more agile fighter who's not intimidated by size or brute strength.

Over the course of the last three years, Kalli's gotten plenty of practice fighting bigger opponents. There were a few scrapes she and Quinn barely survived. Every single encounter taught her an invaluable lesson about fighting. Lessons her father never learned.

Lessons he will never learn now.

She watches with detached interest as Dimitri pulls himself out of the snow and tries to take a step on his broken leg. It gives out, and he barely catches himself with his other legs. He's still growling, still trying to make himself look big and intimidating, even though his tail has crept between his legs and his body is shaking from pain.

Her ears are still up and there is no snarl on her lips. There's no need. She doesn't need to posture or intimidate. She knows with absolute confidence that she is stronger than this bigger wolf.

Casually, she circles him, noting the way he stumbles as he attempts to keep her in view. She uses that time to push power into her aura and after she's done a complete circle, she pauses, waiting for Dimitri to attack. She even sits and tilts her head at him inquiringly, as if she's a pup wondering why her elder isn't playing anymore.

She could be the aggressor, but she'd much rather make him come to her. She can see his aura glowing, but it's nowhere near as powerful as hers.

Her taunting actions are enough to make him attempt another bid for dominance. He pounces, using his front feet to propel him. It's an ungainly move and even if she had been a lesser wolf, it wouldn't have gotten him far. She remains sitting, letting him come at her. There's an audible crack when their auras meet and because hers is so much more powerful than his, he's the one who bounces away.

A gasp goes through the audience, and she hears them murmur to each other. She can't be bothered to listen to what they're saying. It's too soon to turn her back on Dimitri. He might be on his side panting, but she knows he's not done yet.

He shifts back to human and sits up. This doesn't end the battle. Nothing ends it until one of them is dead. But shifting between forms is unusual.

Interested in what his ploy might be, she shifts as well and steps closer. She's forced to pull her aura back in so she can get close to him. But she keeps enough distance so she can react if he tries something.

"How did this happen?" he demands. His strangely mild outrage would be more fitting if he were a teacher finding out that a student cheated on an exam instead of facing down a daughter who is beating him in battle. Even now, as he gingerly moves the leg she broke, he can't believe she's winning.

"This happened because you're arrogant." She doesn't feel any anger, hate, or triumph. Even now that she's on the cusp of ending her father's life, her emotions are muted. Strong emotions have no place in her calm, controlled mind.

"But . . . you're you and I'm me," he protests, obviously at a loss for how his daughter could have possibly bested him.

A soft pity fills her. "I'm the result of two powerful blood lines. Did you think I was weak all those years I lived here? I deliberately hid myself. I didn't want this." She waves her hand to encompass the circle and everyone watching them.

"I ran away to be with Quinn but also to keep you safe, you old fool. You should have let us go. Let us live our lives and be happy. I knew that was unlikely, but I wanted to give you a chance. But you didn't take what I offered and now you get to suffer the consequences of your actions. All this is because of your biased, narrow-minded focus."

"No," he whispers, comprehension finally dawning on him. "This isn't right. This isn't how I die."

"I'm afraid it is," she counters. She points to the crowd gathered around them. "You can't cheat here. Can't have one of them drug me. No magic collars or bars to keep me in check. There is nothing between us but air. Nothing is holding me back but the fact that I want to be sure you understand how all this happened. How you made all this happen."

To further make her point, she flares out her aura, and it knocks him back. He cries out in surprise and pain. Panting, he stays flat in the snow, looking up at her with an expression that's a combination of disbelief and outrage.

She shifts back into her wolf form and stalks closer to his head. He tries to shift, but the agony of his broken leg makes it hard, and he's only partially shifted when she closes her jaws on his throat and rips him apart.

He dies quickly, his blood bright on the crisp snow all around them. She spits out the bit of flesh from her mouth and then looks around.

Quinn is standing next to Memphis, holding open a jacket for her. His face is bright with love and relief. She shifts the moment she gets close to him. They kiss as he wraps her up in the jacket, already warm from his body heat.

"I woke up to the sound of Dimitri screaming. Then I hurried out here to find you kicking his ass," he tells her. "I didn't think you could get any more beautiful. I was wrong."

"NO!" a scream makes her turn quickly, ready to face a new threat. But no one comes at her. She watches her mother drop to her knees next to Dimitri's dead body.

Her face is nothing but anger and anguish. "How could you do this to me!"

At first, Kalli thinks Angelina is referring to her, but then she realizes that the woman is talking to Dimitri. Lifeless eyes stare up at his screeching mate. They don't blink or flinch when Angelina brings both fists down on his chest.

Behind Kalli, Quinn wraps his arms around her shoulders and draws her close to his warm body. He shakes his head as they watch Angelina have a mental breakdown. "I knew she was crazy, but I didn't think it was literal."

"I think it's been a long time coming," Kalli comments without inflection as she watches her mother rant and hit the man who she spent her adult life with. It might be a stretch, but Kalli wonders if living a loveless life has led Angelina to this horrific breakdown.

She glances around at the faces of the wolves watching the spectacle. In one fell swoop, she's executed her father and broken her mother's mind. Neither task was hard, which only proves how fragile the Volk pack was.

They might have sold everyone else on the idea that they were rich and strong, but if your foundation is rotten, the building cannot stand.

"Well, hell, girl, you've got some damn fine moves!" Memphis crows. "I'm sorry I ever doubted you."

Giving Memphis a genuine grin, Kalli shrugs. "I know how to pick my battles."

"And how to fight those battles," Lex adds with an approving nod.

"Lider?"

Kalli turns her head to take in the wolf who's trying to get her attention. She recognizes him as one of the wolves that cares for the children of the pack. Nathan Volk taught her math and helped her build a model of an atom. Now he stands in front of her, head bowed, hands clasped at his belly, his aura pulled so far into him that there's no shine to him at all. The picture of submission.

"What?" Kalli asks gently.

"We need to know what you want us to do, Lider," he explains, risking a glance at her face before refocusing on the ground at his feet.

She feels Quinn tense behind her. As the victor, it's her right to claim the position of lider. The Volk pack could be hers.

Taking a moment, she looks around at all the wolves that have drawn close to her, leaving Dimitri's body to freeze in the snow. Angelina now collapsed next to him sobbing.

Some of these wolves were deliberately cruel to her or Quinn. They enjoyed their position of power to hurt and taunt her. Their expressions range from nervous to openly defiant. A few look like they're ready to declare *Unichtozheniye Vyzov* the moment her twenty-four-hour grace period to recover is over.

Or perhaps they're contemplating assassinating her in her sleep. Either is a real possibility.

As her gaze goes from face to face, all the anger she set aside to do battle fills her. What's interesting is that it's not the hostile faces that are sparking her rage, it's the relieved faces. The ones that look eager to have her as lider. It's the faces of those who were kind while she was a child. They did their best to show her love and affection, even when her parents refused to bother with either.

Fury almost overwhelms her. They might have been kind, but they all stood by and let Dimitri's cruelty stand. They remained silent when he decided who could live and who would die.

Every one of them is as guilty as Dimitri. Even more so because she knows in her heart that they disagreed with Dimitri but let him carry on anyway.

Not a single adult here has her sympathy. No one here deserves her care.

Standing tall, she addresses the crowd, her face pitiless. "I am NOT your lider! I will never be lider to cowards. I would not lead a pack of curs who stand by and let babies be executed. I refuse to defend a pack where children are used as pawns, traded between packs as if they're commodities. I'm not Volk because that very name stands for practices that should have been discarded by our grandparents."

Nathan makes a distressed sound and flinches when she trains her eyes on him.

"But you won," he reminds her unnecessarily. "You're supposed to be in charge now."

He sounds plaintive and scared like a child who's been told his parents are abandoning him. A spark of shame hits her, but it's quickly extinguished when she notices several of the Volk wolves looking at her with lustful expressions.

She just won a *Unichtozheniye Vyzov*. She has mating scars on her neck, and yet these men can't keep control of themselves even as their former leader is stretched out dead at their feet.

"Lider Kalliope," Nathan starts again, as if he can argue her into taking the position. "You are—"

"The answer was no," Quinn cuts him off before she needs to. He raises his voice and addresses all the wolves gathered.

"Alex and Ryan risked their lives to defy Dimitri while everyone else stood by and waited for Kalli to be raped and me to be executed. Those two wolves have earned their place as part of Kalli's pack. None of you have. It's that simple. You had your chance, not just yesterday, but for years. Years!" He shouts out that last word, his agitation showing as his aura lights up. "You never stood up for anyone then, so Kalli will not stand up for you now."

With that, he picks her up and carries her back into the house. She snuggles into his hold and nuzzles his neck with her nose.

"Well said, my love," she whispers as voices rise up to convince her to reconsider. Both ignore them.

They're almost to the porch when Memphis stops them, holding Kalli's clothes in his hands. She accepts the clothes from him as Memphis sounds a low whistle.

"Darn girl, you've impressed the hell out of me, and that's not an easy thing to do."

"Wait until you see my encore," she quips, making Memphis bark out a laugh.

Lex steps up to stand next to Memphis. "There's less than an hour until sunset. After sunset, we'll figure out how we are all getting back home."

"I like that plan," Kalli murmurs. "Home sounds good."

Memphis nods and Kalli thinks he even looks a little misty-eyed. "You two go in there and snuggle with your vampire for a while. We'll urge the wolves to leave and bury the body."

"Except Alex and Ryan," Kalli insists quickly. Memphis's expression softens. "They're my pack now. I'm responsible for them."

"Of course not Alex and Ryan," Lex is quick to agree. "They're your wolves, Kalli. I wouldn't make them leave."

Relieved, she nods her head and lets Quinn carry her over the threshold as Memphis and Lex start shouting at the crowd. Quinn kicks the door shut with his heel, and Kalli breathes out a sigh of relief.

It's over.

It's all finally over. Time to start a new chapter in their lives. A new chapter that includes the wonderful vampire still dead to the world in the bedroom.

"Put me down," Kalli instructs. "I want more food, and then I want to talk to our vampire. He's not going to wiggle out of his obligation this time."

Soren wakes to find Kalli and Quinn sitting on the bed on either side of him. They're staring down at him with matching, solemn expressions. They're both fully dressed, and Kalli is holding a mug of coffee. Quinn's arms are uncharacteristically crossed over his chest, as if he disapproves of something.

"It's about time you woke up," Quinn comments. There's no humor in his tone to soften his expression.

"The sun must have set," Soren murmurs, and tries to sit up.

As if rehearsed, Kalli and Quinn each put a hand on his shoulders and keep him on his back. They don't apply much force, but they don't have to. He's willing to do as they ask, even if that means remaining in a vulnerable position while they loom over him looking grim.

"Do you need blood?" Kalli asks.

Soren doesn't answer right away, preferring to do an internal check instead of giving a placating response. Even after hours spent seeing Kalli through her heat, he's mildly hungry but nowhere near ravenous. "I'm fine for now. But I'll need some within the next few hours."

"Memphis should be back soon with a vehicle to get us all to Fairbanks. After my heat started and we had to hole up here, Lex went back to find the demons. He took them into Fairbanks and rented them rooms. He said they were pretty understanding about the whole thing. He also said they did a good job hiding. None of the

Volk found them. Lex said if he hadn't seen them sneak off, he might not have found them himself."

"I'm glad they're unhurt," Soren comments, eyeing his wolves with concern. *Why are they acting so distant?*

"Both demons are rested so they can take to portal us whenever we're ready," Kalli elaborates. "All we need to do is meet them in Fairbanks."

The unchanging expressions on his wolves' faces at the prospect of returning to his home turns his next statement into a question. "That's good?"

Quinn doesn't say anything, and Kalli's only answer is to set her mug down on the nightstand. Then they go back to staring at him. His worry is turning into alarm.

"What's wrong?"

"Nothing's wrong, exactly," Quinn states. "But we've decided we're tired of waiting for you."

Alarm is rapidly becoming panic. He can't keep the worry out of his voice. "Waiting for me? Is this because of the sun? Please, *cariad*, that's not something I can help."

Kalli and Quinn exchange confused expressions. They have one of their familiar silent conversations, then turn their gazes back on him. Both are staring down at him with unyielding eyes.

Kalli speaks for them both while Quinn gives a sharp nod at her words. "We've been waiting for a month. We were ready, but you dragged your feet. We've decided that ends now. You're making us flock before we leave this cabin."

Because that isn't what he expected to hear, it takes several seconds for him to puzzle out her words. Then his heart almost bursts with love and adoration as her meaning becomes clear. He feels a grin split his face as his eyes bounce back and forth between his wolves.

"Perhaps I was being too cautious," he allows. "But I didn't want either of you to decide out of fear or because you felt I was the better option. But I see that wasn't it at all. You two have chosen me, and I couldn't be more thrilled."

Quinn gives him an approving look. "About time you realized that."

"We should do this right," Soren continues, already making plans. "Let me take you home. I'll order an exquisite meal with candles and flowers. I'll make the moment perfect. I could even hire a photographer to take pictures of us. Nice ones we can frame to remember the event. And we could . . ."

His words trail off when he realizes both wolves are frowning at him.

Kalli shakes her head. "Nope."

Quinn shakes his head as well. "No way."

"But why ever not?" Soren asks, wondering if he misunderstood her speech. Did she use the word flock and not mean it? In a split second, he goes from elation to depression.

"No, Soren, you don't understand." Quinn states, then looks over to Kalli to continue.

Kalli doesn't miss a beat. "We do this here and now. We're not going to let anyone else interrupt us. No more heat. No more *Unichtozheniye Vyzov*. We become a flock now."

That catches Soren's attention. "*Unichtozheniye Vyzov?*"

"Oh, I challenged my father to a one-on-one combat and killed him," she explains with a negligent wave of her hand.

"What?" he shouts out, startling both wolves.

"That was over an hour ago," Quinn adds and then breaks out in a chuckle. "You slept through it. Kalli was brilliant. Dimitri never had a chance."

"I . . ." Soren doesn't even know what to say.

It's his job to protect his flock and yet here they are, telling him that they already faced down their most deadly adversary and won. If that isn't a sign that they want him for himself instead of the protection he can provide, then nothing else is.

When both wolves' eyes widen and Quinn leans in to examine his face, he knows his eyes must have gone blood red.

"What the hell?" Quinn murmurs as he reaches out to touch Soren's check, his finger coming back smudged with a pearlescent, dark liquid. He rubs it between thumb and forefinger, then looks backup at Soren with amusement. "Leave it to a vampire to cry sparkly, black tears."

"That's so goth," Kalli comments with a small grin. "If the humans only knew, some of them might go crazy about it."

That makes Soren huff out a laugh. He ignores that comment and focuses on the more important thing. He can't wait any longer

"*Cariad, annwyl.*" This time when he sits up, they let him. He grabs them both, hugging them tightly. "If you're both willing, then nothing would make me happier than making you two my flock right here and now. We'll have a proper Alighting Ceremony later."

"Ohhh, an Alighting Ceremony. That sounds so exotic," Quinn teases. His grin disappears when Soren aggressively pulls him close for a kiss. By the time the vampire's done, Quinn looks slightly dazed.

"An Alighting Ceremony is a bit like the vampire version of a wedding celebration. We can say the vows now and celebrate later."

"Best idea you ever had," Kalli mutters, making Soren chuckle before kissing her. He can feel her aura flare with passion as they kiss.

Reluctantly, he ends the kiss and then pushes them out to arm's length, examining their faces.

"You are both sure about this? There is no going back afterward." Soren knows he's doing a poor job of warning them because his smile won't go away.

Kalli brushes aside his warnings. "Yeah, yeah, you've told us."

"Repeatedly," Quinn adds. "Do either of us strike you as individuals who change their minds after picking someone?"

"You make an excellent point, dear Quinn," Soren agrees. He takes one of their hands in each of his. "Close your eyes, my darlings," he orders. "Take deep breaths. This won't hurt, but it'll feel intense."

Taking his own advice, he shuts his eyes and focuses. When vampires are reborn, they gain some inherited instincts. How to bind a flock is part of that. Natural compulsion takes over where knowledge ends and soon, he feels power flowing among the three of them.

First, he plants a piece of his soul in each of them. Most vampires can only create a flock one at a time and would need months to recover in between. But Soren is powerful, and although it's difficult, he's elated the pieces of his soul are accepted and flourish within both his wolves.

The next part needs to be done delicately or he could hurt them. Practicing more finesse than at any other time in his long life, Soren carefully carves off a bit of Kalli's soul and pulls it into himself. Kalli gasps at the sensation but doesn't jerk or cry out. Then he does the same to Quinn, who tenses but doesn't make a sound.

The moment Quinn's bit of soul is in Soren, he feels their triumvirate snap into place. He can feel their emotions and at the moment, all he's getting is satisfaction and love.

"You belong to us now," Quinn states softly. Soren opens his eyes to find Quinn and Kalli gazing at him with matching expressions of joy. "We're a triad of two wolves and a vampire. This feels so perfect."

Kalli gives a slight nod of her head. "Yes, you're all ours."

The warmth of the connection with his wolves makes his whole body flood with heat. He hasn't felt like this since he was human. It's a delicious sensation and if he could, he'd strip Quinn and Kalli naked and hold them close for hours on end. "I can't think of any two wolves I would rather be owned by."

"Let's get our vampire home," Kalli comments. "We need to feed him and then clean up the house."

"Do you think we should order extra blood for him?" Quinn asks, casting a concerned look over at Soren. "It's been a hell of a few days."

For the first time in his life as a vampire, two people are talking about him as a beloved partner and treating him as if he's a helpless infant. It's both amusing and slightly annoying.

He gives them both a stern look. "Soren will take care of his own blood consumption," he announces.

Quinn pats him on the head and smiles. "Home first, attitude later." Quinn whispers loudly to Kalli. "Looks like someone might need a nap."

That makes Kalli laugh, and Soren gives up his dour expression and grins. He'll accept the head pats and silliness because his life suddenly became perfect.

Several months later

Kalli stares at the website for Central Oregon Community College as Ryan exclaims, "It's perfect. Don't you think?"

After they all got back from Alaska, Ryan and Alex settled into Soren's house with little difficulty. At first, they flinched whenever Kalli talked to them. They also treated her with the kind of over-the-top deference Dimitri always demanded.

Even now, after two months of all of them sharing a house, and Kalli never once raising her voice or losing her temper, Alex and Ryan are just starting to relax. Occasionally, they'll still get a little skittish around her, and she's forced to remind herself that it might take them years before they start treating her as a friend and equal instead of an all-powerful alpha who might punish them on a whim.

Ryan continues talking as she examines the website. "And I talked to the student liaison. They said that they have plenty of older students coming in as freshmen. It's not weird that I'm almost twenty-seven. What do you think? This way I can go to college but still stay close to the pack, and I don't have to live anywhere else."

It's hard for Kalli not to smile at Ryan's enthusiasm. It was only a few days ago that Ryan found the courage to approach Kalli with the request to go to college. Among the Volk, education wasn't seen as particularly important, so it was rare for anyone to go to college or trade school. When Kalli readily agreed to let Alex attend a few seminars on real estate, it gave Ryan the courage to ask about college. Kalli didn't even hesitate to say yes.

Besides, Soren had already explained that he expected to finance everyone's college education on whatever subject that interested them. When Kalli mentioned how expensive education could be, Soren gave her a stern look.

"It's not a loan, it's an investment," he told them. "I don't care what any of you do, but I want . . . no, I *need* you to be happy. If college will help that happen, then it's my privilege to provide it." Then he reminded her that she promised to stop arguing about money.

She caved after that. It makes Soren happy to provide, and it's not as if he doesn't have plenty of resources. And if the situation were reversed, she'd happily pay for Soren to attend a university without question.

Despite how uncomfortable it makes her, Alex and now Ryan, will get an education at Soren's expense. Quinn patted her on the head and told her she was being a "good wolf" for letting them go to college. She rolled her eyes and let it go.

One thing that makes her feel better is that with only four wolves total in the pack, there's no reason to hold anyone back. It's not as if they are dozens of wolves all vying for limited resources.

Right now, she's taking a few online classes herself for banking and economics. She's not sure she's interested in getting a degree, but the idea of being able to help Soren with his businesses makes her feel accomplished and, in a small way, makes her feel like a contributing member of the household.

"I think staying local is a great idea," Kalli agrees, giving Ryan a big, encouraging smile. Any hint of doubt from her will crush him, so she's careful to always be enthusiastic about his choices. "And the college looks good."

"Kalli?" Alex calls out from the front of the house.

"We're in the den," Kalli shouts, and Alex comes bustling in, holding a box.

"I picked them up today," he announces, and sets the box down on the couch next to Ryan. Kalli was leaning over the back of the couch to see Ryan's computer screen over his shoulder. But now she straightens up and gives Alex a quizzical look.

"Picked what up?"

"The Annwyl Pack shirts," Alex announces, beaming at her. Because they are a new pack, Kalli had to come up with a name. She tried to get the other wolves to weigh in on the subject, but they all steadfastly refused. It was entirely up to her to figure out what they were going to call themselves.

Every pack needs a name, not only for identification, but to help with bonding and cohesion. They might be small, but Kalli knows that all of them need to feel like they are a real pack. An official pack name can go a long way toward reinforcing their legitimacy.

When she thought about what she wanted this new pack to represent, she decided it needed to be the opposite of Dimitri and the Volk. Cruelty has no place in her pack, so she settled on *annwyl*, beloved, in Welsh. It's the term Soren has spoken to both her and Quinn so many times, and the first time she said "Annwyl Pack," out loud, it felt right.

The other wolves love it, and Soren was touched that she picked a Welsh word instead of going with something from her family's Russian or Greek heritage.

Kalli loves how Annwyl rolls off the tongue. One night, as they brainstormed, they came up with the pack logo. Unlike most other packs, it isn't an image to intimidate like a snarling wolf or gruesome icon. It's simple and meaningful: a stylized black wolf paw inside a red heart.

When Alex made a strange face at it, Quinn asked if he didn't like the logo. His insightful answer surprised both Quinn and Kalli.

"I love the logo," Alex told them quickly. "It's perfect. It's a modest and flawless representation of Kalli and the pack. She might look small and weak, but she's far more powerful than anyone would expect. Even her own father. The fact that we are picking an image with a heart on it might seem like we are emotional, but really, is there anything more powerful out there than love? We're all here, safe and with bright futures ahead because we fought for love. Fought to be with the partners we were meant to be with. Maybe other packs will follow our example."

Kalli couldn't agree with him more, and the pack's name and logo became even more meaningful.

She honestly didn't expect that they would do much with the pack name or logo. It's there because they needed to feel connected. But now, apparently, the Annwyl Pack has matching shirts. She's drawing a line if they want to form a baseball team. She hates baseball.

Tearing open the box, Alex pulls out a bright green shirt with the red and black logo boldly printed in the center, with Annwyl written below. He holds it up to his chest and grins proudly. Something occurs to Kalli, and she snorts out a laugh.

"What?" Alex asks, looking a little hurt. "You don't like them?"

"No, it's not that," Kalli assures him quickly. "I just realized that people will probably think we run a dog rescue or something."

Ryan grins shyly. "We kind of do."

That makes Kalli burst out laughing. The fact that Ryan can joke like that with her is a big step, and half her laughter is delight at his growing courage, more so than the silly quip.

"Good one, Ryan," Kalli compliments him.

"Thanks, Benadur Kalli," Ryan says with a chuckle.

"Brat," Alex says with a smile as he tosses the green shirt at Ryan.

Because Kalli picked a Welsh word for their pack name, they all decided to stay with the Welsh language theme. After consulting with Soren, they started referring to Kalli as Benadur, chieftain in Welsh. She'd rather not have any title at all, but some things are too ingrained to get rid of.

In truth, the more Welsh the pack uses, the more pleased it makes Soren. It was Quinn who explained to her that using the language of his ancestors makes Soren feel like he's part of the pack instead of on the periphery. That revelation meant Kalli is more willing to let the others call her Benadur as long as it made Soren smile.

They even picked out a Welsh pet name for Soren: Dyn Mawr, big man. They call Memphis: Dyn Tew, thick man.

The only other person they've chosen a pack nickname for is Lexington: Tywyllwch, darkness. Kalli finds it fitting, if not disturbingly accurate. But then again, Lex is an unnerving guy who seems to visit far too much. Soren explained that after Kalli ruthlessly demolished Dimitri in combat, Lex has a strange, platonic crush on her.

Kalli deals with it all by mostly ignoring Lex unless he talks directly to her. Which seldom happens.

"Here's yours, Kalli," Alex says as he tosses a shirt to her. She grabs it and holds it up, happy to have one in navy blue instead of the other brighter colors.

"What going on in here?" Quinn asks. He puts himself behind Kalli and draws her back into a tight hug.

"We got shirts," Kalli says with a grin and holds hers up so Quinn can see.

Quinn grins. "Oh, cool! We're official now. We've got shirts!"

Alex takes the teasing good-naturedly. "You're just jealous because I thought of it first."

Quinn looks over at the box. "I'm jealous because you got a green shirt. Are there any more coming? All the rest in here are blue or red."

Kalli slips out of Quinn's embrace as the three men banter back and forth about shirt colors. She thinks about grabbing a snack from the kitchen and then settling down with her laptop to start on a spreadsheet Soren asked her to put together.

She was never that interested in math in school, but now that she's applying it to practical things, she finds it enjoyable and fascinating.

Soren comes out of the kitchen with a concerned expression on his face. Her heart kicks up, and she reaches for his hand. "What's wrong? Are you okay?"

He pulls her into a quick hug. "I'm perfectly fine, *cariad*."

She hugs him back. "That's good. Then whatever it is can't be too big a deal."

"I'm afraid it concerns you and the Volk," Soren says. She stiffens, and he reluctantly lets go when she pulls away.

"Tell me," she demands.

"Better to show you. Alex picked this up from my lawyer in town while he was running errands." He takes her hand and leads her down to the basement. At his desk is a stack of documents, all of them official looking.

Considering the number of businesses Soren owns, it's common for him to get stacks of paperwork from his lawyers and accountants on an almost weekly basis. One document is sitting off to the side, and that's the one that he picks up and hands to her.

She stares at it, uncomprehendingly. There's a lot of legalese but her name is there, added to the text several times. Helpless to make heads or tails of the confusing document, she looks up at Soren and shrugs. "I think you're going to need to interpret for me."

"It's the oil rights that made your pack rich," he explains. "This document transfers ownership to you. *Cariad,* you're almost as rich as me now."

Blanching, she shoves the document back at Soren. "I don't want it."

He takes it back and sets it down. Then he draws her into his arms. "It's not a matter of what you want. It's done. Everything is in your name. We can give it away to someone else or to a charity, but for now it's yours."

"Why would they do that?" she asks, not expecting an answer, but Soren knows more than she realized.

"After I read the paperwork, I contacted the lawyer who prepared the documents up in Fairbanks. He's a wolf in the Amarok pack. He said the Volk basically disbanded after we left. There's still a group living on the property, but it's mostly made up of single males. There are only a few mated couples and no children."

Kalli shouldn't care, but she asks anyway. "Where did they all go?"

"That's where it gets interesting. It turns out they came south. Those that left Volk all came down here."

"Here, as in the lower forty-eight?"

"Yes, but more specifically, here as in Bend," Soren explains gently. Guilt makes her stomach roil with nausea. Accurately judging her expression, he sits down in his desk chair and sweeps her up onto his lap.

It feels good to cuddle close to him. She closes her eyes and relaxes into his embrace, letting the smell and feel of him comfort her.

She can feel their soul bond when she concentrates. Soren assured her that over time, she wouldn't need to concentrate, and she and Quinn could use the bond to even talk. For now, she focuses on the bond and draws strength from Soren's quiet, peaceful mind.

When he talks, she feels the rumble in his chest as well as hearing his voice in her ears. "I know you've felt conflicted about refusing to be lider. When you told me what happened with the rest of the pack after you killed Dimitri, what did I say?"

"You said a lot," she mutters grumpily. "You gave me an entire speech."

To her frustration, Soren didn't express an opinion on her choice to denounce everyone in the Volk pack. Even when she asked him flat out if he thought she did the right thing, he told her it wasn't up to him to decide that. Only her. Right or wrong can be hard to judge in situations this complex. He reminded her that the wolves of Volk have many options. Coming from a once prestigious pack, they will be readily accepted by other packs, even if they aren't bringing wealth with them.

That fact that she refused to take over for Dimitri doesn't mean they'll be homeless or leaderless. It only means that she's shifted the hard choices onto them.

As when he gave her the speech the first time, he doesn't let her get away with any prevarication this time. "I think you know which part of my speech I'm referring to."

Her brief bout of petulance vanishes. "You said that my decisions don't need to be set in stone. I can change my mind."

Rubbing a hand in a circle on her back, he keeps his voice soft and kind. "That was one of the hardest lessons for me to learn over the years. When I was growing up, things were absolute. There was only one religion; everyone else worshiped false gods. There was only one way to grow food; everything else was foolhardy. There was only one way to raise children; otherwise, you will have spoiled, insolent children and later, sinful adults."

"You're talking about way back when dinosaurs roamed the earth," she teases him.

"Hush, sweet wolf," Soren reprimands with a smile. "You're not going to distract me with humor. As I was saying, everything changed after I became a vampire. After I was turned, whole new worlds were opened to me. There's so much diversity out there that the idea that one group could get everything 'right' is preposterous.

Eventually, many realize that the words *right* and *wrong* need to be replaced by the words *choice* and *consequence*."

"Are Quinn and I part of that choice and a consequence?" Kalli asks him. She needs reassurance and isn't sure how to voice her need. But now that they share parts of their souls with each other, Soren knows what she requires without the need for words.

"You are. The choice was to have you in my flock or not. The consequence was lonely simplicity or complexity with love. I know half the reason you refused any contact with people from the Volk over the last month is because you're worried it will upset me. As I've told you numerous times, you can be Benadur of a pack of four or four hundred and that won't change your status in my flock. You are mine, and I'm yours. Nothing can alter that."

"But if my pack gets bigger, sometimes I'll have to be Benadur first and your flock second," she points out, anxiety making her sit up and frown at him. "Won't that bother you? It was originally only me and Quinn. You didn't sign up for anything else."

"I'm not some insecure youth to feel dismissed because you have duties. The fact that you are Benadur doesn't detract; it only adds. Now I get you, Quinn, and an entire pack to care for. This doesn't cause me distress. Don't you realize yet, Kalli? With this added burden of more wolves also comes additional affection and satisfaction. That's the choice and consequence here."

Then he makes a scoffing sound. "Besides, I entered into our relationship with my eyes wide open. Your aura is much too bright for you to remain packless. I knew once you and Quinn were no longer forced to hide that other wolves would seek you out. There is no way you wouldn't draw a pack to you. This isn't a surprise to me, and it certainly isn't something I've been dreading. I'm excited to be a vampire among wolves."

"Really?" His words are making her realize she can have it all. Soren and a pack. She thought he was only trying to comfort her before and that he would eventually come to resent the pack for demanding her time and attention. Now she sees that Soren isn't "putting up" with a pack, but actually looking forward to being part of a community.

"Annwyl is going to be the shining example of what all packs should be," Soren declares, and she can tell by his expression that he's already plotting and planning. "There's a property for sale close to here. It used to be a small resort but folded a few years ago. We could buy that; it shouldn't take much time to make it an excellent home base for a pack. There's a main house and a few dozen cabins scattered around the property. It would be an excellent place for people to live if they don't want to be on their own. And we could . . ."

She listens with half an ear as Soren lays out plans for the Annwyl wolves. Choices and consequences filter through her mind.

The choice was to flee with Quinn. The consequence was that they found Soren. The path to love and security was rocky and rough, but courage saw her and Quinn through. And now that the former Volk wolves are displaying enough courage to move south, she'll accept her responsibility as their Benadur.

Bravery isn't always epic battles with monstrous foes. Sometimes it's facing one's past and finding forgiveness.

One year later

From: Stephen Marks
To: Soren Bowen
Subject: Tiffany and Delilah

Soren,

As you might have guessed from our silence, Delilah has become reluctant to try being turned. Your speech the night we negotiated the use of a demon spooked her enough to request we look for other options. At present, we are introducing her to other vampires to see if any of them might find her suitable for their flock. If we aren't successful, we will revisit having you turn her. This might only be a delay in your promised duty, so please don't think that you have been released from your pledge. If necessary, we might trade in your 'turn' for something else, so be prepared if we bring a different human to you for turning.

On another topic, I heard that one of your flock is the alpha of a wolf pack. Good luck with that. Those wolves congregate in large communities and are rather lacking in the concept of privacy. I wish you the best but would never want my flock to be distracted like that.

You really are unique among vampires. I hope your flock appreciates that.

- Stephen Marks

The email from Stephen is a relief. Although Kalli and Quinn seemed accepting of what he was forced to promise to get to them, he dreaded the day he had to fulfill his obligation to Delilah. Now that he's been granted a reprieve, he fervently hopes that some other vampire decides Delilah would make a perfect flock member.

He thinks about the last line of Stephen's email: *I hope your flock appreciates that.*

What Stephen and most other vampires will never understand is that having a flock member with a pack attached hasn't lessened anything for Soren. He has the family he never expected to have.

The wolves from Volk and other packs that have joined Annwyl over the last year have readily accepted Soren among them. He's been hugged, touched, and talked to as if he were another wolf, a novelty for a vampire. He's treated with the same care and kindness that Kalli insists the wolves use with each other. He expected the pack to be wary of him, but the opposite is true, and he couldn't be happier.

He held an infant the other day. A baby only a few hours old was entrusted to him while the mother was cared for by Dr. Seaward and his naga wife. No one protested. No one screamed in horror at the vampire holding the child. And when the baby looked up at him with solemn, dark eyes, Soren's heart melted. It was only with great reluctance that he gave the baby back.

The occasion was monumental for several reasons. The first baby born in the Annwyl pack, and the first infant Soren has held since he was turned. He ended up having to find a quiet place to shed a few tears when he found out they gave the baby a traditional Welsh name: Rhys.

Soren types out a quick reply to Stephen and is clicking send when Quinn dashes down the stairs and closes the door quickly, but quietly. Sitting back in his office chair, Soren watches as Quinn presses his ear to the door and listens. Then he looks up and finds Soren watching him with a quizzical expression.

Grinning ruefully, Quinn straightens up and shrugs. "Kalli's on the warpath," he explains. "One of the youngsters in cabin twenty-two accidentally set it on fire. Everyone's fine, but the cabin's going to need some major work before it's usable again."

Now Soren can understand why Quinn is hiding. Lately, Kalli's been easily pushed into a temper. Although she's never cruel, an angry Kalli can be intimidating and even uncomfortable to be near if her aura flares unexpectedly.

Both Quinn and Soren have found the best tactic is to make themselves scarce and give Kalli time to cool down. When they do approach her, they make sure to have one of her favorite sweets in hand. That usually brings a smile to her face and . . .

Something occurs to Soren that makes his heart speed up, and adrenaline hit his system. "Quinn, is it just me or has Kalli been unusually quick tempered the last few weeks?"

That makes Quinn pause, a thoughtful expression taking over his face. "Now that you mention it, it seems like the things that she normally brushes aside are bothering her more lately. Do you think she needs a vacation? She won't like that idea, but we could try anyway."

Soren grins at him. "If I'm correct, she's going to be forced to take time off in a few months."

Puzzled, Quinn tilts his head. "Why would you . . .?" Comprehension hits Quinn, and his face lights up.

Suddenly, Kalli is there, throwing open the door and storming into the room. Her face is flushed, and she paces the room as she talks.

"How do you set fire to a cabin that doesn't have a fireplace? Explain that to me. They decided to light candles and turn off the lights. They had power, but they turned off the lights and used candlelight because they wanted to know what it would be like."

She doesn't wait for Soren or Quinn to say something. She throws up her hands and makes a frustrated sound.

"There is a reason electricity was invented—because using fire for everything is a bad idea! Then they decide to fall asleep with candles lit everywhere. Guess what happened? One of them got knocked over and set the whole damn cabin on fire. Those two should have known better! I let them live alone in that cabin with the understanding that they would be responsible adults. Well, you know what? Their adulthood is officially revoked. They're going back into the dorms!"

She stops pacing to pull in a lungful of air, probably to continue her angry rant, when she stops and stares at him and Quinn. He's probably wearing the same dopey expression on his face as Quinn.

Unable to resist any longer, Soren jumps up and folds Kalli into a hug. She gives a little hiss, sounding like an angry cat, but doesn't fight the embrace.

"You're beautiful," he murmurs.

Quinn wraps his arms around her from behind, trapping her between them. "Gorgeous," he agrees.

Her anger evaporates, and she relaxes into them. "Are you guys horny?" she teases. "You know you two can fool around without me. I won't get upset."

That makes Soren chuckle. "We know, but it's not about that. Or rather, it's another consequence."

"Consequence?" she echoes with confusion. "What are you talking—"

She gasps and pulls away from both of them. Placing both hands on her stomach, she stares down at herself. Her eyes go unfocused, and her aura brightens momentarily, then a huge smile unfurls across her mouth. Her eyes are shiny with moisture when she looks back up.

"I'm pregnant," she declares.

The news doesn't surprise any of them. Kalli want into heat last month. A natural heat. Her wolf decided life was safe and secure enough to push her into a heat that left both him and Quinn exhausted but deliriously happy. Because she didn't get pregnant from the drug-induced heat in Alaska, no one really considered she'd get pregnant this time.

Looking back, Soren realizes they were being foolish. It makes sense that a natural heat would be more likely to produce offspring.

Kalli shoots an anxious look at both him and Quinn. "We don't know who the father is."

Soren's taken aback by that statement. Why would it matter who the father is? This child belongs to all of them. Then he remembers Dimitri and his obsession with bloodlines. Smiling gently, he pulls Kalli and Quinn close to his body.

"While it is unlikely that I would be the genetic father," Soren explains, "it doesn't matter because this is the child of my heart."

"I love this baby, and I haven't even met them yet," Quinn comments, and tears start rolling down Kalli's face. Soren knows they're tears of joy, but it's still hard to see his stoic Kalli crying.

"Easy, *cariad*," Soren murmurs. "All is well, and soon your pack will grow by one more beating heart ready to give and accept love."

"And that's the difference, isn't it," she says softly, burying her face against his chest as Quinn places a kiss on her neck, right next to his mate mark and a fresh bite from Soren.

"What is the difference?" Soren asks.

"Love," she says quietly. "This baby will be born to duty and obligation, but also love. That's what was missing from Volk and what makes Annwyl strong and enduring. With love comes acceptance and forgiveness. Love helps us be patient, and it sets us up to want the best for each other. Somewhere in our past that got lost."

"But not any longer," Quinn comments.

"Not any longer," Kalli agrees.

"Annwyl," Soren breathes. "The Beloved pack."

"And now every pack is going to want a vampire too," Quinn teases, lightening the mood.

"Well, they'll have to find their own, because this one is claimed," Kalli states with mock fierceness, hugging Soren tightly

Soren wouldn't have it any other way.

Dear Readers,

Thank you for reading *Two Wolves For Soren.* There are more books in this series and a free novella! You can find all the links on my website:

www.RKMunin.com

I hope you enjoyed it enough to leave a review! As an indie writer without the support of a publishing company, I need all the help I can get. Your good reviews keep me writing.

If you have any questions, comments, or suggestions feel free to contact me via email: author@rk-munin.com

Cheers,
Rye

www.ingramcontent.com/pod-product-compliance
Lightning Source LLC
Chambersburg PA
CBHW060434310726
48977CB00001B/188